NAIROBI NOIR

EDITED BY PETER KIMANI

BROOKLYN, NEW YORK, USA
BALLYDEHOB, CO. CORK, IRELAND

Published by Akashic Books
©2020 Akashic Books

Series concept by Tim McLoughlin and Johnny Temple
Nairobi map by Sohrab Habibion

ISBN: 978-1-61775-754-9
Library of Congress Control Number: 2019935269

Akashic Books
Brooklyn, New York, USA
Ballydehob, Co. Cork, Ireland
Twitter: @AkashicBooks
Facebook: AkashicBooks
E-mail: info@akashicbooks.com
Website: www.akashicbooks.com

To Anne M, the desert rose from Murkutwo

ALSO IN THE AKASHIC NOIR SERIES

MUMBAI NOIR (INDIA), edited by ALTAF TYREWALA

NEW HAVEN NOIR, edited by AMY BLOOM

NEW JERSEY NOIR, edited by JOYCE CAROL OATES

NEW ORLEANS NOIR, edited by JULIE SMITH

NEW ORLEANS NOIR: THE CLASSICS, edited by JULIE SMITH

OAKLAND NOIR, edited by JERRY THOMPSON & EDDIE MULLER

ORANGE COUNTY NOIR, edited by GARY PHILLIPS

PARIS NOIR (FRANCE), edited by AURÉLIEN MASSON

PHILADELPHIA NOIR, edited by CARLIN ROMANO

PHOENIX NOIR, edited by PATRICK MILLIKIN

PITTSBURGH NOIR, edited by KATHLEEN GEORGE

PORTLAND NOIR, edited by KEVIN SAMPSELL

PRAGUE NOIR (CZECH REPUBLIC), edited by PAVEL MANDYS

PRISON NOIR, edited by JOYCE CAROL OATES

PROVIDENCE NOIR, edited by ANN HOOD

QUEENS NOIR, edited by ROBERT KNIGHTLY

RICHMOND NOIR, edited by ANDREW BLOSSOM, BRIAN CASTLEBERRY & TOM DE HAVEN

RIO NOIR (BRAZIL), edited by TONY BELLOTTO

ROME NOIR (ITALY), edited by CHIARA STANGALINO & MAXIM JAKUBOWSKI

SAN DIEGO NOIR, edited by MARYELIZABETH HART

SAN FRANCISCO NOIR, edited by PETER MARAVELIS

SAN FRANCISCO NOIR 2: THE CLASSICS, edited by PETER MARAVELIS

SAN JUAN NOIR (PUERTO RICO), edited by MAYRA SANTOS-FEBRES

SANTA CRUZ NOIR, edited by SUSIE BRIGHT

SÃO PAULO NOIR (BRAZIL), edited by TONY BELLOTTO

SEATTLE NOIR, edited by CURT COLBERT

SINGAPORE NOIR, edited by CHERYL LU-LIEN TAN

STATEN ISLAND NOIR, edited by PATRICIA SMITH

ST. LOUIS NOIR, edited by SCOTT PHILLIPS

STOCKHOLM NOIR (SWEDEN), edited by NATHAN LARSON & CARL-MICHAEL EDENBORG

ST. PETERSBURG NOIR (RUSSIA), edited by NATALIA SMIRNOVA & JULIA GOUMEN

SYDNEY NOIR (AUSTRALIA), edited by JOHN DALE

TEHRAN NOIR (IRAN), edited by SALAR ABDOH

TEL AVIV NOIR (ISRAEL), edited by ETGAR KERET & ASSAF GAVRON

TORONTO NOIR (CANADA), edited by JANINE ARMIN & NATHANIEL G. MOORE

TRINIDAD NOIR (TRINIDAD & TOBAGO), edited by LISA ALLEN-AGOSTINI & JEANNE MASON

TRINIDAD NOIR: THE CLASSICS (TRINIDAD & TOBAGO), edited by EARL LOVELACE & ROBERT ANTONI

TWIN CITIES NOIR, edited by JULIE SCHAPER & STEVEN HORWITZ

USA NOIR, edited by JOHNNY TEMPLE

VANCOUVER NOIR (CANADA), edited by SAM WIEBE

VENICE NOIR (ITALY), edited by MAXIM JAKUBOWSKI

WALL STREET NOIR, edited by PETER SPIEGELMAN

ZAGREB NOIR (CROATIA), edited by IVAN SRŠEN

FORTHCOMING

ACCRA NOIR (GHANA), edited by NANA-AMA DANQUAH

ADDIS ABABA NOIR (ETHIOPIA), edited by MAAZA MENGISTE

ALABAMA NOIR, edited by DON NOBLE

BELGRADE NOIR (SERBIA), edited by MILORAD IVANOVIC

BERKELEY NOIR, edited by JERRY THOMPSON & OWEN HILL

BOGOTÁ NOIR (COLOMBIA), edited by ANDREA MONTEJO

COLUMBUS NOIR, edited by ANDREW WELSH-HUGGINS

JERUSALEM NOIR, edited by DROR MISHANI

MIAMI NOIR: THE CLASSICS, edited by LES STANDIFORD

PALM SPRINGS NOIR, edited by BARBARA DeMARCO-BARRETT

PARIS NOIR: THE SUBURBS (FRANCE), edited by HERVÉ DELOUCHE

SANTA FE NOIR, edited by ARIEL GORE

TAMPA BAY NOIR, edited by COLETTE BANCROFT

NAIROBI

A104

KANGEMI

KAWANGWARE

KILIMANI

KAREN

KIBERA

NGONG
FOREST
SANCTUARY

GIRAFFE
CENTRE

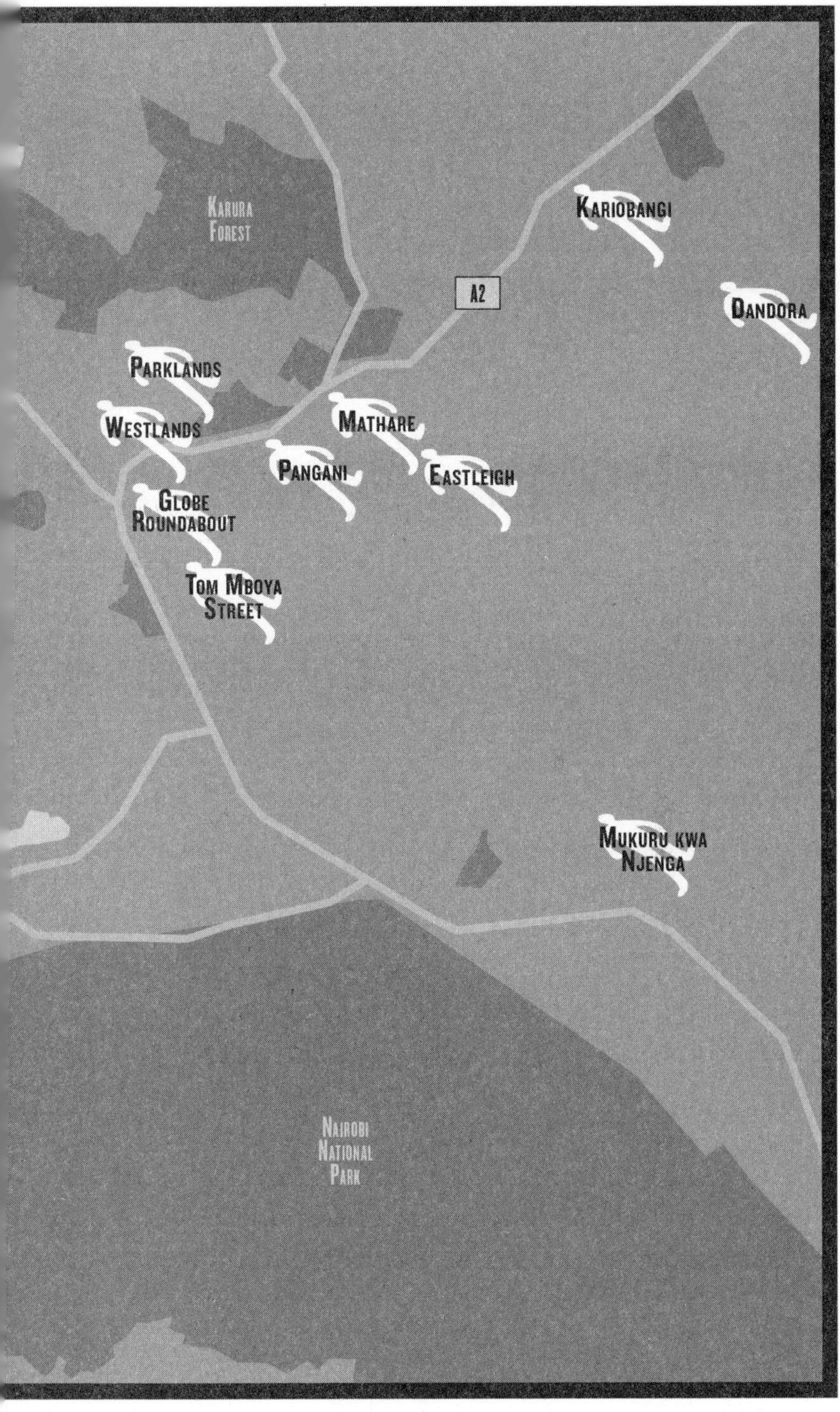
Karura Forest
A2
Kariobangi
Dandora
Parklands
Westlands
Mathare
Pangani
Eastleigh
Globe Roundabout
Tom Mboya Street
Mukuru kwa Njenga
Nairobi National Park

TABLE OF CONTENTS

PART III: THE HERDERS

INTRODUCTION
CONCRETE JUNGLE

Nairobi, *shamba la mawe*—Nairobi, the stone garden—is a pithy formulation intimating the city as a place of pleasures and perils. Its colonial founders declared it their Eden, the garden where they found easy nurture, living close to nature. They christened it the Green City in the Sun. It was this allure that, centuries earlier, drew Maasai herdsmen to the space that they knew as *Enkare Nyrobi*—the place of cool waters. They found enough water and pasture for their animals.

Over the past one hundred years, Nairobi has evolved from a supply depot for railway workers to the largest metropolis in East and Central Africa, with an estimated five million residents. This has come with a unique set of challenges: water is always in short supply, power blackouts are rife, and traffic jams are so bad, even lions come out of the wilds to marvel at the snarl-ups! This is no exaggeration; Nairobi is the only city with a game park, and the kings of the wild occasionally stray on major city highways to kill boredom . . . as do pastoralists who insist the city occupies their grazing fields. A place of hunters and herders is a good way of thinking about it.

The Maasai were not the only community displaced to make room for what became the White Highlands, the centerpiece of the colonial agri-based economy. Other communities were similarly dislodged from their ancestral lands in central and eastern regions of the colony, where they had been converted from self-sustaining herders and hunters into rent- and tax-paying subjects of the Crown. This precipitated an exodus of villagers into the new, segregated city where suffrage, labor, and residence were assigned according to racial hierarchy: whites, Indians, Arabs, and Africans, in that order.

Nairobi remains one of the most unequal cities in the world. The western part of the city boasts a United Nations headquarters—the only one located in the so-called *developing* world—with heated pools and other trappings of comfort. On the other side of town, in the Kibera slums, hundreds of thousands are hemmed into a few hectares of earth, without running water or electricity, so dwellers have invented "flying toilets." Nothing lofty, really, just a mound of shit wrapped in polythene and hurled to the farthest reach of the arm. And in keeping with the spirit of the city, which means finding lucre even in the most propitious of circumstances, slum tourism has become quite popular in Kibera.

The journey toward a just, multiracial, multiethnic society, as you, dear readers, will attest from this collection, remains on course, the most abiding evidence being the seamless, if unintentional, infusion of *Sheng* throughout many stories in this collection. This hybrid Kenyan patois, fusing Swahili with other indigenous languages, was the by-product of the quest by youngsters in Nairobi's Eastlands area to communicate without their parents—with whom they shared very modest dwellings—getting in the way.

By incorporating words and expressions from other Kenyan languages, the youngsters were making a salient proposition: out of the old, they would create something new; out of the many languages, they would make one collective whole, and claim it as their own. It is this principle that *Nairobi Noir* affirms; from the chaos that marked its origins, a thriving city has emerged.

Today, huge swathes of the city resemble a construction site. As I went to work, soliciting and editing contributions from writers within Kenyan and beyond, diggers were revving to tear down old estates in the Eastlands, which are no longer able to contain the ballooning population. More affluent suburbs, such as Westlands, were also in the process of reconfiguration from residential to office blocks. Other estates, such as Kileleshwa, once a leafy suburb, were being remodeled to accommodate large apartment blocks that ensure neither the sun nor the green are visible to its dwellers, calling to mind Bob Marley's "Concrete Jungle":

> No sun will shine in my day today
> The high yellow moon won't come out to play
> I say darkness has covered my light
> And has changed my day into night . . .

In that sense, *Nairobi Noir* is an act of excavation, rediscovering the city's ossified past and infusing life to preserve it for future generations. It is also an act of celebration, reminding readers of the brilliance of the best-known writers to emerge from this part of the world, and heralding the birth of new writers whose gifts, we can safely predict, will shine brightly in the years ahead.

The oldest writer in this anthology is eighty-one, the youngest is only twenty-four; if there is any inference one can draw from this demographic it is that this anthology offers an entire spectrum of Kenyan writing: the past, present, and future. If we can allow one extravagant claim, a collection of this nature is unprecedented in Kenya's literary history.

Although the range of issues explored in this volume is as diverse as its contributors, it all gestures toward a common theme. In this concrete jungle, the hunters and herders live on. As do the hunted . . .

The wealth of Nairobi, no doubt, is its people. One visual that defines that wealth is the muscled men who sit out in the sun, bare-chested, at Gikomba market, knocking scraps of iron into shape. By nightfall, the hunk of iron is miraculously hewn into bright-blue tin boxes, sturdy *jikos* that make the tastiest *nyama choma* in the world, among other innovations.

That's the Gikomba of my childhood, though it hasn't changed much. The well-built men still sit out in the sun— *Jua Kali*, scorching sun, is also the name of the market—but I suspect it's the sons who have replaced their fathers. And the rhythmic gong goes on uninterrupted, pulsating with life to power the city, and by extension, the nation's economy.

Such analysis proffers an interesting paradox: the minions toil under a scorching sun all their lives, putting extraordinary efforts to earn their day-to-day, ordinary living; those in the "leafy suburbs" burrow in a labyrinth of concrete, where the sun never shines.

How do we account for this phenomenon? And how have the conditions of the workers remained unchanged, despite the passage of time? The answer, perhaps, lies in these pages. The opening story is set in Eastleigh, once a bustling middle-class suburb inhabited by Arabs and Asians in the city's segregated past. In recent decades, these demographics have been largely replaced by ethnic Somalis, earning Eastleigh the moniker of "Little Mogadishu," following an influx of refugees from Somalia's conflagration. At the heart of this story is a quest for belonging: the pain of homelessness and the angst of being a constant target of bribe-taking, gun-toting policemen.

The last story in the collection is set in Mukuru kwa Njenga, to the east of the city, where more policemen are on the beat with one solid idea on their minds: how to make an extra coin—by any means. The persistent police presence in these stories highlights Nairobi's noir character: law and order, crime and punishment, in a province regulated by complex characters who create problems for law enforcement. And policemen who are complicit in violating the law.

The stories in between course through the city, excavating refreshing perspectives on race, caste, culture, politics, religion, and crime, among other themes, in ways that will surprise the reader, just like they surprised me. The Green City in the Sun may have turned into a concrete jungle, but it is still enchanting. And the spirit of its forebears, the hunters and the herders and the hunted, still lives on . . .

Peter Kimani
Nairobi, Kenya
October 2019

PART I

The Hunters

SHE DUG TWO GRAVES

BY WINFRED KIUNGA

Eastleigh

Her brother's body was found in a dark alley in Eastleigh Section One, near the old post office. His torso was a collage of torture marks and bruises, already dark blue against his light-brown skin. Were it not for the notable birthmark on his neck, Ahmed would have been unrecognizable. It was the local imam who saw the body as he was going to make the morning call to prayer.

"*Eebe naxariiso!* Allah, have mercy!" he screamed, waking up the sleepy neighborhood. Most of the tenements lit up and a few faces cautiously emerged from the small barred windows.

"What's going on?" asked Fartun, the number one Eastleigh gossip. Everyone called her CNN, a title she accepted. No one answered. The streets were now empty as the imam had hurriedly left for the mosque to avoid the police. He had firsthand experience with their brutal force.

Fartun quickly put on a hijab and ran down the stairs, making an awful lot of noise as she heaved her body against metal doors when she briefly paused to catch her breath on every floor. She was the only one courageous enough to leave the confines of her apartment at that hour. She had to get the latest information, she always argued. Neighbors depended on her to bring fresh and juicy news every day. Two stray cats were gnawing and fighting over the body but Fartun's approach scared them off. They stayed close by, though, their yellow-green eyes creating an eerie feel in the dark and smelly alley.

After poking and inspecting the body like a seasoned mortician, Fartun shouted her discovery to the waiting faces up above: "It is Ahmed!"

"Which Ahmed?" someone inquired.

"A fair question, Imran, as Section One has over a thousand Ahmeds. It is Ahmed Farah, brother to that pleasant woman called Fawzia, the refugee who refused to spit on her former husband when he begged her to take him back. If I was her, I would have spit on his henna-dyed beard. I hear that he pleaded with her like a dog and—"

"Relevance!" Imran interrupted, halting what would have been a long story of Fawzia's entire marital history. "We are only interested in the body and the cause of death."

"Stop badgering me. Are you not the one who wanted to know whose body this is? Don't interrupt me when I am adding details to the story. Don't you know that a good story must be embellished, seasoned a bit with other niceties to keep listeners engaged? I am not called CNN for nothing. I do my research, I dig deeper, and I unearth all the details."

She paused to let that sink in among her attentive listeners above. Most people regarded her as a gossip, but Fartun considered herself a community reporter.

"I heard that this young man was among those arrested last week by the antiterror police unit. I need to talk to a few people to figure out exactly what happened."

At that, everyone retreated to their apartments. They knew that Fartun would go out to gather more "intel," as she usually referred to her gossip, and would update them before sunup.

* * *

When Fawzia received news of her brother's brutal murder, she lay prostrate on her carpet, crying and rocking sideways in deep anguish. Her grief came in torrents, like a dam that had burst its banks, spewing the slush that had accrued on the bottommost part of her being. There was no grip, no foothold, so she let the floodwaters engulf her body and soul. She sank in the miry depths, and for the next hour she just lay there in the obscurity, in the nothingness. She awoke from the hollow pit, eyes swollen like Sodom apples, head throbbing like Burundi drums. She rose slowly and walked toward the mirror. Just two hours ago, before the news about Ahmed, the mirror had reflected a beautiful woman with sparkling eyes. That aspect of her life was a lie, always fleeting. Her true reflection was what she saw now—a crushed woman whom calamity had trampled on, over and over. Happiness was elusive; it came rarely, like Atacama Desert rains.

Now tragedy had completely overshadowed her recent accomplishment. Just three days before, she had bought her own apartment. Now, looking around at the place, a sense of despondency overcame her again. Why even bother? There was no man to share her home with, no husband to make *basta* for, and no children to liven the huge space. Due to her childlessness, her husband Ibrahim had given her *talaq*, usually considered a disgraceful means of divorce in Islam.

But she had not always been barren. When the doctor announced that she was pregnant with twins at the turn of the century, the women at the Dadaab refugee camp where they were living at the time began saying that she was as fertile as Mahmoud's camels. Mahmoud was a Somali refugee whose camels had had twin calves four times. Camels seldom bear twins, so it was a rare phenomenon and one that had amazed the whole camp. But her luck was abruptly changed one fateful night. Instead of double cries expected from a healthy set of twins, there were two small bodies on the doctor's operating table.

Neither of the twins survived due to intrapartum complications related to female genital mutilation (FGM), a procedure that Fawzia, like other Somali girls, had undergone when she was eleven. The doctor at the camp hospital had tried deinfibulation in the hopes of saving the babies, but it did not work. Postpartum hemorrhage further prompted him to remove her uterus to save her life. This was the worst possible outcome, of course. Without a baby in her arms, what was she? *Who* was she? Among Somalis, a woman is only worth her children. Minus a womb, she was as good as dead. She wanted to punish the good doctor for saving and killing her at the same time.

Her husband gave *talaq* even before she left the camp hospital. There was no *iddah*, the waiting period intended to give the couple an opportunity for reconciliation and to confirm that the wife is not pregnant. For the months that followed, Fawzia was the object of ridicule from the very neighbors who had broken into ululations when they had learned of the pregnancy. It was her best friend Marian who eventually saved her. Marian now lived and worked in Toronto after getting resettled through a scholarship. She had heard of her friend's predicament and had committed to removing her from the deep mire she was in. She sent Fawzia an e-mail.

> My dear Abaayo,
>   I cannot believe that you did not tell me of the calamity that has befallen you. Am I not your bond sister? Did we not play on the same streets in Kismayo? Didn't our families leave our motherland on the fateful night of guns?

Did we not survive the treacherous journey to Liboi and finally to Dadaab? Did we not share our shah, our anjera, our buskut? Did we not go to the same school? Were we not subjected to the knife on the same day? Did they not remove our "thing" by that same knife? Did you not weep with me when my brother Karim died of cholera?

Why then would you, Abaayo, not allow me to weep with you? Why would you deny me the opportunity to hold you, so that your tears can fall and form trails on my hijab?

I have sent you 1,500 Canadian dollars. I want you to leave Dadaab, travel to Eastleigh, and stay with my sister Ayan for a while. Register as an urban refugee with UNHCR at the Nairobi office. The money is for you to start a business. I recall that you trained at the camp to be a masseuse. Remember how other girls frowned at the course, saying that it was a dhillo, a whore's job, to touch another's body? And how you didn't care what people thought about it? Why is it that now you believe in the blinkered words of the doom prophets at the camp? What happened to the strong woman I once knew? Have misfortunes put a veil on her face and faith?

I may not be able to actually cross the ocean and the vast lands that separate us. But I will do anything for you, as long as I am able to. So take the money and run. Run from those big-lipped women, run from that dog Ibrahim, run from the mockery. Who are we, if we do not put our feet into the waters? How will we discover new lands, new frontiers, if we grow afraid of the waves?

I dare you to find joy in the unknown.

Your four-leaf clover,
Marian

Fawzia remembered how Marian was always there for her. She shouldn't forget to e-mail her and let her know of Ahmed's death. She needed somebody who would grieve with her without judgment.

Relatives had already prepared Ahmed's body for burial when Fawzia arrived at her father's home. As a woman, she could not be involved, but she knew the process since she had been part of prepping her mother for burial a year before. She remembered how she and her aunt had closed her mother's eyes and mouth, straightened her limbs, and then gently washed the body with warm water as they recited prayers. Once they were done and the body had been sprayed with a perfume called Adar, they wrapped it with white cotton cloths from head to foot. It was such a tender process, one that allowed the living to show love, one last time, to those who had gone back to Allah.

Now, as the men took Ahmed to the mosque, Marian wished that she could be allowed to say *janaaso*, the goodbye prayer for him. She wished that she could be there to bind his body in the green cloth with Allah's name stitched in gold yarn. She wished she could see her brother's face, just one more time. But women were not allowed to attend the funeral or the burial, so she stayed at home. She was jealous of the linen, the grass, and the soil that would cover Ahmed's body. It would be closer to him than she would ever be.

They had been close friends growing up, even though Ahmed was five years younger than Fawzia. He was born on the road between Liboi, a town on the Kenya-Somalia border and the Dadaab refugee camp. A Médecins Sans Frontières doctor assisted in his delivery. The doctor was part of a refugee rescue mission after a resurgence of conflict in Somalia in

July 2006. Ethiopian troops, sponsored by the United States, had entered Somalia to buttress the Transitional Federal Government (TFG) in Baidoa. Sheik Hassan Dahir Aweys, then leader of the Islamic Courts Union (ICU), declared war against Ethiopia and forced civilians to join the bloody conflict. Thousands fled to neighboring countries, especially Kenya, which was already hosting over four hundred thousand refugees at the time. Fawzia's family was among the hundreds of refugees that arrived at Dadaab on July 29 of that year.

They had grown up in the camp, playing *shax* and *Layli Goobalay*. Sometimes people thought they were twins as they were always together. As teenagers, they discovered they had different dreams: Fawzia wanted to be an entrepreneur and Ahmed wanted to be a doctor. Fawzia did not like history and often quoted Thomas Jeffeson: "I like the dreams of the future better than the history of the past." She was not proud of her conflict-ridden nation's history, or her people's. Ahmed, on the other hand, believed like Marcus Garvey that "a people without the knowledge of their past history, origin, and culture is like a tree without roots." So he read about Somalia, the land of his fathers, and about Kenya, his adopted motherland. It is not a wonder then that when Fawzia invited him to Eastleigh, he—the history buff—wrote to her in response:

> My dear *walaashaa,*
>
> You say that you don't like the past, yet you are living in a place that reflects where our fathers came from. Eastleigh is referred to as "Little Mogadishu" because 90% of the people who live there are Somalis. And doesn't that place remind you of the stories that mother used to tell us? Of mosques, of bazaars, of women dressed in hijabs, of orange-bearded men spitting on the streets during Ra-

madan? Doesn't the call to prayer, doesn't the gathering of faithfuls for salat, remind you of home—the home we may never see?

I know you don't like history lessons, but I have to share this. When you invited me, I decided to research the place I would be moving to. Guess what I learned? It was not always called Eastleigh. In the late 1900s, it was divided into Nairobi East and Egerton Estate demarcated as a "whites only" zone. The original owners were European and South African investors who made very limited developments in the area. Egerton was blandly structured, with streets named after important colonial personalities such as the first Nairobi superintendent, James Ainsworth. Nairobi East was also unexcitingly organized in a grid with streets intersecting numbered avenues. Those are the same vibrant streets you see today.

It was not until 1921 that the colonial government integrated the two suburbs into one. Having realized that few Europeans wanted to settle in the area, the colonial government opened it up to Asians. When Allidina Visram, a rich Indian trader, moved into the area, he made substantial investments that spruced it up, and before long Eastleigh began to be referred to as "Little India," evidenced by still-existing street names like Moghul Lane and Saurashtra and Ganges roads. You thought we were the first ones there, eh?

Soon after Independence, Asians began to leave and Kenyans—most of whom had been living in the area unofficially despite the segregation—began to buy plots and sections in Eastleigh. Most European and Indian street names were removed. Now we, the Somalis, are the kings of Eastleigh. From the look of things, we are here to stay *and to expand. Soon, Father's shop will be a full-blown mall. And you, with your business acumen, will run things after he is gone.*

So, would I like to come to Eastleigh? Hell yes! I can't wait to walk on those dirty streets and to jump over the potholes. I can't wait to hear the businessmen and women calling the customers: Yimaadaan oo iibsadaan! It will give me a sense of home, of how Mogadishu, the real Mogadishu, used to be, or I dream will be.

See you next month!

Your favorite walaalkiis,
Ahmed

O Ahmed! She cried at the memory of him. Of how fun it was to have him living with her as he attended Eastleigh High School and later the University of Nairobi. Of his impromptu history lessons. Of his innocence and playfulness. It was just her now. And her father. She grieved for him, for his fragile heart that had lost a wife and three sons. Two had died in a tragic car accident on the Garissa-Nairobi highway. The last born had just been murdered by the Kenyan police. Somalis generally believe that life and death are in the hands of Allah and therefore the cause of Ahmed's death was "by God's will," but Marian refused to accept it as such. Ahmed's death was by human hands and she vowed to avenge him.

When Fawzia heard that a news van had been spotted near Madina Mall, she took a *boda boda* from Abdiwalla's food kiosk where she had been getting information from Fartun on Ahmed's death and instructed the driver to drive like the wind. None of the few passersby were willing to be interviewed so Fawzia volunteered on condition that her face would be blurred on TV. The minute the camera was pointed at her, she started like a magpie. She did not even wait for a prompt from the reporter. She had already prepared what to say.

"You want to know about what's going on? I will tell you. After the Kenyan government ordered the UNHCR to stop registering urban refugees and asylum seekers and for all urban refugees to move to the Dadaab and Kakuma refugee camps, the harassment of Somali refugees intensified. Even when some human rights groups fought for refugees, even after the court blocked the government strategy—albeit temporarily—it did not stop the police from harassing us, especially those living here in Eastleigh."

"Are all refugees being harassed or it is just Somalis?" asked the reporter.

"Mostly Somalis. In this day and age, being Somali is a crime. They ask you for your ID, but even if you have the necessary documents, they still arrest you. They pack you into the police vehicles and take you to Pangani where they grill you for hours, calling you a terrorist. If you are a businessperson, they call you an al-Shabaab financier. If you don't bribe them, they bring you to Kasarani for three days for further screening. Some people disappear, especially young men, or reappear dead, with torture marks."

"Are you claiming that the police are brutalizing young men?"

"*Jijazie!* Must I cook and chew the food for you?"

The reporter looked like he wanted to crawl and hide under the camera. But then he just smiled and went on: "What happens if one doesn't have an ID?"

"If you don't have an ID, and you claim that you are a

refugee, they force you to go to Dadaab. Have you ever been to the camp?"

The whole crew shook their heads. The interviewee had become the interviewer.

"Uuumm . . ." the reporter started, trying to regain control.

"Let me tell you, Dadaab is a hellhole. It is already over-crowded and yet they want refugees living in towns to go there and congest it further. It is like adding stew to an overflowing pot."

"Are you a refugee yourself?" asked the reporter.

Fawzia looked at him with contempt. "*Kwa nini?* Do you ask so that you can arrest me too? So I look like a Somali, eh? You people from *bara*, you see a woman in a hijab, and im-mediately you assume they are from Somalia. *Ptttt!*" She spat on the ground. "You are just like the police. This interview is over!" She turned to go.

"One more thing, madam," the reporter appealed. "How do you think all this will affect the economy of Eastleigh?"

"Look around. How many businesses are open right now? How many people do you see out shopping?"

The camera panned around to show the empty streets.

"People are withdrawing money from the banks, closing their businesses, going back to Somalia, or to Britain for those who have relatives there. People are leaving."

And indeed, the Eastleigh buzz and vibrancy which were usually created by the thousands of customers who come from all over East Africa and the Middle East crisscrossing the nar-row dirty streets to buy clothes, curtains, carpets, electron-ics, and jewelry in the huge malls and wholesale shops nuz-zled between colossal hotels and lodges were now greatly dimmed.

* * *

Ahmed was dead, but Eastleigh's avenues and streets were full of his steps.

See! That is Muratina Street, formerly called Ainsworth. Remember I e-mailed you about it? Did you know that muratina is home brew? The Kikuyu used to believe it was medicinal. He would point at every street and give its history. Everywhere she went, Fawzia heard him. The air echoed his voice and laughter over the heckling of the remnant merchants and the chaotic traffic. She did not know whether to be glad or sad about seeing and hearing him everywhere.

A week after Ahmed's burial, Fawzia was at the halal market when she bumped into a young man.

"*Waan ka xumahay!* I am very sorry," she said. The man crouched to pick up the mangoes that had fallen when they'd collided.

"No problem, Madam Fawzia."

"Do I know you?" She squinted her eyes to look at him more closely. She had definitely seen him somewhere. Not once but twice. Near Amina's kiosk where she bought her spinach and *sukumawiki,* and at the Pumwani bus station.

"I cannot tell you my name. But I am here to help you."

"I don't understand. Help me how? And why?"

The young man finished gathering the mangoes and stood up.

"*I raaca.*" Follow me. He whispered, "We must avenge Ahmed."

To follow or not to follow? Her instincts said run, but curiosity won. She walked behind him, watching his nonchalant steps with unmasked interest. He didn't glance back to see if she was coming or not, but when they approached the Olympic shopping center, he stopped and waited for her to catch up and walked beside her. Fawzia was glad that not many people knew her here; otherwise they would have wondered who it was she was walking with. To anyone who didn't know her, the stranger beside her would look like her protective brother. They stopped at a food kiosk and he ordered soda for both of them.

"A Fanta Orange for my sister and a Sprite for me. Anything else for you, *abaayo?*"

She shook her head.

They sipped their drinks in silence. Finally, she could no longer take it and the questions came out in bursts: "Who are you? How do you know Ahmed? Why do you want to help me avenge him? And how do you intend to do that—what's in it for you?"

He was not at all uneasy with the barrage of questions. He continued to sip his soda while he observed the passersby. "I am a soldier. I am a *gaajo.* A sword. I pierce the heart of the Kafir."

Fawzia felt dizzy with fear and terror. She clutched the cold soda bottle so tightly that her fingers went numb. Right in front of her was an al-Shabaab soldier, the most feared terrorist group in East Africa. And he was offering to avenge Ahmed. Why? Was Ahmed part of them? Were the police correct in calling her sweet, nonconniving brother a terrorist?

"No, he was not. Your brother was not one of us."

He can read my mind! she thought to herself.

"Let me expain. Why are we here? While our main objective is to overthrow the Western-backed government in Somalia and make our motherland an Islamic state, and to be recognized as having made significant contributions toward revitalizing the global Islamic caliphate, we also want to punish the Kafir. We have watched for a while now as our people are ill-treated in this land. And while we are grateful that many have found a home here, we are also infuriated that they want us to pay with our blood. Don't you think that kindness should be extended without punishment? Why do you think our rights are being violated by the very people who should be safeguarding them? Because Kenyan politics and general worldview are viciously controlled by a Christian—a Kafir philosophy—that is antagonistic to Islam, the true religion. And Kenya is a ripe ground for our wrath. They have agitated us and our people, but above all, corruption has paved the way for us to establish ourselves and spread our roots.

"About Ahmed, we had not yet approached him, but he was a perfect candidate for our *hijra* recruitment because of his medical training, though I suspect he would have hesitated. He was too fascinated with this nation—its history and future—for our liking. Yet we still want to avenge his death. You don't have to be part of us for us to support you. You have the motive, we have the means.

"You don't have to answer now. Go home, think about it. If you decide not to utilize us, no problem. You will never see us again, or anyone affiliated with us. However, you will be in our good books if you say yes. What do say you? Will you go home and think about it?"

She nodded, not in agreement, but in fear.

"I will contact you in a week."

"How?"

"I will find you. I am trained to find you."

On the massage table was Nairobi County Deputy Police Commandant Humphrey Ambayo. He had been delivered to her by a beautiful woman who Fawzia had never met. The woman's head was not covered and she was dressed provocatively. *She must be one of them*, Fawzia thought. Only four months after the initial contact with the young man, the object of her bitterness and hate was on her table, lured there by a stranger who the commandant knew as Malaika, a "masseuse" in Fawzia's spa.

"*Mkubwa*, boss, just relax . . ." Malaika cooed at the big-bellied man.

"You know, I am not in the business of being touched by hands other than my wife's," Commandant Ambayo responded with a nervous laugh.

"So you are a massage virgin?" she asked in feigned pleasantness.

"Yeah." He laughed again. "But I am glad to be breaking that virginity with you. In fact, I would not mind breaking your real virginity." The commandant rose from the table and sat upright, his belly folds cascading like a judge's wig.

"We will see, sweetheart. It depends on many things. Like how fat your wallet is, and how willing you are to share its contents with a poor girl like me."

"My wallet will be as fat as you want it to be." He spread his body again on the table, facing down, and waited for her soft hands.

"This will be a one-hour massage. I will start with a *pinda* routine which involves the use of heated plant pouches, sort of bean bags to relax you."

"Hope you are not planning to burn my nice skin."

"Nope. Actually, there will be no skin irritation. The bags will defuse any negative energy that is often the cause of health issues. Your stress levels will go down. The plant scents will not only cleanse you through the skin but the nose as well."

"Great! Let's do this."

"I will also light a candle that will melt and turn into a

scented oil that I will apply on your body, and then give you a massage inspired by Swahili techniques. I will finish with a face massage."

"Quit talking and just do it! I can't wait any longer."

"Okay, big boss." She draped the warm towel over his derriere, dimmed the lights, and began the massage. Over the soft music, Malaika whispered: "You are still tense. Maybe we should have a conversation as I do this so that you can relax your muscles."

"Okay. We can talk about a *clande* visit to Naivasha, just me and you."

"Or we could just talk about your work. I saw you on *Citizen News* talking about the antiterror swoop in Eastleigh. You look so handsome, so confident, on TV."

Commandant Ambayo blushed at the compliments.

"These Somalis are all terrorists! They should be killed or deported," she added with contrived annoyance.

"*Aki!* As the head of this operation, I show no mercy. My troops have been working day and night to flush out these animals."

"How do you know which ones are innocent and which are not?"

"All of them are guilty. If they are not terrorists, they are sympathizers or financiers."

"What about refugees and Somali-Kenyans?"

"If someone is a refugee, they should be at a refugee camp. Those insisting on living in the city have money. That is why I ensure they pay for their stay. I collect rent from them every week. Even Kenyans of Somali origin. Have you been to Eastleigh? They own such huge malls. These Somalis have lots of money and we all know they don't pay taxes. I just want a share. I am Nairobi's landlord,

I am their Caesar." He chuckled at his own brilliance.

"Good for you! You deserve that share."

"You are my kind of girl. You understand how this country works. People say we are corrupt, but in essence, we are just taking what should be ours."

She wanted to snap his neck and kill him right then. Instead, she rubbed her fingers to control the anger and massaged the small of his neck. She had to be patient. She was instructed not to kill him—that was not her task.

"This feels really good."

"Perfect. That's what I want to hear. Your muscles have relaxed. No more talking now. If you can, try to sleep"

After that, she did not break contact with his body, not even to change position or get more oil from the candles. Keeping a steady rhythm was important. She wanted to create a hypnotic effect, and this worked before long. The commandant was soon snoring serenely.

When he awoke, the commandant was tied to a metal chair with nylon ropes. He was completely naked, as he had been on the massage table. Was this part of lovemaking? He had heard of erotic practices which involved dominance, submission, bondage, and even sadomasochism. He was willing to explore this new frontier, so long as it was with Malaika. Just thinking of her lips, of her musical voice, of her hair which flowed like a *mami wata*'s, of her curvy hips, made him shake with anticipation.

But where was she? And why must they have their *clande* in such a dark, musty room?

"Malaika! Where are you? If you have to tie me up, at least chain me to a comfortable bed."

His call came back as an echo against the bare walls, accompanied by unhurried steps made by a hooded figure, and the creak of a trolley against the floor. Something told him the massage was over and this subsequent phase was not about pleasure.

"What the hell is going on?" the commandant asked fearfully. He looked around for his gun. He remembered placing it inside his trouser pockets at the massage parlor, but none of his stuff was here. He cursed at his folly. "Whoever you are, release me now or you will experience the fullest power of the law!"

When the figure was close, he realized it was a woman in a burka. He broke into a scoffing laugh. What did this woman think she could do to him? He was the deputy police commandant!

The woman was unfazed by his outburst. She stopped the cart right beside the table and removed the burka, exposing a beautiful but cold face.

"My name is Fawzia Sheikh Farah."

"Am I supposed to know who you are?" he asked. The icy eyes that met his squinted glare sent a tremor down his naked spine.

"I am Ahmed Farah's sister."

He thought hard. That name was familiar, but he couldn't place it. He shook his head.

"Wrong answer!" she snapped. "So, you don't remember my brother, even after you sanctioned and witnessed his torture? You don't remember ordering your men to dispose of his body like a dog's in Eastleigh Section One? You don't remember declaring him a suspected terrorist on national television?"

Commandant Ambayo's memory was jogged. It was that university student who they killed to send a message to the

Somali community, to instill fear among the young men.

On the trolley were surgical gloves and a tray full of acu-puncture needles. Fawzia, wearing a pair of the surgical gloves, picked up a needle and raised it, letting it gleam against the light. The commandant shook with fear. He was trypanophobic.

"Acupuncture is used in traditional Chinese medicine to deal with various types of pain. It is believed that energy cur-rents are accessible through 350 points in the body and inject-ing needles into these points with correct variations brings the body into proper balance. However, instead of reducing pain, these needles, if wrongly used—by untrained hands such as mine—can be the devil's pitchfork."

She tenderly touched the commandant's skin, soothing and cajoling with a sweet but diabolical tune. And just when his muscles relaxed, she dug the needle into his body with a single swing of her hand. The scream came from the deepest pit in his stomach and cut through the air like a sharp dagger. The man's pain did not upset her as she had thought it might. Instead, her anger and bitterness ached with desire to inflict even more suffering.

For the next hour, she tortured him needle by needle, each of them ploughed into his skin in spurts of her own agony. His pleas for mercy, his groans of terror in anticipation of another needle, and the subsequent excruciating cry were a cacophony in a uniform sequence.

Finally she stopped, not because of his petitions, not be-cause she was disconcerted by the depths of her own deprav-ity, but because her arms were tired. She sat down on a chair not far from the massage table and watched the commandant as he whimpered like a dog. When all was quiet, she yanked the pillow supporting his head, placed it over his face, and pressed with all her might. He jerked his head sideways, but the torture had sucked all of his energy and will to fight. His body became limp as he floated to nothingness.

My dear Abaayo,

When you sent me money so I could leave Dadaab, that place of pain and sorrow, you gave me back my life. I know I wrote to say thank you, but I want to say it again: because of you, I was able to start afresh.

I was able to take my brother Ahmed to university, even though he didn't get to graduate. You know he died last year. Allah rest his soul in peace. I was also able to support my father and open a business for him. He turned that small shop into a mall. But he grew weary of this life and Allah honored his desire. He went to be with his fore-fathers a fortnight ago.

As for me, I am planning to once again try new fron-tiers like you once encouraged me. I will update you when I get there, wherever that is.

Aristotle once said, "The antidote for fifty enemies is one friend." That, my four-leaf clover, is what you are to me.

Mahadsanid,
Fawzia

When she was torturing the commandant, Fawzia's vengeful heart had been soothed by his agony. But his groans of pain, his cries for mercy, never left her. She heard them over and over again—when she ate, when she slept, and when she awoke. She saw his defeated form when she finally suffocated him. In her dreams, his body welcomed death in helpless surren-der. How she wished for darkness to cover her, to wipe away memories of the past. She prayed for her soul to be liberated, whether to obscurity or to light. After many moons, a night of shutters, of drawn curtains, did finally come, pulling her into the nothingness that would be her final frontier.

The following day, a short paragraph on the back of the *Daily Nation* read:

> *Woman Hit by Bus on Mombasa Road*
> *A woman died yesterday after being struck by a bus on Mombasa Road. The middle-aged woman had a Kenyan passport in her possession and a one-way ticket to To-ronto, Canada. She was clasping in her hand a crum-pled note which read:* When seeking revenge, dig two graves—including one for yourself.

That same evening, in Eastleigh, Fartun told her neighbors that Fawzia had been killed by the police, just like they had killed her brother.

NUMBER SITA

BY KEVIN MWACHIRO

Kilimani

We were known as the Trinity. We had played with the word *triad*, but when we first heard it we didn't quite understand what it meant. Trinity was easy—we'd always heard it in Mass, and when we started calling ourselves that, it made people uncomfortable. We liked that. One of us was named after their father, one of us was the only son in the family, and one of us had a father whom he'd never met. We are all born in 1973, we went to the same primary school and even shared the same high school at one time. Kilimani or Kili was our home. There was nowhere in this hood that was out of bounds for us. The main roads, side roads, and off roads felt the imprint of either our bikes or our Bata sandals. We ventured to the border of Woodley and Kibera. Though Kibera was another world we dared not tread alone, it was too foreign to our cushioned world. Kileleshwa was avoided—it seemed staid thanks to the government housing that provided a middle-class living to public servants. The other neighboring areas of Valley Arcade and Caledonia flirted into and out of our radius and this was mostly thanks to family visits, and later in our lives during the quest for cheap liquor.

We were Mbiu, Morris, and George. I hated my name. Didn't and don't care for it. George offers nothing but commonness. I was sandwiched between siblings and was often off the radar of family and relatives. George made me even more insignificant, and back then it added to my low self-esteem— George! I couldn't wait to drop it once I turned eighteen. I became Nyanje and told my friends that I was not going to carry the name that came from the land of our colonizer. I was named after my father, who was named after his grandfather whom I'd never met, so were all the other firstborn sons of my uncles and aunts. I was George wa Kilimani because we were perceived to be the poshest relatives and I couldn't be called George wa George! There is George wa Buru who is the coolest of us all; then there is George wa Lenadi (Leonard), George wa Frederick, and George wa Charlotte (pronounced Shaleti). George wa Charlotte we pitied. He was fatherless, but his mother was fierce, feisty, and fun. We loved her, for she was also our go-to aunt. Counselor, confidante, and comfort all rolled up into one. Even Mbiu and Morris adored her. She became their aunt as well. In fact, Auntie Charlotte is the only person in the world whom I still let get away with calling me George. Her eyes carry a mischievous glint whenever she calls my name, and when our eyes meet they go into our place of secrets.

"There are parts of our lives we cannot erase, and no number of seasons will make us forget when we mourned," she once said.

"Like when you had George?" I asked. She always let me speak my mind.

"Like George and other things," she answered, and from then I unearthed George for her and her alone. I didn't feel like I disappeared under the name George with her.

I'm back in Kilimani. Another part of my life that I had buried. It's interesting how life pulls several numbers on you.

I never thought I'd leave this place and consequently turn my back on its memories and its ghosts. This is where I said goodbye to George. It was here that I also said goodbye to the middle-child syndrome. Unbeknownst to me, until my later years, even within the Trinity, I was the "middle" friend. Easily forgotten.

"Take a left on Marcus Garvey and then look for Kamburu Drive. It will be on your left," says the passenger seated next to me. *I know exactly where I am!* I want to shout, I could drive here blindfolded for crying out loud, but I'll play the taxi driver that I am. Rose Avenue has changed. This used to be a dusty Nairobi orange *marram* road. This was *akina* Morris's road. There were more jacaranda trees than roses on this road then. Unfortunately, neither roses nor jacarandas flourish now but tall office blocks have sprouted up on properties that once housed single bungalows and marionettes—or town houses, as they are called these days. Residential flats now have businesses as their tenants. There aren't any kids anymore on these streets, the only ones being mischievous and unruly on these streets are the *matatus* and *boda bodas*, our motorbike taxis.

"You take directions very well, unlike all the other drivers that I've used recently," says the gentleman. I smirk. I don't think he cares for an answer. He is already peering at his phone, probably happy that he has engaged me with small talk. Hoping he has secured a good passenger rating for the taxi app. A typical Nairobi upstart. He gets his haircut weekly, has manicured nails and a naked chin. He is a smart dresser, I admired his tan shoes when he stepped into the car, the trousers case his thick legs and emphasize a distended ass. His plaid shirt stretches over an emerging belly. Ahh, he has a body shape that epitomizes Nairobi success. The *tumbo na tako* syndrome. In this business, you profile your clients perennially. Whom to talk and whom not to talk to, and you pick up on the women who need attention more than a ride. Then there are those who treat you like a chauffeur. The things new money does to you. I find myself clicking my tongue rather loudly. He is new money.

"*Hapa, hapa,*" he barks. "Here at TWR." I stop in front of the gate. "Bless you and goodbye."

"But you haven't paid yet," I point out. He seems to be in a rush. I stop my meter on the app and show him the fare. He quickly flashes a 500-shilling note and hurriedly opens the door.

"Keep the change, my brother," he says. He seems anxious as he heads toward the gate that houses the Christian radio station. As I turn the car around, he doesn't move toward the gate. He just stands there rummaging through his pockets. I can tell he is stalling. I give him his peace and hastily drive off. I know his game. This was my hood, after all. Across the road is a nondescript brothel: Number Sita. Interesting that after all these years it is still there. It has withstood time and still hides its delights. The signboard with the number 6 beside the gate is new. Number Sita. From my rear mirror, I watch the chap cross the road and disappear behind the solid steel black gates. Maybe he'll find his balls! Number Sita still rules men.

"God bless you too," I find myself saying as I break out into laughter.

"We are all going in," said Mbiu. "No ifs, no buts, for we are going to get butt." We stupidly made a pact that this was where the three of us were going to become real men. Circumcision was one thing, but dipping your pen into the inkwell was the more important rite of passage. Number Sita offered the safer option. The hookers at the nearby Ngong Hills Hotel were too expensive. We'd have to buy them beer, probably more than once, and then pay for the room. We were high schoolers and living off our parents' pockets. None of us had a house girl attractive enough to seduce. So, Number Sita it was. We only had three hundred shillings between us. If we were lucky, we might all walk out with a blow job at the very least and still get home in time for dinner. Nana had told us about Number Sita. It was also Nana who taught us how to appreciate the female form and about foreplay.

"You men learn how to fuck from dogs and seem to be content with that," she'd quipped once. We were too embarrassed to admit the truth of her words for we had all watched Morris's dogs mate a few years before. Nana was also the first lesbian we'd met, and we trusted her as she entrusted us with her truth. Who better to teach about women than a woman? We felt so grown-up knowing her. Nana shaved her head clean weekly, wore men's underwear, saying they were more comfortable, was forever in sweatpants and T-shirts that were capped by a threadbare jean jacket, and she always had a basketball with her. She was a point guard with the Posta Panthers basketball team. Nana's feet, hands, and tongue were fast. This was how she managed to survive off and on the court. She was beautiful. Chocolate skin that radiated, a toned body, baby-melon tits, and the kind of full lips that you wanted to kiss and be kissed by. She wore a toothy smile with an attractively centered gap. Her *mwanya*. She whistled like no one we knew, and she always had a tune. We were all in awe of her. She was safe, open, and kind, just like Auntie Charlotte.

I wonder what Number Sita is like now. Are the corridors and rooms still lit with blue and red light? My heart had drummed as we walked into Number Sita that afternoon.

None of us knew what to expect and yet we had to pretend to be men, something we didn't even know how to be. But we had dicks, newly acquired baritone voices, and money! The lady of the house eyed us up and down and smiled as she welcomed us in.

"*Karibuni, wanaume wangu,*" she said. It's like she knew we needed to be addressed as men just to settle our butterflies. We were led into a room stuffed with oversize sofas, Lingala music from a boom box filled the air, and perched on those sofas were girls and women. Stares so seductive and confusing approached us. Some eyes rolled and chose to ignore us, while other eyes waved their lashes, promising heaven. The Trinity was temporarily broken by a mixture of desire and personal confusion. *Kila mtu alikuwa anajitetea.*

I remember each room had a curtain in front of its doors ensuring privacy, yet the walls kept no secrets for you could hear grunts and moans as you walked past closed doors. It was a church of sorts, because I heard God being called on many times. I was led through this labyrinth of pleasure and sin by the hooker I'd selected in the lounge. It was her long, brown, slim legs that drew me to her. She sat alone away from the other women. I was attracted to her even more because she smiled at me, and her eyes stilled me. She seemed safe. Looking back to that day, I think she picked me.

Nana dated a girl who worked at Number Sita. We had never met her. We saw Nana spend evenings and one-bob coins at the phone booth outside the Ngong Hills Hotel chatting with her girl. You could tell if she had been on the phone. She was so dribbly with her basketball and all teeth. At twenty-three she was seven years older than we were and still full of dreams and shamed love. Both she and her sister Betty received an allowance from their father who lived in

America. They hardly spoke of their mother, and we didn't ask. Nana was the first woman we all unknowingly fell in love with. It was strange and not so strange. Unsurprisingly, her ghost always came up whenever I went down on women. She taught us how a woman's body should never be rushed. Tease it, be adventurous with it, take time to discover, and "heaven," as she called it, will open itself up to you. These are lessons that have since brought me lots of pleasure and caused too much heartache.

My phone beeps, bringing me back to my hustle.

I drive toward Woodley Estate opting to avoid the mayhem that is Ngong Road. Kibera and its corrugated splendor usher me into more bougainvillea-lined roads and the dated grayed bungalows of Woodley. It has never lost its simplicity. How it has held up against the encroaching slum and Chinese contractors, one will never know. Maybe it's because most of its residents either work or have a history with the Nairobi city council. I call my next punter.

"Hello, Stesh, this Nyanje from Taxify—I mean Uber." I'm on too many taxi apps, chasing too little money. "Can I get your exact location please?"

Despite Woodley being a sensibly planned neighborhood, there are no house numbers. As I disconnect the call, I'm impressed by the precision of her directions. Maybe she grew up in this hood?

Her house has a silver *mabati* gate. I notice that it is the only property on the road that is, in fact, numbered 21. Number Sita to 21 all in one day, who'd have thought? I smile. The verdant fence and jacaranda tree dwarf the corrugated entrance. Woodley still seems to harbor the best of both worlds. Its residents are what I'd like to call "old" middle class.

Bureaucrats and technocrats who kept the same jobs from college to pension. They were the baby boomers who had a deeper sense of service and witnessed Kenya being birthed. They lived through the swinging sixties; each of our fathers came from this time. They either owned a Peugeot, Renault, VW Beetle, or Fiat. It's the thing you did then.

"*Sasa? Uko poa? Nipeleke hapa* Adams *tuu. Sawa? Asante.*" Adams Arcade Shopping Centre, Ado to locals, is a mere ten-minute walk from where we are. We both know this, but I say nothing. She's the customer. "*Halafu, tufika* Ado *naingia supaa tuu dakika mbili then utanirudhisha hapa home. Sitaka-wia.*" I don't believe a word she says. I'm in for a long wait as she shops.

Stesh is your typical Nairobi girl. Her life is hers, and so is the life of every man who comes her way. She reminds me of Betty, Nana's sister, Morris's secret lover. I only got to discover that they had had a thing many years on. Betty was twenty-two and we were sixteen when they dated. Morris was full of secrets—his and other people's. He was our conscience.

Stesh is a full woman. Her legs make the sweatpants look like tights, and I don't want to imagine the friction being caused as her thighs brush against one another. Her waist resembles that Michelin Man ad and her tits are voluptuous, her hoodie encasing them well. Her weave crowns her head, with tresses that cascade around her face. She's pretty, yet plain. She looks like one of those women who is never seen in public without makeup. Mbiu would like her. He likes this African form of beauty. He often says, "If you are going to climb a mountain, why not climb Kilimanjaro? Hills have no thrills." He thinks of himself as a wordsmith. He is foolish and spews a bravado that I foolishly worship. He apes his older brother in order to hide his poor self-esteem, and we say nothing and let him be the de facto leader of Trinity.

"*Uko, mfit,*" Stesh compliments me. "*Unaenda* gym?" As she asks, her hands quickly prod and paw my biceps. I regret wearing this polo shirt.

"*Asante,*" I respond, not wanting to appear rude. "*Naenada kiasi,* just enough. *Nikujaribu, au sio?*"

She chuckles, and I quickly change the radio station to a Christian one, hoping it will distract her. She chuckles again.

"Even Adam needed Eve. You are gay?" she asks.

We both laugh. She's witty; I'll give her that and only that. I notice her right hand is no longer on me, but resting between her thighs. I'm shocked that it can fit between them considering the girth of those things! I steel my gaze forward, focusing on the hawkers and buyers that line Toi Market. Trying to ignore Stesh, I remember how Woodley was once a clean and orderly neighborhood. It had respect then; now it's a *mitumba,* a secondhand haven, with overgrown hedges and lengths of elephant grass.

"*Kuna joto leo,*" Stesh says. Her voice is attempting to sound seductive. From the corner of my eye I see her hand massaging her thigh. We both know that she's not talking about the weather. And I am back at Number Sita.

"How old are you, *kijana*? Feeling hot today?" asked the hooker who stared at me as she placed her calabash-shaped bottom on her bed.

"*Mimi si kijana,*" I replied with an added gruffness to my voice, trying to mask my nervousness. She was beautiful, sensual, and carried a seductiveness that quickly birthed a hard-on. I was scared that I'd cum even before I'd get to undress. I sat next to her and touched her. Her skin was soft and warm. Her perfume too flowery and she smelled of pomade. I looked her in the eye, inched toward her, and said nothing. The less I spoke the better, and I realized that was the only way I'd win her respect. My mouth needed to get to work. I was about to kiss her, but decided against it; I didn't want to appear romantic. I changed tactic, kneeled before her, and clumsily but forcefully parted her creamy thighs. They were so tender. I quickly saw the surprised look on her face; her eyes widened. I smiled. A wave of calm settled in, tempering my excitement. A surge of raw teenage power took over. *This is what it is to be a man*, I thought.

"*Ya leo ni mengi . . .*" she started to say. I didn't let her finish the sentence, and proceeded to bury myself in her depths, just the way Nana had taught us. "God" came into our room. Her lack of underwear made things even easier. She became even softer.

"Nyanje, *si* you'll help me with my shopping when we *fika* home?" Stesh asks, removing me from Kilimani past to Kilimani present.

"*Sawa*, madam," I respond. Hoping that by calling her *madam* she'll feel old and insulted. She looks like she's nearing thirty. Stesh won't age well, I note.

"*Poa!* Super!" she says gleefully. I am being pawed again. Then the smell comes. The ghosts that perfumed Number Sita.

Almost an hour after our arrival we met outside Number Sita. Morris was already seated on the culvert beside TWR. I nodded at Morris, and he smiled back. I silently sat next to him. Mbiu was the last to emerge. He came up to us and immediately passed his index finger under our noses. We inhaled and said nothing. We smiled, seemingly victorious in our quest. No tales were exchanged. We had become men, or so we thought. How that happened, *if* it happened, only Number Sita knew. Our Saturdays would never be the same. We'd all go back to Number Sita, but never again as a group. We had started building our private worlds. But that day we all walked off victorious, singing Ini Kamoze's "Here Comes the Hot Stepper," though we only sang, "*Na, na, na, na, na, nah.*"

I notice, as we approach the Adams Arcade Shopping Centre, that my palms are feeling clammy. A wave of anxiety crashes into me. Stesh is no longer interested in me and has turned her attention to her phone, which is more responsive than I am. I drop her off outside the Tuskys Supermarket and we agree that I'll let her know where I park. This arcade was our old stomping ground. It was here we had dates at the Taurus Restaurant. We bought our first beers from Tumbo's Bar. There was the corner store that only closed on New Years Day, the supermarket, the post office, the butcher, the bookstore, the antique store, the Metropole Cinema with its cheap action movies, and the area behind the cinema—the spot. I am back in my once-upon-a-time. The only parking spots available are taking me back to the one place that I didn't want to go.

It was Friday night. We were at Adams. We had enough money between us for a beer each and a few sachets of vodka—minipacks, as they were called. We weren't happy drinking inside Tumbo's Bar with the *wazee*, as the old men were unruly and lecherous toward the women in the bar. We stationed ourselves under a loquat tree that was in the recesses of the parking lot. We shared cigarettes, booze, and laughter. Mbiu was in full form that day with another one of his tales, and as always we were his ready audience. From our vantage point we got an unobstructed view of the walkway that lined the shops. We saw Nana and a young woman whom we assumed was her girlfriend. Nana carried her trademark rucksack which probably held her training gear and basketball.

"That's Nana and the . . ." Mbiu didn't finish his sentence. We all knew where we had seen the leggy, slim, curvaceous woman walking beside her. Number Sita. No one said anything, but our silent stares confirmed that we had all bitten from the same fruit. This was one of those times when eyes couldn't hold back secrets.

Nana walked into Tumbo's alone and to our surprise came out with Auntie Charlotte. I ignored Mbiu and Morris. The women's body language seemed comfortable with one another. They seemed to be a trinity too. Auntie Charlotte and Nana's girlfriend walked into Tumbo's and Nana headed around the back of the building. She air-dribbled as she walked, and we knew she was in her happy place. The back route through Woodley was the shortest way home for her. The rear of the building was also where a lot of sex took place and where weed was smoked. It was Ado's main spot, but we weren't yet of age to venture there. We went back to ourselves and let our girl be.

But we also saw Mbiu's older brother and two other men walk out of Tumbo's and head to the back, probably to smoke weed, we thought. We returned our attention to Mbui and his storytelling.

Almost twenty minutes later we saw Nana's basketball roll itself from the back. We had never seen the ball wander by itself. Where was Nana and why wasn't she coming to pick up her ball? We watched in silence as it continued to roll. Then it stopped, along with our hearts. A few minutes later, Mbiu's brother and the other two men emerged from the darkness. There was a shiftiness to their walk, but also a confidence. One of them kicked the ball hard into the darkness. They walked back into Tumbo's laughing among themselves. Mbiu stood up and moved away from us, heading toward the bus stop.

"Morris!" I called. Hoping that he'd know what to do. I noticed his eyes were glassy.

Morris gave a feeble but sharp shout and, to my surprise, chased after Mbiu. I was alone. I found myself running toward Tumbo's and Auntie Charlotte. Safety. I buried Mbiu and Morris after that night.

I now find myself parked under the same loquat tree. There are too many ghosts coming out today. I know I'll have to eventually drive back past to exit. I'm sweating profusely and breathing heavily, and then I'm breaking down. After all these years, I unearth my tears for Nana. It is only when I look up from my steering wheel and through my salted eyes that I notice the basketball courts behind the building.

ANDAKI

BY KINYANJUI KOMBANI

Dandora

I t was the tap on the shoulder that stopped the young man in his tracks, a sharp, urgent tap that bore into his collarbone. The pain shot through his shoulder, and he whipped his head around.

The panting, sweaty face of a shorter, darker man met his.

"Ah! Kocha!" his face broke into a smile.

The shorter man waved his hand as if in surrender. He bent over, his hands on his knees, still panting like a petrified thief who had just survived a mob attack. He coughed and mumbled something.

The young man removed the large headphones that covered half his head.

"I've been . . . calling . . . out for . . . you," Kocha's words came in short bursts. He coughed again. "Those head-phones will be the death of you. Can you even hear a car approaching?"

The young man shrugged and turned his head toward the road. Kocha followed his gaze. He probably got an answer to the question he had posed, because he looked down again and coughed some more.

The road was flanked on both sides by hundreds of traders with wares sprawled on the ground, on wheelbarrows, and on platforms made from materials ranging from pallets, roughly hewn stones, metal frames, and sticks. Only a madman would drive on the road at a speed high enough to knock anyone down.

"Are you okay?" the young man asked Kocha. He pulled a device from his pocket and touched a button.

"*Niko fomu*," I am fine, came the labored answer. "*Za wapi?*" Where are you going?

"*Niko tu hivi, raundi mwenda,*" the young man responded—I am just making my rounds.

Kocha's eyes fell on the bag the young man was holding, then stayed there for enough time to make the young man's eyes flinch. Then both men looked away.

"I've been searching everywhere for you," Kocha told him. Then, after taking a long breath, he continued, "Our game was moved forward to this afternoon. I have to raise a team."

"Wah!" The young man's jaw dropped.

"Yes, you should get a phone, man. This idea of running all over to look for you, *haileti shangwe*. It is not pleasing at all."

If the young man heard the complaint about the phone, it didn't register on his face. He stared into the distance, as if there was a phone for him in the middle of the street. "How many people have you gathered?" he asked.

"Three," Kocha responded weakly.

"Three?" The young man's face looked like he had been hit by the butt of a policeman's G3 rifle. "What time is kickoff?"

"Three o'clock." Kocha straightened up. He was still breathing heavily. With a sweep of his finger, he wiped the sweat off his brow, then snapped the finger expertly to splash the sweat into the ditch next to them. "And you know this is a do-or-die game for us. Will you make it?" Kocha's eyes briefly scoured the bag that the younger man held, before moving up.

Their eyes locked for a moment and then Jobo looked away.

"I have to take care of something first," the young man said, staring past Kocha.

Jobo didn't stop gazing off even when Kocha slid into an alley next to an electrical repair shop marked, *Kaka Fundi wa Radio*. His mind was elsewhere. He was looking past the man and far into the crowd. After a few seconds he slipped his headphones back on and walked ahead, clutching the bag tighter.

Still, he did not move toward his destination. He made a long detour into Grao.

Grao lay smack in the middle of Dandora Phase 1 and 2. A tall stone fence now surrounded the grounds, the product of turf wars between the big church neighboring it and the many land grabbers.

Jobo remembered the fights that had been waged for control of Grao, pitting angry men against each other, each bolstered by teams of hirelings armed with crude weapons. Most times, the winner was decided by the size of the gang he could hire. Having the right land-ownership papers was no evidence of ownership—each party had genuine title deeds signed and stamped by the Ministry of Lands, which they did not hesitate to wave at their opponents.

Currently, the church had hold on the land, courtesy of the area Member of Parliament who had made it a campaign pledge to secure the grounds. The church had quickly put up the fence. But Jobo knew that the ownership was only temporary, until someone with more clout than the MP prevailed. Only time would tell. The cartels were biding their time. It would not be a surprise to soon see a block of houses being built, using stones from the wall. This was Dandora.

How his brother Roba had found himself among the marauding gangs one afternoon remained a story to be told for generations to come. He had been hanging out at base when someone came in with the news that there was some quick money to be made. All one needed to do was obtain any ugly-looking weapon that would scare people away. The prospect of earning five hundred shillings was too tempting, and Roba found himself shouting himself hoarse at another group of youth, daring them to come closer if they wanted to meet their maker. It was after a lot of shouting and daring that he had been told the other side was paying a thousand shillings, and he immediately switched sides.

Oftentimes, those confrontations did not turn violent. After all, the gangs knew their rival gangs and would meet in the estates after the financiers had departed. At other times, though, especially when the gangs were from other estates like Kariobangi and Huruma, things could indeed turn violent.

The police, who mostly just hung around watching the gangs threaten each other with fire and brimstone, would swing into action if the situation became bloody. When this happened, the estate would shut down.

Jobo was startled out of his reverie by the sight of a ball zooming toward him. A series of loud gasps escaped from the nearby football field. The ball was coming straight at his head.

Instinctively, he bent down. The ball whizzed by, just an inch from his head. He somehow stopped it with his right foot, bouncing it over his head and over to his waiting left leg. Then he flipped it to his right leg and hit it back into the field, all this time carefully watching the bag in his right hand.

"Wow!" A wave of admiration crossed the field. A few people clapped.

The field was filled with spectators and football players in kits of different colors. He had been so deep in his thoughts that he hadn't even noticed he had strayed into the field.

He clutched the bag tightly and crossed the road again. He was now facing the direction he had come. If someone was following him, they would realize that he had been walking in circles all along.

He took another quick glance behind him. There was nobody. Satisfied, he slid into an alley.

A few moments later he emerged into a small clearing. On his left side, a black gate stood high in the sky, only matched in height by a wall built with roughly hewn stone. The colorful bougainvillea leaves peered above the stone fence. In many parts, the leaves overhung the wall, crawling almost to his height, leaving an uneven, unkempt shape.

Opposite the gate, on all four sides, were buildings facing the road, away from the black gate. The only way into the compound was the alley Jobo had come in through. Nobody knew who the owner of the plot of land in the middle was. In the estate, there were such pockets of land, marooned for the moment, until someone claimed them.

Jobo picked a small stone and hit it against the wall. Three sharp raps. He glanced toward the alley.

Every time he came here, while waiting for the gate to be opened, he always expected someone to jump in from the alley. He always had a knot in his stomach, which was only unwrapped by a cough on the other side of the fence.

"*Amani*," he mumbled the password. Peace.

There was a slight pause on the other side of the gate, and then Jobo heard a click as a key turned in the lock, then the welcome sound of a bolt sliding out of place. The gate opened slowly and someone peeped past Jobo's frame and toward the alley.

"You are late," the man said plainly, as he stepped back

to let Jobo in. The statement was neither an accusation nor a lament.

"You are lucky I even came," Jobo responded. "There is a game this afternoon. *Tona*."

"*Tona*? So your tournament is more important than us?"

Jobo did not look in any way perturbed. Instead of answering, he pushed past the younger man and walked toward the house. He could feel the guy's eyes on him.

The house was old. It was not like many of the Dandora houses which were multiple stories. Its wall was lined with plaster and smothered with white chalk—if you looked closely you could see the finger shapes of the people who did the plastering.

There was a small compound which could fit two cars, but it was clear that no vehicle had driven into this compound in the recent past. A small, freshly weeded and watered vegetable garden stood where ordinarily there would be a car park. Rows of healthy looking kale and spinach stalks waved cheerfully.

With his left foot, Jobo kicked aside a watering can, perhaps more forcefully than was necessary. The younger man walking behind him clicked his tongue as he picked up the can and placed it aside.

Above the metal door was a small handwritten sign: *ANDAKI*.

"Ah! Finally!" someone said from inside the house even before Jobo went in. He recognized Roba's voice.

Before he could respond, a few other shapes emerged from somewhere in the house. Within a second, the bag was yanked away from his hand and its contents removed. There were four large bowls and two large flasks.

"*Kuna nini leo?*" Roba asked as he smacked his lips. What

is there for us? But he clearly was not waiting for a response. He was already opening the lid.

"You guys are hyenas." Jobo relaxed into a sofa as the four young men congregated around the dining table behind him. The sofa was not comfortable. Age had eaten into the cushions, and he could feel the hard wood press into his bones.

Someone else came from the kitchen with several plates. "*Wazi* Jobo," he complimented Jobo, who received the gratitude with a wave of his own hands.

They ate ravenously, none of them speaking. For a long time, only the chewing and cracking of bones could be heard. It was as if Jobo did not exist.

There were five men in total. The tallest of the lot—the one who had opened the gate for him—was called Bryo. Only his mother called him by his proper name, Brian, and only when she was angry at him—which was most of the time by the way. Bryo was fifteen years old and until recently was in form two at the local secondary school.

Next to him was Max. At twenty-five, Max was the oldest. He was short and dark, and both sides of his face were lined with sideburns most likely shaped at Sams Kinyozi, the barber shop near Grao that everyone went to. Max didn't speak much, but when he did you knew why—he had a pronounced stutter.

Next to Max was Boi. Boi really hated being called that, and always insisted, sometimes using his fist, that his real name was Danson. But everyone called him Boi for as long as anyone could remember. It was one of those pet childhood names that stuck. He was slightly plump, unlike the others who were all lean. Over the course of the week Jobo had heard a lot of taunts about the "man boobs" that protruded from Boi's chest.

Roba was tall and thin, just like Jobo. People always con-fused them, especially because they wore the same hairstyle—cropped short. Most people said that the two brothers had their mother's sharp and fierce eyes, and eyebrows that seemed to curve inward, accentuating their fierce looks. Once, someone had suggested that they shave differently to avoid the confu-sion. But the suggestion died a natural death because neither of them was willing to change his hairstyle.

"*Mzae*, pass me the salt," someone said.

Jobo looked up and saw Max wearing a murderous look on his face.

"*Mzae ni wewe*," Max shot back. "*You* are the old man."

Jobo smiled. He had been told that the previous day, Max had used the fact that he was older than everyone else in the house to win an argument, and now they were using this as an insult.

"Hmmm!" Kim, the guy with one missing tooth, said. "Your mum is a very good cook."

"I will pass her the compliment," Jobo replied. His mum would be very happy to hear it.

Kim continued: "At least this week I can sleep in peace. Last week was something else."

There were a few guffaws from around the table.

"What happened last week?" Jobo asked nonchalantly. He only wanted to make conversation; otherwise it didn't re-ally matter to him.

"The kind of food we were eating, hmm!" Kim answered, "you wouldn't know what it was until you ate it. And at night you couldn't sleep because of thinking, *If I die now, what will have killed me?*"

"*Kwenda huko!*" another man dismissed him. "Don't talk like that about my mum's cooking. We all know your mother doesn't know how to cook, and during her week she had to buy it . . ."

"Ah, that's better," Kim shot back. "Better than to cook *mashakura*."

The room erupted into laughter. *Mashakura* was an increasingly popular yet ridiculed mixture of all imaginable dishes, served in one large plate.

Bryo and Kim picked up the dishes and went to the kitchen. Jobo remembered that the previous day, it was Max and Boi who had cleaned up. Roba wiped the table with a very white cloth.

"You guys have fascinating lives here," Jobo said. "Out there, you are all macho. It's hard to imagine the lot of you washing dishes and cleaning up."

"Life happens," Boi said. "Having to choose between washing dishes and being in a six-by-six hole, I'd rather wash the dishes over and over again." Then he stood and headed into the bedroom.

Jobo walked to the sitting room, where a collage of photos was pasted on a faded notice board. Some of the photos had come off, leaving patches where they had been pinned.

"Why do you always look at that photo?" Roba asked him.

"I don't know. It just makes me wonder. Why did this man carry his things? These photos must hold a lot of memories for the owner of the house."

The owner of the house—and Jobo only guessed it because he was the common feature in most of the photos—was stout with a balding head.

"Maybe we will never know," Roba speculated. "It is said he moved with only a suitcase to his up-country home. Anyway, how is the tournament going?"

"We are playing our first game today," Jobo told him, then

added, "That is, if we can find enough players. Kocha was looking for more players today."

"Kocha is so dedicated. Perhaps *too* dedicated. It might disappoint him. And if it does, it will destroy him. Football is all he has."

"Let's hope we succeed," Jobo said. "If this time we make it further up the league, who knows what would happen? You know, they are scouting for talent for the national team."

Roba nodded. "There was a fight here yesterday," he said out of the blue.

"What? Why?"

"People ganged up against Boi."

"Why would they do that?"

"Boi is not one of us. Everyone hates him and he knows it."

"What do you mean *one of you*? Aren't you all here for the same reason? To stay safe and alive?"

"Yes we are, but all of us are here for the *wrong* reason."

Jobo wanted to react, but stopped when he noticed that his brother was going to say something more.

"The rest of us are victims of mistaken identity, Jobo. But he is a *mgondi*."

"He's a gangster?"

"Yes. Remember the petrol station that was robbed in Westlands a few months ago, where four attendants were shot dead? He was involved."

"Wow. Do the mothers know?"

"They do. He is only here because his mother is from Dando and a member of Mama Bora, otherwise we'd have thrown him out of the Andaki."

Jobo looked away. "You don't throw people out of the Andaki. That is why it's called Andaki. It's a safe house."

Roba turned his head down.

For a long time in Jobo's life, he had seen Roba as the big brother—the dependable bully, the one who harassed him all the time but also defended him from other bullies in school, the one his mother always trusted to take care of him. Now, to see him broken, cloistered up at the Andaki, was something nobody wished to behold.

Jobo removed the headphones from the machine. Another Kalamashaka song was playing:

Nakumbuka saa mbili usiku nikiona
ule mzee akishikwa koo,
balaa! Nashindwa, nikimbilie nani,
jambazi, hapana!
Polisi, hapana!
Watanitia pingu hata bila sababu.

I remember at eight o'clock seeing a man being mugged.
I wondered who to run to,
the thugs? No!
the police? No!
They would put me in cuffs even if I was innocent.

The three men were silent.

"These musicians were always ahead of their time," Max said.

Everyone nodded in agreement.

"But they lived in better times," Bryo added as he walked to a water dispenser beside the dining table. "At least those days all you feared from the police was being handcuffed. Nowadays, if they come for you, *ni kukang'wa*." He flashed his forefinger across his neck to gesture slitting.

"So what do you guys do every day, holed up here?"

"Nothing much," Kim said. "We play games, sleep, watch movies, and sleep some more. I know you are about to say that we must be living the life, doing all those things that our mothers would be haranguing us about at home, but nothing is further from the truth. There is nothing worse than being holed up here."

Max came in at that moment and jumped in: "There is a dartboard outside that we can't play lest passersby hear us. It is a prison without the wardens—"

"You boys need to stop whining," Boi's voice cut in. He was standing in the doorway, arms akimbo. "Would you rather be dead?" The silence was enough to answer him. "Because that is what awaits you outside, beyond the gate."

Nobody spoke.

"Yes," he was now emboldened, "you should be on your knees, thanking God for everything, and praying for more miracles—like for the owner of this house not to decide to bring it down and build apartments like the rest are doing. You need to pray for the women of Mama Bora to be more united and for them to continue to make more money to pay for the rent and food. Otherwise you will all be felled like houseflies."

When he was agitated, his "man boobs" shook even more. Jobo would have smiled were it not for the gravity of the situation.

When he saw that his words had hit home, Boi exclaimed, "*Haiya!* Why are you not on your knees?" This relaxed the air, and a few people smiled.

"I didn't know you to be religious," Roba said.

"I am not religious," the young man responded. "I mean, not in the way other people are. But I have seen things that have shaken my entire belief system. How come, out of all my friends, I was the only one spared? Why me?"

"Someone said that everyone has a day written down when he will go," Kim said. "That was perhaps not your day."

"Or there is this thing about purpose," Jobo said. "They say everyone has a purpose—maybe you have not achieved yours."

Boi looked at each one of them with his piercing eyes. "Why did Kisii spare me? Why didn't he shoot me like he shot the rest, yet all of us were lying down waiting for the bullets to splatter our brains away?"

Jobo noticed that everyone looked toward the door. The mention of the name *Kisii* had a drastic effect on everyone in Dandora.

Jobo had never met Kisii. Not many people had seen him. It is said that the only people who had seen him did not live to tell others what he looked like.

That is why those who have been through the other end of Kisii's gun and lived to tell the story were treated specially here, as if they had just returned from the world of the dead.

Kisii was loved by few and hated by many. His reign of terror over Dandora and other Eastlands estates had spanned more than ten years. Jobo started hearing about him when he was still in lower primary school. If a child misbehaved, the mother would threaten to call the policeman Kisii and the kid would behave instantly.

Eastlands had been, for a long time, home to many vigilante groups; from the 42 Brothers to, lately, the Mungiki. The latter was a semireligious outfit that had, in the early days, aims of taking the people back to their traditional culture. But it is said that the group, known for their dreadlocks, morphed from cultural-religious to a political outfit. And when the politicians were tired of them—or achieved what they wanted—they turned their backs on them. Now its members had to go underground because the police came at them with guns blazing.

For some, Mungiki was evil incarnate—they controlled everything from shops to the public transportation system. Before you brought your *matatu* (public service van) to any route, you had to give them protection money. And each day one had to pay money to their agents, failure to which your *matatu* would be burned to ashes. For others, Mungiki was the savior—in an area unpoliced by the government, thugs had reigned supreme. The Mungiki as a vigilante group was said to reduce petty crime in the estates. And it was said that none of its members went home hungry—they would ensure that those who could drive got *skuodi*: a short round-trip assignment to a vehicle while the official bus driver took a lunch break.

Jobo remembered hearing the clip of a government minister on TV declaring a shoot-to-kill order against the Mungiki, which had grown so huge that it even distributed electricity stolen from the national grid. "We will wipe them out. I cannot tell you today where those who have been arrested are. What you will be hearing is that there is a burial tomorrow. If you use a gun to kill, you are also required to be executed."

Perhaps Jobo was too young, then, to understand the gravity of the statement—he only heard about it from his schoolteacher. But he was not too young to experience the impact of it. Kisii was born out of it. For a lot of young people in Dandora, it was a case of when, not if, Kisii and his people would come for you.

So the Mungiki went underground. They no longer paraded around with their trademark dreadlocks and snuff-sniffing ways.

When they came for Roba, Jobo was in school, so he was

spared the trauma. Apparently, one of Roba's friends had been implicated in a mugging. What Roba told Jobo later was that his friend Jack had bought a secondhand phone, and it turned out that the phone had been stolen, so the police tracked it. When they arrested Jack, they made him name his best friends, just before killing him. And Roba's name was saved in the stolen phone.

Jobo was told that it was his mother's cries that stopped the policeman from shooting his brother. At the last moment, Kisii had decided against killing Roba. "Get out of here. *Rudi ocha*. Go back to your ancestral home. If I see you here again, I will shoot you. You hear?"

It is said that a petrified Roba nodded desperately, and then remembered something, "*Lakini afande, sina ocha . . .* I don't have an ancestral home, I was born here and my mother was born here as—"

This infuriated the policeman so much that he cocked his gun and aimed at Roba's head, which elicited another anguished cry from the mother.

"Wait! Don't shoot! I will take him. I will take him back home."

People in Dandora still speak today of Jobo's mother's bravery. Who would dare grab Kisii's pistol?

And that is how Roba found himself in Andaki.

Bryo had a different story. He met an uncle of his on the way to school. The uncle, who seemed to be in a crazy rush, gave him a bundle to keep in his school bag. "I will come for it later," the uncle said before running off. Bryo was to learn later, when the police came to pick him up at school, that underneath the banana leaves and wrapping paper was a gun, and that they had shot his uncle dead.

Bryo wasn't on the list of people the police were eyeing.

Still, he had to leave because he had been entered into Kisii's notebook.

Very few people knew about Andaki. If Roba had not been taken to the safe house, neither he nor Jobo would have been aware of its existence.

Jobo knew that Mama Bora was a group drawn from the women of Dandora. What he did not know was that each month they contributed toward rent for Andaki. It served the people who had no up-country home to go to when ordered so by the police. And each week, one of the women whose sons were at the safe house provided food for all the occupants.

> *Bullets hu-fly*
> *babies hu-die*
> *mothers hu-cry*
> *na siku zina pass by.*

> *Bullets fly,*
> *babies die*
> *mothers cry*
> *as days pass by.*

"Hey! I got to go now!" Jobo said, standing up suddenly as if the song were a wake-up call. "The game awaits."

"All right, Roba," Kim replied. He walked into the kitchen and brought out the bag of dishes.

"As always, we are very thankful," Bryo said as he stretched out his hand for a fist bump.

The bag was lighter.

Joba glanced at Roba as he prepared to leave. His brother stood as well and led him out.

"All the best," Roba said. "Perhaps you will get your big

break soon. And get us out of this estate once and for all."

Jobo nodded. "Kocha told us that you never know who is watching the tournament games. It could be one of those scouts."

Roba opened the gate and ushered Jobo out. But a rush of footsteps made them pause.

Before they could react, there was a blur of fast movement and the gate swung open wider. Roba immediately fell to the ground. There was another flash of movement and Jobo felt a gush of wind as a blow connected with his stomach.

"Stupid! *Lala chini*! Get on the ground!" came a rough order.

Jobo looked up, still grimacing in pain. There were six or so men—he was not sure—standing over the two boys, each holding machine guns at the ready.

He did not need to be told who they were.

"Lie down with your hands on your head!"

The boys quickly obeyed.

From the corner of his eye, Jobo saw the men move into the house. But then they disappeared from his line of vision. He was about to raise his head to see what was happening when the sole of a shoe rammed into his skull.

"Stupid!" someone yelled above him.

He actually felt his brain move even as a thousand stars flew inside his head. He shut his eyes tightly to ward off the pain.

"*Wacha ujinga!*" he heard Roba's urgent whisper. Stop being stupid.

In another minute Jobo heard a series of loud crashes and shouts from the house. Someone screamed.

And then suddenly a gunshot split through the air. Jobo pushed his face deeper into the concrete.

Orders were barked.

"*Lala chini!*" Lie down!

"*Toka nje!*" Get out!

"Where are the others?"

Jobo felt several bodies falling next to him, and heard their groans as they hit the ground

"Here is the last of the lot," someone said a moment before another body hit the ground. "Stupid fool, hiding in the ceiling. What kind of low-life criminal are you?"

They were ordered to lie on their stomachs but with their hands on their heads.

Jobo could not resist it anymore. He opened his eyes slowly. They were surrounded.

"*Vijana!*" Young men! "*Leo mtajua cha mtema kuni.*"

They had said that when you see Kisii, you will know it. From the way the rest of the officers looked at him, it was obvious that the man who had just spoken was the squad leader.

Kisii.

He was middle-aged with a slight build. On his head was a red cap. He wore a leather jacket a size too big, blue jeans, and Sahara shoes.

"Did you think you would hide here forever?" he spat. "Haven't you ever heard of the long arm of the law? Well, today you will know. You better start saying your last prayers."

He cocked his gun.

"*Afande,*" Roba spoke up, his voice shaking, "please spare my brother here . . . he was just bringing us food . . ."

Kisii folded his hands. "Bringing you food, eh? Bringing food to a bunch of criminals is the same as *being* a criminal. He will go the same way as all of you."

This was happening. He was going to be shot dead in cold blood.

"*Afande*, we have surrendered," Bryo's trembling voice said. "You can arrest us and we face the law."

One of the other policemen laughed heartily. "Arrest you? Keeping you alive will only increase the costs. And you know the government is cutting costs."

"All these boys are innocent, sir," Boi spoke solemnly. "Let them go. They have never harmed anyone. Just follow the law."

"The only law we know is the law of the Lord Jesus Christ," Kisii told him. "We don't judge people. All we do is to arrange for them to meet the Lord." He laughed loudly.

Jobo thought about the tournament. He saw Kocha peering earnestly at the gates of Grao, hoping to see him emerge. He thought about the Kalamashaka song:

> *Mungu wangu niokoe*
> *tabu uzitoe,*
> *roho yangu na ipone.*

> *Save me, my Lord,*
> *end my troubles,*
> *so my heart can be at peace.*

For some reason, Jobo's heart stopped fluttering in his chest. Even when he looked up and saw Kisii with a pistol aimed straight at his head, he did not flinch.

A police radio crackled.

Kisii pulled out a phone from somewhere inside his leather jacket, and with the one free hand he pressed a few buttons. His fierce eyes never left Jobo even as he placed the phone to his ear. "You boys," he said, "I keep telling you. When I warn you to go up-country, I really mean it. Do you think I enjoy shooting you?"

"No sir," came the chorus from everyone on the floor.

"Then why don't you listen to me?"

The person on the other end of the line seemed to have answered, because Kisii turned away and began listening. "Affirmative," was the only word he said, then he disconnected the phone and pushed it into the pocket. *"Asiyefunzwa na mamaye hufunzwa na . . . ?"* he asked them as he pulled the safety catch.

Nobody answered the saying, until one of the other policemen finished it: *"Ulimwengu."*

He who is not disciplined by his mother is dealt with by the world.

"Okay," Kisii said, glancing at his colleagues, "we are a merciful lot, so we will give you one more chance. Get up and run for your lives."

What? Just like that?

Jobo heaved himself up, and then he saw that Kim and Roba had done the same. But the rest of the boys continued lying on the ground. He hesitated.

"Don't!" Max whispered urgently. "Don't run." He was no longer stuttering. "They want us to run, then they will shoot us in the back and tell everyone that we escaped from lawful custody."

Jobo looked at the policemen and saw them exchange glances.

Kisii took a step toward Max. Then he bent over and pressed the gun into his forehead. "Young man, you are so clever, eh? You think anybody cares how you died?"

"What is that?" another policeman called out, looking toward the gate.

Kisii stiffened.

A loud wail cut through the air. It was a woman's voice. "UUUUUUUIIII!"

"UUUUUUUIIII!" came a different voice.

"UUUUUUUIIII!" another voice joined it.

And suddenly the whole air was filled with dozens of cries: "UUUUUUUIIII! UUUUUUUIIII!"

The voices were coming closer. The policemen looked at Kisii indecisively. He stood up and turned toward the gate, his pistol straight in front of him.

They pushed him back into the compound. Dozens of women screaming, "UUUUUUUIIII!" pushed him even farther aside as they took a moment to survey the scene. "UUUUUUUIIII!"

"You will not kill our children while we watch!" one woman screamed at a policeman.

He took a step back. Then all the policemen took a step back.

The women came where the boys lay. They lay spread-eagled, shielding them.

"Shoot us first!" another woman dared the policemen.

The policemen looked at Kisii with consternation. For the first time he had a stupefied expression on his face. The women continued screaming.

"UUUUUUUIIII!"

"UUUUUUUIIII!"

More women were screaming outside. And more women were coming into the compound. And more women lay over the boys.

Kisii lifted his pistol in the sky. Jobo shut his eyes tightly.

Bullets hu-fly
babies hu-die
mothers hu-cry
na siku zina pass by.

When Jobo opened his eyes again, he saw that Kisii still had his pistol in the air. He thought the man was going to shoot in the air to disperse the women. Instead, he walked slowly toward the boys on the ground. The women hugged them tighter and let out louder screams.

Slowly, Kisii crouched low. "I'll be back," he said softly to Jobo. And then he stood up, made a lighthouse scan of the compound, and nodded to the other policemen.

They all walked out slowly

na siku zina pass by . . .

Author's note: This story contains quotes from songs by Kalamashaka ("Taf-siri Hii," "Niokoe") and G.rongi ("Kichungi").

A SONG FROM A FORGOTTEN PLACE

BY TROY ONYANGO

Tom Mboya Street

In the deep recess of the street, close to where the narrow road hesitates, before melding into a large potholed road, sits a woman in rags and spiky hair that stands on her head like a pineapple crown. She pulls a thin strip of the blanket that reeks of stale urine to cover her bare arms. The midmorning cold bites her skin and her face is ashen. She breathes through her mouth and pulls the blanket harder, the yank precipitating a yell from her twins, like a philharmonic orchestra.

She tries to quiet them by pressing their faces against her bosom and soothing: *Shhh, shhh.* The cold has found their bones, and the twins' cries hit a crescendo competing with the cacophony from the cars in the street. But the babies' cries are a shrill addition to the bedlam on Tom Mboya Street. Exhausted, she lets them wail and her eyelids flutter a few times before they shut. And she is *gone.*

In the time she has been here, she has learned to block out the monotonous chant of the hawkers, the hooting of the buses, the loud Afrobeat music seeping from the stores that sell not-so-original designer jeans and misspelled Timberland boots, and she roams inside her head. An uncaged animal running free in the wild. She has learned that in there, she can be her former self—the Claudette before Laban: bold, carefree, happy, whole, without any of the harsh judgment that the world has cast at her feet. Without the guilt of being labeled a bad mother. Bad woman. Bad *everything*. Bad. The word bounces on the walls of her world, ricocheting until all she hears are the syllables tumbling and knocking her thoughts, but she finds a place to tuck it. A place she forgets exists within her as soon as the deed is done. The place she has put Hawi, her daughter.

Hawi, who she knows is long dead—legs up, head down—drowned in a toilet bowl. By her. *Rain, rain, go away. Come again another day.* But the rain hasn't stopped beating her from that day. The water falling on her body like acid needles, burrowing into her skin and corroding the flesh away. The bones coming to the fore and even that's eaten away by the water that falls from the sky in dribs and drabs until she feels she *is* Hawi, and she is drowning. Like how she was that day when Laban walked in, found her singing, safe in her world, with Hawi turning purple-blue as toilet water flowed from her nose, mouth, ears, and eyes. Like how she feels every time she thinks about the life she had with him. When it was just the two of them, loving recklessly, fucking anywhere, going to dingy clubs that smelled of sweat and stale semen, drinking bottles and bottles of whiskey and vodka. But that was before life happened and events snuffed the joy out of them, leaving only shells of their former selves, clinging to memories eroded by time. Tolerating each other and calling it love. The love life before Hawi. Before the drugs. Before . . .

The crying of the twins still pierces her thoughts, but she trains her mind again to deliberately focus on the sound of feet as they shuffle past her, all in a bid to get somewhere or nowhere. Feet that rush past her every day, ignoring her, mocking her, raising puffs of dust from the pavement and dumping it on her. She hates those feet. Eventually, she slips back into her paradise: an unlimited supply of marijuana mixed with grass, cow dung, and soaked in diesel; cheap alcohol brewed in the back rooms of truck repair shops by women who add their ARV stock to the mixture; no children crying or drowning in toilet bowls; and no city council *askaris* rushing after her with big *rungus* that hit her skull and her back with the sound of a coconut falling on a rock. No policemen who arrest her and threaten to put her before the judge, only to bring her to the back alleys filled with heaps of garbage and take turns with her. Definitely no burly, unruly boys who are not yet men with eyes the color of hot glowing coals who will never give her drugs without money unless she agrees to let them fuck her whenever and wherever they want. No gang leaders who ask her to pay tax for the space she sits on every damn day or else they'll insert dirty Sprite or Tusker bottles in her cunt! (Their words.) Lastly, no men, definitely no men to tell her what to do or what is good for her. She loves it in there.

In there. Where she finds herself by losing her body and taking on whatever form she wants. In there, where she does not have to listen to Laban tell her, "Claudette, the cocaine is bad for you and the baby." *Is it not you who introduced me to it?* she always asked him, without speaking the words. Laban, always the one to touch the flame of the fire first, tell (beg) you to touch it, then pull his hands off, and when the skin on your hand starts peeling away, the pain cutting through your body in waves, he would say, "You shouldn't have touched the flame in the first place. Can't you see it is fire? It burns."

Fuck it!

There is no room for Laban *in there.* In here.

The sound of a coin falling into her metal bowl startles her from her reverie, and she opens her eyes to see the twenty-shilling coin do its little dance, spinning and wobbling, before settling at the bottom of the bowl; her first reward of the day. She looks up to thank the kind person who has been extravagant enough to hand her a morsel when everyone else has been treating her like she is part of the dirt that covers the ground, part of the wall caked with mud dumped there by The Feet on rainy days.

A man who looks like he could appear in a paint ad meets her eyes and nods. Her chapped lips part to say, "*Asante*," but her gum is heavy and her teeth cling to each other like someone glued them together. The man is long gone, and by the time she manages to squeeze out her thanks, it is swallowed by the dark fumes emitted by the *matatu* parked nearby with the *tout*, a boy who doesn't seem to be anywhere above fifteen, shouting, "*Kayole hamsini!*" The man's whiff still clings to the coin as she thumbs it from the bowl and tucks it underneath her breasts. At least now she can get something for the twins to eat. Their crying has died down, and Adonai sucks on his thumb as he scratches his scalp. Lamek has closed his eyes with his head in between his mother's thighs. The biting cold rages on.

The street is awake. The hooting of the cars. The clopping of pointed heels on the pavement. Nigerian, Congolese, Nigerian, South African, Nigerian music, competing over which is the best. She has always preferred Congolese music; the way it springs from a place of warmth and tenderness like a beanstalk breaking through the soft earth. Then it rises and rises, growing and filling the whole room with the sweet melody that makes the body jelly and the bones rubbery and one finds oneself moving his waist, legs, and arms as if possessed by a gentle, cultured demon (but still a demon all the same), and one can dance and dance and not feel the sweat trickling down the ridge of his back or feel his legs stiffen at the knees because he's tired. One ignores all that. Lingala flows and erupts within the body. Not that thing that Laban insisted on listening to. That. That—

Claudette, can you feel it? That's Coltrane.

Claudette, you HAVE TO listen to this. Buddy Rich.

Oh Claudette, my love, Miles Davis is a fucking god!!!

The sound of the streets again, splitting and searing and tearing through the thoughts of her moving to Kinshasa or Lubumbashi. That was the dream before she met Laban and fell madly in love. She was nineteen going on twenty. Flesh clinging to her bones in all the right places. Skin glowing like models advertising cocoa butter on TV. Her heart was still untrained, untaught, untamed, and when she saw slim, tall, dark Laban walking down the street, she knew, even before he turned his full body and looked at her, that she would marry him. They would be different from those couples who tried to change each other and ended up fighting all the time. They would love each other, always. They would travel the world together. Accra, Dakar, Lilongwe, Windhoek. Finally, they would settle in Kin la Belle. Ha, Kinshasa.

She closes her eyes and tries to find herself again in a dingy sweat-filled club swaying her hips to Franco or Madilu or M'bilia Bel, but the song of the street is impatient, nagging, restless. A preacher with a man's body and a woman's voice shouting to no one to change their ways or forget about the Kingdom of God. A politician with the voice of an ungreased wheelbarrow lying to his followers on a television inside the barber shop right next to where she sits, staring at her, like someone expecting manna to fall from heaven. The people gobbling the lies and shouting their support. They have been promised money. *What currency is sufficient to buy the truth?*

The truth. Does hunger know or care for the truth? Empty rumbling bellies are not filled with *truths*, they are given food. Food bought with money. Money that has been scarce, especially when the politicians are using every avenue to get campaign money.

Down the street, a few meters from the old red-and-white building, the city council *askaris*, clad in their gray khaki uniforms, are rounding up hawkers, idlers, loiterers, and daytime prostitutes. Women with children dangling from their hips and fear balanced on their heads run toward her. She sees the three *askaris* before they see her and she gathers the twins in her arms, blanket dragging on the ground. She disappears into the alleyways, walking until she finds herself at the edge of the city center. The tarmac melts and a black river flows in its place. Still, she runs. She knows what they will do if they find her.

She remembers clearly how the bald one with a leathery scar on his forehead pulled her from the streets one evening. It was a Sunday, she recalls, for the streets were deserted and the churches were full all day. He wasn't supposed to be there on a Sunday evening. Just as she wasn't. The council *askaris* never worked after the sun had folded up and hidden from the city. She heads down a small road whose name she has forgotten. They never roamed when the neon lights flooded the streets, blinding her. But *he* came that day. He pulled up in the dirty white van. She is still running. She saw him late. She takes a bend upward and finds herself back on Kirinyaga Road. He grabbed her by the arms, bundled her like a baby, and threw her into the back of the dirty white van. A lorry brakes hard at her feet. Inside the back of the van, the smell of death. She can see Odeon now. They drove for so long. She stops, the twins heavy in her arms. He opened the back of the van, got in, and closed it. She looks at Adonai whose face is crunched into a fist. She only started crying when he stopped grunting. Adonai and Lamek, nine months later, with the help of the man who sold scrap metal, dog food, and human body parts under a bridge the Chinese had finished building. She half floats, half glides as if she has lost all sense of direction.

She is back on Tom Mboya Street, farther down near the club whose male patrons dress in women's clothes and the women dress like men and the tall green building that can be seen from almost anywhere on this street. She resents this side of town for it is full of street boys who would do anything to get their next meal (throw plastic bags full of feces, inject you with a syringe full of blood they claim is from an AIDs patient, push you in front of a moving bus, gut you with a serrated knife). She would never harm anyone just to get something to eat. She would use her babies to beg from strangers before she would even think about hurling a bag of shit at someone. She has to find a place to put the twins down before her arms fall out of her shoulders.

A man in flowing jet-black dreadlocks that fall on his thin shoulders walks past her carrying a woman's handbag like it belongs to him. He smiles at her. She looks away. Farther down, a wail pierces the dense air. *Mwizi!* She sits down and closes her eyes. *Nisaidieni jameni.* A song she has heard more times than she can count. A song of lost dreams. *Kibeti yangu.* A song from a forgotten place. She knows and the lady knows, too, that no one can help her. The people gathered around her are both witness and accomplice to the vile act. They stand and shake their heads and say, *Nairobi ni mbaya.* They all know Nairobi is the mouth of a shark and none of them would dare go against the gangs unless one has a death wish. The city is full of bloodthirsty vampires and the bright neon lights can't keep them at bay. They lurk in the shadows—Tom Mboya Street, Luthuli Avenue, River Road—and when they smell the blood coursing through the veins of their victims, the heartbeat a drum singing their songs, they pounce and drink from the first jugular they find. That is the city, and no amount of wailing will help.

She closes her eyes. The *askaris*, the hawkers, the bright neon lights, the man with flowing dreadlocks and a wide smile, the woman's cries—they are all gone.

At the farthest end of the street, a woman sits and doesn't see the three men approach. She doesn't notice them because she's in her own world. The world she has managed to build inside her head. The world where there is no pain. Pain in the lower part of the abdomen from the policemen who come to her every night and take turns with her. Pain from the city council *askari* with a leathery scar on his bald head thrusting and her begging him to stop. Pain from pushing the twins out of her nine months later. The twins who now sleep peacefully under the blanket that she uses to cover her body from the cold. She is in a world that has no cold, when she feels a cold hand on her shoulder. She opens her eyes, blinking to adjust to the world with pain and cold, and is alarmed to find three men staring down at her. She lets out a scream, for she thinks it is the city council *askaris* she evaded earlier.

"Claudette?" The voice of a man she had forgotten existed. She stops screaming. A man she once loved. A man—"Claudette." The voice, calm like the sea on a warm, sunny day. She looks into his face. And into the face of the other two men with him. She cannot recognize one but she knows the other. From where? He is the one who dropped a coin in her bowl earlier. The coin that she can still feel cold against her nipple because she had forgotten to buy the twins something to eat. He is the one she thought could appear in a paint ad. *Is he one of Laban's friends, maybe from the band he was in?* Laban. Yes, Laban. The memories start rushing in and her head hurts. She avoids his gaze which feels like it is peeling away all the walls she has put up and can see her for who she truly is. But Laban lowers himself onto the ground and reaches his hand toward Claudette. Claudette who has her eyes closed and her teeth clamping down on her lower lip. She is gone. *Rain, rain, go away.* Laban leans closer and the stink from the blanket stings his eyes and nose. He has his arms around his Claudette. Junior and Slim Jack stand nearby and watch as tears flow freely from his face.

Laban has finally found his Claudette.

MATHREE

BY MAKENA ONJERIKA

Globe Roundabout

I f there is one issue I have with Klemo, it's that this guy can never let you tell a story properly. He always has to insert himself somewhere. I tell him, "Dude, wait, I'm getting there."

He pushes his spects up on his nose and taps Fat Toni. "Listen to this guy. Is there a time when his stories are not pointless?"

Fat Toni lifts his Tusker and gives it a long kiss. He burps. "Dudes, I'm done thinking hard stuff till Monday morning."

We are at our usual joint, sitting on the wannabe terrace above the sidewalk on Kimathi Street. Outside, Nairobians are speed walking toward bus/*mathree* queues. A Kenya Bus is dragging itself down Kimathi toward the Hilton Hotel, changing gears like a guy suffering from asthma. And fat nimbus clouds are holding a *kamkunji* above, debating when to piss on Nairobi.

"Mike testing, testing, one, two, three," says some guy in the church upstairs. Soon they will start pouring buckets of cold prayer on us, as in, *Jesus Christ, deliver those drunkards downstairs.* I swear.

Klemo signals for another round from this new waitress he's trying to square. He makes sure to flash his watch, a serious wall clock.

It's early. The only other guys in the bar are two tables

away. There is a fool over there loudly declaring Man U will beat Arsenal in the game this weekend.

"Let's talk about something else," I say, and knock my Tusker on their Tuskers, cheers. "How's that mama of yours, Klemo?"

His face drops. Last week, his main chick found a suspect phone number in his pants pocket. The scars all over his face are exactly why I don't date chicks who wear fake nails. Dangerous shit. I've pissed him off. Good thing Fat Toni and his potbelly are between us, to keep the peace. This guy seems to add more weight daily.

"Just finish this story fast," says Klemo. "I want to talk some business with you guys."

12:05. It's not even lunchtime proper, but I am the only one in the office doing any work. Since eight, everyone else has been pushing papers, playing solitaire on their comps, and kick-starting the weekend. Brian and Carol, sitting behind me, haven't stopped arguing about Goldenberg and who stole the money. I don't know how many times Brian has said Kamlesh Pattni was the mastermind, with Carol opposing him from all angles. He taps my shoulder and says, "Jaymo, *kwani*, you're being paid extra? Learn to relax, man. It's Furahi-day. *Ebu*, help me out with this woman."

Carol, who would be superfine if she just never opened her mouth and showed those brown teeth, jumps on me with her argument: "Kamlesh is just a scapegoat. Where are the cases against people like Moi, for example?"

They can relax and talk politics, of course; they are old-timers on this job, and no one is giving them 24/7 CCTV. I say I don't know, it's not like I have a TV set to follow news anyway, but before my eyes are back on my comp, Mr. Kajenjo is shouting my name across the office.

Somehow I don't panic. I walk over to the door of his glass office. He puts his hand on my shoulder. "James, how long has it been since you became permanent?"

Next to this guy, I'm both vertically and horizontally challenged. "Two weeks, boss," I say. Imagine, I even smile.

He dims his eyes and squeezes my shoulder. "Is that why you've started sitting on your buttocks?"

He doesn't even tell me what the issue is, that I messed up the job for our Westie client. He just starts slapping me with words. And when this guy decides to work on you, *walai*, it's like you are a shirt he's washing. He soaps you up proper with hard soap, he *suguaz* you, he wrings every drop of dignity out of you, and then he throws you on a line for everyone to see. The whole time he is demolishing me I'm thinking about this story Klemo likes to pull out when we are giving chicks vibes at the club: "You see Jaymo here, this guy was a ninja back on campus. One time a lecturer was thinking he's a *makmende*, saying how he couldn't believe any of us airheads had managed to get into Campo, and guess what Jaymo did? He just shouted, *Shut up*, kubaf!"

In front of the chicks, I like to maximize on that story, but honestly, I don't remember anything like that ever happening. Then again, on campus I was mostly high on weed.

Kajenjo keeps shredding me and I keep bleating, "I'm sorry, boss. I'll go fix it immediately, boss."

That's what tarmacking for two years does to you. After choking yourself with a tie and suit and displaying your certificates from office to office until your shoes run out of sole, you press delete on all that campus nonsense.

Kajenjo finishes with, "I'm giving you an hour to fix this, James, an hour. Otherwise . . ." Pause. Have you ever eaten bread and water for one year—breakfast, lunch, and supper?

How about playing hide-and-seek with your landlord?

12:15. I remove myself from the office immediately and head toward Old Nation to find a number 23 *mathree* and get myself to Westie ASAP. Man, I'm shaking all over.

The city council has gone for lunch so hawkers have emerged and are in full-swing business on every centimeter of the sidewalks.

"Fifty bob. Bras, panties, everything fifty bob."

Some guy grabs my arm. *Ati*, "Brother, buy something nice for your girlfriend." I slice him with dagger eyes.

Seriously, do Nairobians leave their houses to come block the street, watching naked chickens on skewers going around and around in Kenchic and McFrys windows? And isn't my stomach talking to me this whole time: *Jaymo, why don't you buy yourself a chicken quarter? A man can't work properly without fuel, bana.*

I tell myself mind over matter, mind over matter. It's already 12:25.

But what do I see when I get to Old Nation? Empty number 23 *mathrees* packed bumper to bumper with their slide doors yawning. It's like a vehicle bazaar: blinging chrome wheels, supersized posters of Eninem-Shakira-Tupac plastered on the bodies, and inside, four rows of seriously uncomfortable seats and wall speakers pulsating with the latest pop hits. The drivers are sleeping in their front seats and the *kangees* are yawning, eating, fighting, and doing everything except trying to fill *mathrees* with passengers. The only ones working are this pair next to the first *mathree* in the line. They are shuffling words like pastor and translator in a Pentecostal church: "Westie (ten bob), Kangemi (twenty bob). Westie (ten bob), Kangemi (twenty bob). Get in we go (chap, chap, we go)." At this rate, how long will it take to fill a fourteen-seater? Jesus!

This chaos is mixing up my brain. A beggar boy is shaking a tin with three coins at me. The blind man holding his shoulder says, "*Saidia maskini.*" Honestly, I feel for this guy. Nairobi is hard. If this wasn't Tom Mboya Street, I would contribute a ten-bob at least, but there is no way I'm removing my wallet down here. You see people walking fast like their shadows are running away from them, but 50 percent of this crowd is just waiting to permanently borrow your wallet. The boy keeps shaking his tin, and I keep ignoring. I fix my eyes across Tom Mboya Street, at the signboards on the *mathrees* packed inside the Koja roundabout. *Limuru. Kinoo. Banana. Kabete.* All the places I don't need to go to today.

A honk, a screech, someone's buttocks slap the tarmac. *Uuuwii.* A *mathree* driver has almost hit one of the pedestrians trying to cross the Koja roundabout.

"*Kubaf! Nyang'au!*" shouts the *karau* trying to control the traffic swinging around Koja. He is walking through the traffic like black Moses, baton raised, white *kofia* on his head, reflector vest throwing flashes.

All this time, the sun is shaving my head and sweat is doing chromatography around my armpits. It's already 12:35 and the two Westie *kangees* are trying to smooth-talk me to board their *mathree*. *Ati,* "The other passengers are on the way." And my name is Michael Jackson!

Then, a *mathree* headed to Kinoo shoots out of the Koja roundabout and cuts in front of the Westie *mathrees*, its *kangee* shouting, "One person, forty bob!"

These are the moments I think weed really pulverized my brain. How had I not thought of taking a *mathree* going to Kinoo or Kabete or Kangemi or a million other places on Waiyaki Way and getting off at Westie? I elbow some guy out of the way and climb in.

Bad, bad idea.

First, the only empty seat is on the back row, between this big guy and a high schooler in some ugly uniform, right where your head bangs on the roof when the driver decides to fly over bumps. Second, anywhere past Westie is up-country, so people are acting up-country-ish, i.e., there are two smelly chickens staring at me from under one of the seats and a *gunia* of cabbages rests squarely between me and the empty seat. Third: I ask myself, *Jaymo, why are three guys wearing heavy-duty jackets in this heat?* And look at the way they've planted themselves strategically in this *mathree*. There is the big guy in the back row, another guy with a square head in the third row from where he can put the *kangee* in a nice chokehold, and the third guy, sitting in the first row behind the driver, is concentrating very hard on a newspaper, yesterday's.

I tell myself, *Jaymo, here, just subtract yourself.* See, last month, Fat Toni's older brother was in a *mathree* on Ngong Road when three thugs with guns diverted the *mathree* to the Ngong Forest. Those thugs cleaned everyone out. Fat Toni's bro made it home in socks and boxers. And here I am, carrying the 20K phone I bought only last weekend. But before I can backtrack, the *kangee*, who is being clobbered by Westie *kangees* for diverting their passengers, jumps in and slaps his hand on the roof.

I say, "Boss, let me get off."

"You see what they have done to me," complains the *kangee*. Someone's whole hand is stamped on his face.

The driver steps on the accelerator and I have no choice but to climb over the sack and two chickens and plant myself in the back row.

"Then put me down when we hit traffic," I tell the guy.

The high schooler twists her lips at me. Here I am, trying

to create some space between me and the big thug, but the chick won't move even an inch. I push her with my shoulders and ignore the teeth-kissing and murmuring.

The big thug is inspecting me thoroughly and I am hoping he can see my shirt collar is frayed and my shoes have known a hard life. At this point it's between fire and fire. Getting off and finding another *mathree* will eat up my time, but getting hijacked . . .

Now, here is the thing about Nairobi: every time I'm going to Westie, the *karaus* at the Globe Cinema roundabout are experimenting with the best ways to create a traffic jam: *Let's stop traffic from Murang'a Road for five minutes and then traffic from Tom Mboya for ten minutes.* But not today, when I actually need a jam. Today, Tom Mboya Street is wide open all the way to the Globe Cinema—buildings are flying past the *mathree* and the cinema is coming closer and closer. The driver is feeling happy with his life. He tunes the *mathree* radio to K___ FM, landing us right on Usher going, *"Yeah, yeah, yeah."*

The high schooler decides even her, she can sing, *"Yeah, yeah, yeah."*

The big thug coughs and I can feel him eyeing her through me. He spits out the window. Man, this stress is not good for my health.

I almost shout *Hallelujah!* when I see one of the *karaus* at the Globe roundabaout raising his hand and stepping onto the road to stop vehicles coming from our side. I am thinking, *Now I can get off,* but then our *kangee* is announcing, "If there is anyone who hasn't buckled their seat belt, you are getting arrested alone."

Ah, shit. We are going to stop right in front of those *karaus.* Forget getting off this *mathree.* I start looking for my seat belt. The one I find refuses to go into my socket. Turns out the high schooler has somehow managed to tie my belt. I say, "Excuse me, you have my belt."

She shakes her head. Just shakes that head with the eyes wide apart like a sheep. Meanwhile, one of the *karaus* is walking around vehicles and looking in through the windows. So I force her belt into my socket and hope the *karau* doesn't notice. The first and last time I was at the Central Police Station (weed plus fighting in a club), I came out with broken ribs. But if I touch this chick, she will start screaming and people will descend on me with their fists: *Young man, what are you doing to an under-eighteen?*

The *karau* nods at the driver and walks around the *mathree*, tapping its body with that black stick that traffic *karaus* always carry around (is it for beating people or what?). Where my heart is at this point, don't even ask. Half of my brain is thinking, *What if I get caught?* The other half is thinking, *What if he notices the thugs and radios the Flying Squad so they can come spray bullets into everything and everyone?*

The *karau* reaches the back row window and lifts the rim of his *kofia*. "*Habari yenu*," he says, and it's a shock 'cause I can't remember a *karau* ever greeting me. He continues tapping his stick on the *mathree*, goes around and ends up at the window next to the *kangee*, where he shakes the *kangee*'s hand. And we are off again.

"You see that," says the big thug, and I agree with my head even though I'm not sure what I'm supposed to be seeing. He starts lecturing me about how things have become bad in Kenya since the Moi days. "Now everyone is eating bribes, left, right, center."

And I am stuck there pretending to care, because the *kangee* shakes his head when I ask to get off.

"Boss, wait until University Way. That's the next stop," he says, starting to collect fares.

A drop of sweat meanders down my back. It's now 12:43,

but of course, this day can get worse, much, much worse. My phone starts ringing. People are looking at me, wondering why I am not answering it; I am looking at them, stone-faced. Do they know how long I took to save 20K and buy this thing? After four rings it goes silent. The radio presenter breaks in. "*You are listening to K___ FM, entertainment all the time. This is ___, helping your lunch go down smoothly. And the question of the hour is, should we have a Kenyan national dress?*"

The big thug is now shaking his finger at the speaker on the wall of the *mathree*. "All these problems in this country and this is the only thing they can talk about? *Bure kabisa.*"

When my phone starts ringing again, he says, "*Si* you pick that phone?"

I fish it out, planning to kill Klemo or Fat Toni if it's one of them. Kajenjo's secretary says, "Hello? James? Mr. Kajenjo would like you to come back to the office."

My lips unzip in a Colgate smile. "The issue is resolved?"

"The client has canceled our contract." She hangs up.

The high schooler now thinks she is Beyoncé: "*Tonight, I'll be your naughty girl . . .*"

And the *kangee* is waving the two hundreds, five hundreds, and 1K notes he has collected and folded over his index finger. "Where do you people expect me to get change for all these?"

I am feeling dizzy. Contract. Canceled.

"*Deree, ebu* pause at that Shell I get change," says the *kangee* to the driver. He signals me to start moving forward so I can get off, but now I don't know what to do. Going back to the office means I am 100 percent fired. I check my watch: 12:50.

I give myself a quick pep talk: *Jaymo, these guys may not be thugs at all. Stay on the* mathree, *bana. Grow some balls and get to this client ASAP.*

The *kangee* wants to shoot me with his finger when I hand

him my full fare. "Boss, is something wrong with that head? *Mara*, you're getting off; *mara*, you're staying."

I have a good answer for this fool, but first I need to get to Westie. We swing around the St. Paul's Church roundabout but before we hit Museum Hill, the high schooler has unleashed her lunch—fries and sausage in a Kenchic bag. And she starts chewing loud enough for me to imagine her tongue rolling the fries and sausage into *bolus* at the back of her throat. I'm seriously not feeling well, but the squarehead thug in the third row is complaining about how much change he has received. Didn't the *kangee* say the fare is thirty bob?

The *kangee* is taking no nonsense. "Town to Kinoo, thirty bob? Those are jokes."

Spittle lands on my face from the right. "Thievery. You people are the ones killing this country. You said thirty bob."

And now, people who already received their change are remembering very loudly that the fare is thirty bob. I watch the thug in the first row carefully folding up his newspaper. He slides it under his jacket and turns to look at the other two thugs. It's obvious he is the boss here, the way he is no-smiles, calm. His hand is still inside the jacket. I watch that hand. My heart is beating like a Chuka drum. *Ngu, ngu, ngu.* I know what's about to happen.

"Wait, wait," Klemo cuts into my story, literally, with his hands. "That makes no sense at all. First, what is a high schooler doing in a *mathree* at twelve, one, instead of being at school? Second, why would anyone hijack a *mathree* to Kinoo? To steal chickens?"

And that's not even the weird part of this story. I need another Tusker. The waitress swings her hips as she comes over and Klemo licks his lips. He really thinks he's taking this one somewhere?

I take a sip of the Tusker, for strength. They won't believe me, but I just say it: "I'm focusing on the thug in front, waiting for a gun to appear, but then I hear a sound on my left, a bleat. The high schooler is bleating like a goat, and on top of that, I look down and she has goat legs."

Klemo is laughing the spects off his face. "Jaymo, seriously, just stop. Where did you get this story?"

Fat Toni has folded his arms over his potbelly. This is his thinking mode. "As in, Legs. Of. A. Goat?" he asks.

Klemo slaps the table as he laughs harder.

I don't know why I am telling them this story at all.

Imagine this: We get to Westie and I find myself alighting the *mathree*, following the goat girl like a zombie, with zero control over my body. I can hear words coming out of my mouth, begging people for help, but it's like my voice is outside my body, far away. Of course, no one helps.

And the chick isn't a chick anymore. She explodes out of the uniform and becomes this animal, covered in black, shiny hair. Hips materialize on the sides of her body, as in those giant-size *madiabas* that move out of sync with the mamas who carry them. I know today is my day; I have met the devil; I'm finished. When she checks on me with a glance over her shoulder, she is smiling and her lips are red, that scary red that makes chicks look like vampires. *Walai*, now she is bending the space around her: buildings, roads, people. I don't feel well, *majamaa*. I think I have vomited. I think I am praying. Forget the fact that I haven't seen the door of a church since before campus.

And then suddenly we are in some forest. Don't ask me how. All I know is I am feeling seriously cold, like to the bone. It's nighttime somehow, and the chick/woman/thing is glowing. She stops, and I know this the moment she will kill me.

"You will taste good," she says. She opens her mouth, her big, black hole of a mouth, and goes for my head. Her teeth dig in, crushing my brains. I scream. (You don't remember you're a man when someone is eating you, *bana*.)

Next thing I know, I am in Kinoo and the *kangee* is preparing to slap me: round two. "This is not a bedroom. You don't have a bed in your house?" he asks.

This is all very funny to Klemo. He is almost falling off his chair with laugher. Tears are making rivers down his face. The *fala*.

"Let me guess: when you checked your pockets, you didn't have your phone or your wallet," says Fat Toni.

The pain of thinking about that phone is too much. 20K gone just like that. Plus the 1K I had for surviving this week, my ID and ATM card (although there is nothing but air in my bank account).

When Klemo is done laughing, he claps me on the shoulder. "Sorry, bro. That's life in Nairobi. At least you didn't get hurt. Say thanks to God."

Part of me knows I was drugged in the mathree. There was no chick/woman/thing trying to eat me; part of me is impressed with these Nairobi thugs and their methods, like how did they drug me; and part of me is scared shitless because that chick/woman/thing was too real. I sip my Tusker to push it all down.

For some minutes we are all quiet. We listen to the Man U fool two tables away insisting that the score this weekend will be Man U 6, Arsenal 0; that Ferguson is greater than Wenger; Wayne Rooney should be footballer of the year. Serious verbal diarrhea. Then the volume on the TV goes up, and I see the waitress pointing at it with the remote. Seven o'clock news.

Some political activist is giving a speech: "*It is the youth of this country who suffer the most because of corruption . . .*"

Man U guy whistles at the waitress. "Woman, are you okay in the head? You think we came here to listen to politics? Put SuperS . . ."

I don't know why, but I hate this guy like a problem. Maybe it's the five bottles of Tusker I have downed. Or maybe it's remembering what happened at the client's when I finally made it there two hours later, groggy and with a headache the size of a hot-air balloon; how much I had to beg to get that contract back; how I kneeled before that boss lady. Maybe it's having to walk all the way back to town to get another shredding from Kajenjo, plus a warning letter from HR. Or maybe I just need someone to hate right now.

"*Kubaf*, shut up!" I shout.

Eight pairs of eyes zoom in on me. Man U guy is already getting out of his chair. "You, *nyang'au*, what did you say?"

"You are a total *kubaf*!"

Aah, now this feels right. It's been a seriously long time since my fist connected with a face.

PART II

THE HUNTED

BLOOD SISTER

by Peter Kimani

Karen

T hey say when life offers lemons, you make lemonade. And what do you make if it brings a *mzungu*? *Mzungu* mix? That sounds like *mchuzi* mix, a spice that Kibra folks love to death. They put it in *sukuma wiki,* which they eat from Monday to Monday, as *mchuzi mix* comes in beef, chicken, and pork flavors, turning the veggies into meats. As we have come to learn, especially from our politicians, not everyone can afford meat, *na kumeza mate si kula nyama!*

I hope you don't mind my politicking. I'm still smarting from my dalliance with politicians in the last general election. I was appointed a youth leader in our ward, which means I was awash with cash. My goodness, I had never handled so much cash in my life. We were supposed to dish it out, like *njugu karanga,* but I kept a tidy amount for myself. When I am dead broke, I recall the smell of the new bank notes. It makes me feel rich again.

But the story that I want to relate is about the *mzungu* who came into my life after the polls. If truth be told, I quite liked the idea of mixing her up to produce a *mchuzi* child, a mixed-race tot . . . Only that, as I came to learn, Jackie wasn't the type to bear children. Certainly not with a man from the other side of the valley.

Which is interesting, for I naively thought her mission was to bridge Kibra and Karen, since the two areas fall under one constituency, Lang'ata—and Kibra is the hotbed of Lang'ata politics. Anyway, I don't want to politic. I want to tell you about Jackie, the *jungu* who came into my life and, my goodness, those were the days of our lives!

Listening to that, one would think I am an old man in his sixties! Well, at thirty-two I consider myself an old man. Come to think of it, I *am* old enough to be a grandfather, what with the haste with which our generation, *vifaranga vya kompyuta*, is producing.

Before Jackie came into my life, she was preceded by yet another *jungu*, a grizzled old bird that, looking back, was my true kismet. Let me explain: I was what folks in Kibra call a hustler, which means I could be found everywhere and anywhere, doing nothing in particular.

My gang and I were at the base chewing *veve* and listening to *dobba*, when someone alerted us about a *jungu* taking pictures of the ghetto. I might not have made much from the season of politics, but I was enjoying the dividends of being a youth leader. With a mound of *veve* jutting through my cheek, my gang and I arrived where Mama Camera, as everyone came to call her, was issuing her disposable cameras to children.

Mama Camera, wearing flip-flops and dark glasses, told the children to take pictures of their day-to-day life. She said the photos would be used in a project called "ShootBack" and the best images would be included in an exhibition in Europe.

But before she could finish her sentence, I demanded to know who had authorized her to come to Kibra. She appeared puzzled by my question. I also saw her lip tremble. Trust me, I am the rude boy of Kibra, and I can be nasty when I mean business. The way I spat out the question must have warned Mama Camera that I could bring *diambo*.

"You think anyone will let me into your country wearing

flip-flops and allow me to dish out cameras to ghetto children to spy on us?" Before she could answer, I prodded on: "And what nonsense about pictures of ghetto life. You want to sell our pictures to museums depicting us as monkeys?"

For a while, Mama Camera made no response and I presumed she hadn't heard me. I was about to repeat my question when she broke into a wan smile and motioned me to draw closer.

I drew closer. My main motive was to scan her properly. I was just twenty-five, an age when everything lay in the realm of the possible. I wanted to *sorora* if she had any valuables that I could snatch. And if the old bird sat badly, as people of Kibra say, *unavuka naye!* Cross with her. I mean, I had a classmate who specialized in European female pensioners and his pictures on Facebook showed he was permanently on the beaches of Malindi. So I wouldn't be the first graduate from Matope High School to end up as a male prostitute.

Anyway, I flashed a smile and Mama Camera flashed her fake smile back. When she removed her dark glasses, tears stood in her eyes. "You are too intellizent to wazte your life in ze zlum," she said in her accented English. My heart instantly went out to her.

Here was an old bird who couldn't even speak proper English dreaming of changing Kibra! I'm talking about a hundred years of history since the British brought our Nubian ancestors from the Sudan as army reserves, and left them marooned there. And here was an old German bird from Leipzig who thought she could solve our problems by *sambaza*ing disposable cameras! It was like the foolish tourist mauled by a lion when she offered him a biscuit in the Maasai Mara!

There are folks who say I am hard on the outside and soft inside, like a coconut. But I seriously pitied this mama. I wasn't touched by the sadness in her eye, but by the folly of her conviction that she could change our circumstances.

The *veve* steam in my head lifted somewhat and I asked softly how I could help her. "Zenk you, zenk you!" she said tearfully. "You will be of tremendaz help to me . . ."

I became her point man in Kibra when she came for her "ShootBack" nonsense. I evolved from her translator to security man and, ultimately, her KYM. That means *Kanda Ya Moko*, the handyman. But I didn't use my hands on the old German bird. I still had some pride.

Within a few weeks, all the kids brought back their film which I helped select, not because I understood anything about photography, but because Mama Camera said I understood life in Kibra better than she ever would. So together we went to this fancy studio in Karen and I recall feeling suddenly self-conscious about my smell—the sweat, the dust on my shoes, *yaani*, u-ghetto pouring out of my every pore. But I bore it all, carefully scanning from one frame to the next, until some thirty reels, each comprising some thirty-six exposures, were reviewed. Out of these, I picked what stood out.

Mama Camera appeared quite pleased with my selection. But it's the Kibra youngsters who were the most pleased, as all the selected images were blown up large, then mounted on fancy-looking frames and delivered for exhibition one evening near the chief's camp.

You should have seen the glow in Mama Camera's eye. She wore a blue print *kitenge* dress and made a small speech to convey her joy working in Africa—never mind that she was in a tiny spot in Kibra, not the fifty-four states that make the continent. When I was asked to address the gathering, I panicked because I hadn't had my usual fix of *veve* or *ndom*. I mean, I would never address such a *kirindi* without some steam. So I trembled slightly before an idea swung in rapidly. I clenched a fist and punched in the air:

> *"Vijana hoooeeeee!*
> *Kina mama hooeeee!*
> *Wazee hoooeeeee!*
> *Watoto hooooeeee!*
> Power to the people!
> Power to the people!"

Apparently, that's all I needed to jazz up the crowd. Almost every Kibra resident I encountered that evening wore a big grin. Seeing a fellow neighbor making a mountain of *sembe*, children bathing in the open, a carpenter at work, *kina mama* plaiting hair, a little girl lighting a *jiko*, a mongrel watching over some drunk—all these images brought them so much happiness. I couldn't really understand why. Perhaps it was the joy of seeing themselves through the eyes of someone else.

What most folks found hilarious was the picture of a man with a flying toilet, the black polythene back neatly clasped in hand, like a javelin. The man's face was a mask of concentration: he seemed aware that one minor slip of the finger and his cargo would come unstuck, with devastating results. The man's upper lip was curled in an impish smile, perhaps imagining what the mound in hand would do if it hit a target. I don't want to sound vulgar but this was the shitty life that is Kibra.

Mama Camera returned the following day to report that our maiden exhibition had been a resounding success. I was obviously taking pride in her work, despite my initial protestations. The measure of her assessment was that she, and by extension I, had been invited to curate the photo exhibition at the nearby Karen Blixen Museum. And Mama Camera was of the view that we should make this more than just an exhibition; we should auction the pictures as well.

Something tugged in the pit of my stomach. Wasn't that the fear that I had expressed when I first confronted Mama Camera? Did she think I had the memory of a fly? She checked herself just in time and clarified that the proceeds would be used to fund the next round of "ShootBack." Another portion of the proceeds would be used to set up a studio that I could run, to ensure future projects were handled by the youth of Kibra . . .

I must confess I was a little conflicted, even distracted, when I went to the Karen Blixen event, thinking I had sold my soul to the old German bird. Isn't that what they call *divide and rule*? Because I had a stake in her business, I was less likely to bring *siasa*.

But that was only the beginning . . . that was the night I encountered Jackie, the Englishwoman.

"*Habari rafiki!*" Jackie gushed, offering a soft, moist hand and a business card with the picture of a shrub, the insignia of the University of Anglia, where she was completing her doctoral study. She was in Kenya for her field research.

Days later, I typed, deleted, typed, deleted. How does a black ghetto boy ask out a rich white girl? Her reply came in gray-blue ink, a drip of the color of her eyes. *I know Kenya produces the best tea in the world*, she gushed. *I would be absolutely delighted to share a cup with you.*

There was more to share. We both shared a country of birth.

"My umbilical cord is buried here," she said to convey her connection to my land.

"Does that make you Kenyan or English?" I asked.

"That's for you to find out." There was a playfulness in her tone. I was absolutely delighted.

The afternoon tea soon grew to evening wine, afforded

by KYM assignments from Mama Camera that miraculously arrived every second Friday, just before the close of business and the start of the growing business between Jackie and me.

Our first trip together, to Karen Connection for drinks, was by *mathree*. I quickly established that Jackie was not using the shared taxi for lack of money; she wanted to polish her Kiswahili. And *mathrees* have lots of people interested in chatting up a pretty white girl.

I noticed a chipped tooth as she spoke. Her words had a biting effect on me; you seldom encounter white folks who want to speak Kiswahili; the more likely scenario is that of locals adopting fake, false, and forced foreign accents, like the talking heads on Capital FM. Not that I cared, I am a Jambo FM fan.

On the third Friday since our *matatu* ride, I tasted the wine on Jackie's tongue, touched her blond hair. "Fake blond," she clarified. She felt comfortable enough not to fake anything.

I clutched her hair again, and whispered in her ear: "Let's take a ride."

"I don't think I'm wearing the right underwear," Jackie giggled.

"I would rather you wear nothing," I said.

She was quite tickled. We were at her rented apartment in Karen. She led me through a maze of rooms until I was fearful I could not find my way out. Where most Kibra folks hibernate in ten-by-ten hovels, here was a single individual living in a house the size of Hilton Hotel.

The wine on her tongue was fading, like vapor rising off tarmac after the rains. There was promise of more rain down in the valley. "You are colonizing my breasts," Jackie swooned with pleasure, when she finally revealed the naked truth.

"For Africa and Asia," I mumbled with a mouthful of nipple. "The two continents impoverished by the Empire."

Jackie snuggled closer. She wanted me to slide into a tube before the ride.

"Am I your first white girl?" She expected me to say: *Am I your first black guy?*

But I did not. I rolled over. Our bodies lay side by side, like the rail tracks that cut through Kibra and Karen. Jackie was a vessel with two compartments; one for blacks, one for whites. She was doing a head count of the passengers getting on board. I limped off, the nipple melting in the mouth hardened into a bitter lozenge. I spat it out. I heard the rattle of the Mombasa train hurtling down Kibra. The train faded away. Marvin Gaye haunted on Capital FM.

"What's going on?" Jackie asked, cheerfully imitating the song on air.

I turned on the lights and faced her. "You aren't me taking for a ride, are you?" I asked.

"I thought you wanted a ride," she replied.

Jackie left for England soon after. I was troubled by the memory of our encounter. Her clean white skin was blinding. I mean it. My eyes could see in the dark. And I was depressed for having failed to rise to the occasion, weighed down by the historicity of the moment. How could I, a poor black boy from Kibra, lay an Englishwoman? I had failed to rise to the occasion when Kenya needed me. Retaliate for the rape of my country by hers. Only that Jackie is half-Kenya—a KC, Kenyan cowboy, as we call the tribe.

The news that I was dating a white girl reached Kibra even before I limped back there, wounded by my failure. And Kibra being Kibra, my private humiliation had turned into a great public triumph. All the fine lasses from Kibra, even those considered *mababie*, wanted to be with me. I mean, really cute girls who spoke English through their noses. One girl's father even had a car, which he cleaned and polished with such dedication every weekend, I think he spent more time fondling the vehicle than his wife. It was an old orange Volvo. Franco's rhumba would boom from the car's pimped-up speakers, as the man whistled along. He must have been very absorbed in his labors for he seldom realized he had lathered the car twice before, or even that his pants had dropped down an inch to reveal the crack in his bum.

Pash was the name of the girl from that family. Together, we made some fine music. I guess had I run for public office that year, the Jackie effect would have secured me enough votes to get into Parliament! Forgive me if I sound conceited, but I think I would have laid any girl I set my sights on at that time. I was on the top of my game, thanks to Jackie.

I came to learn a good number of the girls believed it was a matter of time before I traveled to England to join Jackie, so they all wanted to remain in my good book to stand a chance of traveling with me, perhaps as a second, third, fourth, or fifth wife!

But that did not happen. Instead, Jackie returned to Nairobi. She sent an e-mail announcing, rather formally, that she was back in town and wondered if we could reconnect. I panicked. By now I was living with this fine girl who I had put in the family way. I should clarify up front that I did not invite her to my house. I just found that some of her clothing had been smuggled into my hood, one garment at a time, until her entire wardrobe—which wasn't much—had been transferred to my humble abode.

Mwari, for that was her name, had gone about her business without any idea that she was expecting and only learned about it when she started experiencing morning sickness. She seemed to react particularly badly to the smell of onions, so we soon started having meals without them. Then she said she couldn't stand *dhania*, so that too was off the menu—a sign of what marriage tastes like. I silently vowed I would kick her out if she claimed she couldn't stand *mchuzi* mix.

Then Jackie came back into my life, after a mere four months away. The Jackie of the past had always taken me to her place in Karen. But the new Jackie said she wanted to come to my hood in the ghetto. She wanted not just to learn Kiswahili, but my culture as well.

I ruminated over the matter. Jackie coming to Kibra would obviously cause a riot among the girls, but I now had a girl in my nest. My life was already getting complicated. That night, I told Mwari: "The Englishwoman is back."

Mwari was quiet for a while and I thought she hadn't heard me. Then she said in a clear, firm voice, "Tell her to come meet her cowife!"

Problem solved! I wrote Jackie that night and said she was free to visit.

By morning, Mwari had changed her mind. "Tell her I am your sister," she said.

"But brothers and sisters don't do the things we do!" I laughed.

"I am serious, Bobo," she said. Mwari rarely called me by name. It was always *babe, sweets,* or other endearments. Occasionally, she would address me as Bob or Bobby. Never Bobo. "When she takes you to England, she will not suspect a thing if you say you are inviting your blood sister."

I burst out laughing.

"This is no laughing matter, Bobo. I am coming to England with you."

"Who says I am going to England?"

"Why is she back, if not for you?"

* * *

I was equally curious to find out what had brought Jackie back to Nairobi, and into my life. I was certainly happy to have another chance to give her the thing, show that she no longer freaked me out.

Mwari's acting was sterling. She made Jackie some *pilau*—this time she coped with onion without a whimper—and enacted a very convincing "sisterly" performance. When Jackie inquired who between us was older, Mwari blurted that we were twins, then laughed out loud when Jackie appeared to consider that possibility.

"We were tight like twins," Mwari said with a smile, flashing her two long fingers stuck together.

"You never mentioned you had a sister," Jackie said, after we retreated to her old apartment in Karen.

"You never asked me," I replied defensively.

"Fair enough," she smiled, flashing her broken tooth.

We were lying side by side, cuddling.

That night, I gave it to her like nobody's business.

"Mr. Bobo Shanti," she cried out, "you are thrashing me like the Nubian drums . . ."

The friendship between Mwari and Jackie blossomed. They met frequently, sometimes without me, and both seemed to have endless things to talk about. When I asked what they were up to, Mwari called me to silence, pointing to a small Sony recorder on the table. Jackie was recording their conversations.

On a trip to Jackie's apartment in Karen one evening, I stumbled upon the recording device. I held it in my hand and marveled at its small belly that had been fed for days, without filling up. Jackie was in the shower. Without event pausing to think, I pressed play. Mwari was recalling our childhood together: "*My brother Bob was aborted seven times by our mother. She had wanted to kill the baby and herself because Father had fled with another Nubian woman. Although I am younger than Bob, I knew this from Mother. When she was angry, she cursed, 'I should have aborted you properly on the eighth time'*—" I turned off the recorder at Jackie's approach, and lay on the bed and considered the fabricated biography.

I noticed how Jackie's tenderness toward me increased with the passage of time. I knew she was taking pity on me, and I took pity on her because she was being manipulated by Mwari.

Things got a little awkward when, between bouts of lovemaking, Jackie would ask about random events that Mwari had shared with her. And since I didn't want to betray Mwari, I feigned reticence about the past.

"Bob, you must see a counselor if you and I are going to remain together," Jackie said one morning. "You have to deal with your past traumas."

I told her I wasn't sick.

"Are you kidding me? You manifest all the symptoms of post-traumatic stress disorder," she burst out. "If you didn't know, denial is one of them!"

"I am not denying anything," I responded earnestly. "Trust me, I know myself . . ."

"Yes you are," Jackie declared. "I have been studying each of the images that you selected for exhibition. They mirror the narratives that Mwari has told me about you. In fact, her insights have been revelatory. The photos are perfect mirrors of trauma and memory using autobiographical trope . . ."

Jackie spoke *kizungu mingi* until I wasn't sure she was even talking about *me.*

"You are not who you think you are," she said with finality.

I shook my head and walked away.

"What nonsense have you been feeding Jackie?" I confronted Mwari.

She stared at me as though I were a space alien. "I thought you asked me to act as your sister," she said.

"What *upuzi* have you been feeding her? She thinks I'm a walking dead. Killed at birth."

Mwari was quiet for a moment. "That was just *pandisa*. Did she think it was true?"

"You don't know these *jungus*," I sighed. "Don't give her any more cock-and-bull stories."

"You mean I should tell her I am your wife?"

"You are *not* my wife!"

"Booobooooooo . . ." Mwari wept.

I slammed the door and took off to Karen. That night, Mwari went into premature labor. She was all alone. It was the trail of blood that alerted neighbors. The baby did not survive. Word reached me while I was still at Jackie's.

"Mwari just lost our baby," I told Jackie.

She stared at me for a very long time. "You made your sister pregnant?" she asked quietly.

"It-it's not . . . not what you think," I stammered.

"She never told me she was pregnant," Jackie went on. She was quiet, then: "Now everything makes perfect sense." She paced up and down. "I am expecting your baby," she said simply, paused, then: "I will flush it."

The news of Mwari's death came that evening. Three deaths in one day.

I went to the *chang'aa* dens of Katwekwera, on the other side of our valley, and drank myself silly. I wanted to hide from the world. I went through funeral wakes in a drunken stupor. I was in and out of the dens. After the burial, some of my gang from my base joined me in the dens. Other boys from the "ShootBack" project came calling as well. They were there to condole me and the only way they knew was drinking. After a few days, Jackie sent me a thousand pounds with a note that I should seek help. I had enough to drink for a long time to come.

It seems like a long time since I started drinking. I don't need the money to stay drunk. Many offers come from men and women who want me drunk, so that I may regale them with tales of laying white women. The Jackie effect remains strong. I would have forgotten everything about my past but for some silly journalist who called recently.

He thrust a book in my face when he came to talk to me in person and said it was based on my life. Some Englishwoman had published it in London. I glanced at the small picture on the back cover. It was Jackie all right, though the caption said it was *Jacqueline Penny*. Its title: *Dispatches from a Shithole Country*. The cover illustration had the picture of the man with a flying toilet, from our "ShootBack" project.

"This book is full of shit," I blurted, provoking laughter in the *chang'aa* den. Neither the journalist nor the drunks in the den understood what I meant.

"But you should read the book first, before making any judgment," the journalist challenged.

"I can judge this one by its cover," I said.

"How so?"

"I am not who you think I am."

"But how can you predict what's inside the book?"

"Tell them! Tell them!" one drunk coaxed. "Tell them you knew her inside out! You are the master of this story!"

SAY YOU ARE NOT MY SON

BY FAITH ONEYA

Kariobangi

O n the day the sewer volcano erupted, it was not just shit and grimy water that came through Njenga's door in Kariobangi North.

"Mamako ako wapi?"

Njenga stared up at the animal barking down at him.

His mother, Nyokabi, called all of them animals. Their neighbor Nyalego said they were wild animals because they preyed on people.

"A human being would not do what they do to people," they told him.

The animal in question had banged the thin wooden door so loudly that the window rattled. Njenga could swear he saw the mud wall crack too. The animal leaned harder against the door and it creaked open a bit more, knocking over the battered wooden chair that was one of the two mismatched seats in the room. A rickety, stained wooden table and a beer crate completed the furniture. The air still reeked of rotten eggs even though Njenga had tried to clean up as much as he could. Feces still smudged the bottom of the furniture. Ras Kimani was a skinny dreadlocked man with very few teeth in his mouth and even fewer scruples. His matted hair hung limply on his head. Njenga resisted an inane urge to pluck off some of the worn-out dreadlocks that just hung there precariously.

Njenga had seen the man before. He knew his name. Ras came to their house at the end of every week to collect security money.

Njenga heard his mother plead for more time. She asked Ras to forgive her. Njenga hated it when his mother asked for forgiveness. Whose Jesus was this man to be a forgiver?

He had seen Ras squeeze his mother's buttocks and heard him tell her she was lucky she was so beautiful.

Njenga dreamed of the day his mother would not have to worry about paying the bills. But his dreams were punctured by reality.

He glanced back furtively at his four-year-old sister Lois, who was peering through the slit of the bedsheets that divided the single room into two. It seemed like she was shielding herself from something she could not yet grasp, but knew enough to fear.

She shrank back behind the linens, stepping over the *sufurias* they stored near the single wooden bed.

Ras glared down at the scrawny boy who wore an old, tattered, nylon Arsenal T-shirt and a pair of patched-up navy-blue school shorts.

Something leaped up from the boy's eyes and reminded him of his own phantom childhood dream of becoming a football star. But the thought was fleeting and he squished it as one would an annoying mosquito.

"Er . . . Er . . ." Njenga stuttered, the words that had unfurled themselves resolutely from the pit of his stomach now losing momentum and struggling to free themselves from his throat.

"*Aniririra kimwana!* Speak up! Nyokabi *ako wapi?*"

Njenga knew where his mother was but he also knew that Ras would not like his answer. "*Sijui,*" he said, sticking out his chest enough to make Ras notice that the fear that had hung thickly in the air before was now dissolving.

Ras spared a fleeting thought of admiration for the little boy. He could use someone like him. Someone with guts.

"Wacha kunibeba ufala. Na uambie mathako pia aendelee kukimbia kama panya, atajua mimi ni paka size gani."

Njenga was sure he did not want to find out how big a cat Ras was or could become if provoked.

Ras asked him if he knew what they did to people who did not pay security fees, his tone dipping as he bent his six-foot frame down to make eye contact.

"No," Njenga whispered, but it was also a prayer for his mother to be safe.

Yet he knew.

"Let's try this again because I like you. *Unakaa kama boy mpoa. Fan yeyote wa* Arsenal *ni friend wangu.* How old are you?" He gripped Njenga's shoulder.

"Nine," Njenga whispered, the word straining itself from his tight throat. He held the door handle so tightly that it croaked, as if in protest at being made to be part of a conversation it wanted nothing to do with.

Ras moved his hand from Njenga's shoulder. He had squeezed it so hard that Njenga felt tears burn in his eyes. He slapped Njenga's cheek three times, gentle slaps that held the promise of violence.

"Now that was not so bad, was it?" Ras smiled. "So, *ameenda wapi?"*

"Ameenda job."

Ras said he would be back, spitting on the doorstep as he slouched away.

Njenga rubbed the spit into the ground with his shoe and locked the door behind him.

"*Kwa nini amekuchapa?*" asked Lois, her doll eyes wider than usual.

He shrugged and said he didn't know why the man had slapped him.

"*Pole* Njenga." She rubbed his face gently and told him she was sorry.

But a different memory hung in the air, its sting as fresh as if it had just happened. Njenga remembered the last time he had to answer the question about where his mother was. It had been the matron at the Missionaries of Charity Mother Teresa's Home who wanted to know her whereabouts.

Njenga had insisted he did not know. His mother had warned him that the question would come when she took them there a year before. "*Nataka kujipanga kwanza alafu ni-wakujie,*" she'd told them.

She'd promised to come back for them as soon as she'd gotten some money together. She'd spoken as one would about going to the market to drop off a bag for later pickup. She had told Njenga to man up when his lower lip started quivering.

But someone had whispered to the matron that the woman who'd brought two abandoned children to the home was actually their mother.

"People say you look like her," said the matron.

Njenga did not utter a word. He had promised his mother he would not breathe a word about who she was. She was going to come back for them. He knew she would.

Silence.

"*Ni mama yako?*"

"*Hapana.* No."

"*Siwezi wasaidia* if you don't tell me the truth!"

"She is not my mother."

"They said you were stubborn. But that won't help you much. *Nyinyi watu wa* Bhangu *hamtawahi* learn."

He did not breathe a word.

His mother had warned him about the questions that would come.

"*Makûûria kana wî mwana wakwa uuge ndûrî wakwa. Makûria kana nîûrî mami uuge ndûrî. Wauga nînîî mami mekûny-ita mahingîre na ndûkanyona rîngî. Nîwaaigua?*" (My son, if they ask you if I am your mother, say you are not my son. If they ask you if you have a mother, say you don't have one. If you say I am your mother, they will lock me away and you will never see me again. You hear?)

The prick of the words still smarted.

Nyokabi stopped to catch her breath at the bridge over the Nairobi River on her way home.

She looked down at the dark, cloudy river as it flowed spiritlessly underneath the bridge and wondered what stories the water would tell if it were human. What stories would it tell about her?

Nyokabi had once been a dancer at Mahutini Bar in Kariobangi South.

She'd met Njenga's father somewhere between "Afro" and "Vunja Mifupa." He was perched on the *sina tabu* stool at the bar, his short legs dangling oddly from it. He kept shooting glances at her as he caressed a bottle of Allsops. Eventually, he squeezed a hundred-shilling note into her tight shorts, shoving it close enough to her womanhood to let her know the depth of his interest.

He wasn't the kind of man whom she would usually fall for. He seemed to have more problems than she did. He sipped a single beer for too long. It seemed like he needed that money to pay his rent more than he needed to appreciate her dancing, but something about him came across as sincere. Maybe it was the gentle way he caressed his beer bottle. Later, he said it was because he was not much of a drinker. But Nyokabi knew. She knew what such prosaic explanations meant. She fell for him anyway. Maybe it was because he smelled like a goat and she felt like it meant he was not a gangster. All she remembered was that she followed him to his single room in Bhangu and they created Njenga as he squeezed his juice into her. She still remembered his Allsops beer breath on her face.

She didn't see him again until Njenga was three, when he came back to finish the loaf of bread he had started eating and left midway.

He gave her Lois. This time, his breath smelled like Senator Keg, the famous brew named for Barack Obama when he visited Kenya as a Chicago senator.

Nyokabi never heard from him again after this. So she took Njenga and Lois to the children's home. Lois was too little to remember. She had only been three years old, but Njenga knew. She knew this by how his eyes followed her everywhere in the house, as if he was afraid she would suddenly disappear.

She had lost her dancing job at Mahutini Bar after she became pregnant and had never been able to pull herself together after that. She could no longer afford to keep her children and she was tired of their empty stares when she came home.

It had not been easy getting Njenga and Lois back from the children's home. It wasn't until she saved enough money doing casual jobs that she went for them.

She told the matron that it was Njenga's father who'd orchestrated their abandonment at the children's home. That was what won the matron over. They spent thirty minutes singing the "men are evil" symphony with the matron as the main conductor.

"*Aki wanaume . . .*"

"Eii!"

"*Wanaume ni wanyama!*"

"Eeeh!"

"*Aki pole sana* Mama Njenga!"

Nyokabi walked away with her children, Njenga clinging to her arm harder than Lois did.

A sewer rat scuttled across the bridge and she stepped out of its way. Something bad always happened when the sewer burst. The landlord of the apartment complex they lived next to had never bothered to fix the pipes and so every so often they would protest—loudly gushing, and with olfactory pomp.

Today had been a harder day than usual.

Nyokabi was sitting outside at the *matatu* stage near Mahutini Bar when Madam wa Vitz beckoned her. All the wash women called her Vitz because she had a Toyota Vitz and made anyone who cleaned her house clean her car too.

It was not the first time she had cleaned Madam wa Vitz's house. It was their third meeting. Madam wa Vitz never asked her name. Her eyes always slid over their heads as they sat there, like a woman inspecting *managu* at the market. They were all the same, but she wanted the ones without bristles. The *managu* that looked like it had the least problems always won the day. Nyokabi became the *managu* that made it home that day.

She did not give Nyokabi a ride in her Vitz; she gave her the house number and the time she was expected to be there.

Madam wa Vitz had no children. Or husband. Madam wa Vitz had more clothes than Nyokabi and her two children had combined. Madam wa Vitz had more food in her fridge than

Nyokabi and her two children could afford in a single week.

"There are some leftovers in the fridge. They have been there for more than a week. *Tupa zote nje. Sidhani kama nitakula.*"

Nyokabi stuffed the food into her bag when Madam wa Vitz was not looking.

Madam wa Vitz took her to the bedroom for further instructions. It was always the same. Turn the mattress over. Fold and arrange the clothes in the wardrobe. Beat the bedside carpet. Change the bedsheets.

But there was some money on the bedside table. One thousand shillings.

Madam wa Vitz had not left instructions on what was to be done with the cash. The money beckoned to Nyokabi. Beckoned to her as a drunk man would a barmaid.

Nyokabi thought of the things a thousand shillings could do for her. Pay Ras security money. Milk for Lois. Would Madam wa Vitz even miss the cash if she took it? The crisp note was straddled by two hundred– and one hundred–shilling notes.

The week-old food Madam wa Vitz asked her to throw away cost more than a thousand shillings.

Nyokabi tucked the note into her bra and dusted the carpet with more gusto than she had ever done in her last three visits.

But Madam wa Vitz had a CCTV camera in her house that was connected to her phone. She waited until Nyokabi finished her chores before she confronted her: "*Sasa umemaliza?*"

Nyokabi confirmed that she had finished her chores.

"*Sasa unangojea nikulipe after umeniibia pesa?*"

"Madam *nisamehe.*"

But Madam wa Vitz had already called the police and they drove into the compound as Nyokabi murmured a prayer.

Madam wa Vitz said she could not pay someone who had already stolen from her. The officer who got out of the van held a chunk of Nyokabi's buttocks and did not let go until they were seated side by side in the back of the vehicle. He kept his hands on her thigh as he asked her why she was using her breasts to hide money when she could put them to better use.

"Such as breastfeeding you? Did you not suckle from your mother's breasts to your satisfaction?" Nyokabi asked him.

He called her a *malaya* but did not let go of her thigh.

Later, Nyokabi let him pummel her with his manhood. She never reached the police station.

Njenga knew he had to do something about Ras to help his mother. Sometimes he wished he had a huge magnet to use. That way, his mother would not have to worry about anything because he would use it to collect all the scrap metal he could and sell it to Light Industries. That way, his mother would never have to send him away.

"*Enda kwa* Nyalego, *nikirudi nitakuletea kitu poa,*" he told Lois. He knew that if he promised her something nice if she stayed behind, she would be less fussy.

Nyalego, their neighbor, sold fish at Mahutini Bar every evening. She laughed with her belly and had a kind, lined face. Her face was yellow with brown patches, but her knuckles were the color of soot. Njenga's mother told him it was because Nyalego fried her skin with Miss Caroline lightening cream.

Njenga liked Nyalego. She taught them how to clean and eat fish and laughed when they grimaced as she gobbled fish eyes. She even gave them some fish once, but not a second time since his mother took too long to pay.

"*Na usikae sana!*" Nyalego said.

Njenga nimbly skipped over open sewer puddles as he made his way to Kiamaiko. Something bad always happened when the sewer burst. Njenga shook the feeling of foreboding from his shoulders as he bent down to nudge a piece of metal from a lump of mud and faeces.

What if Ras came back again? What would he tell him then?

If he collected enough scrap metal to sell to Light Industries, then he could help his mother pay security fees and buy food. The cling and clang of metal reminded him that he was the man of the house. It was the sound of his dream coming to life.

This time he would buy chicken legs. It had been a long time since they had chicken legs and *anyona*. He felt the taste of the pounded bread in his mouth when he thought about it. He imagined how he would roll it in his palm and dip it in the chicken legs stew.

"*Si wewe ndio ule boy alijifanya ndume?*"

Ras Kimani was suddenly towering over him, asking him if he was indeed the tough guy he had met earlier.

"I'm not asking for trouble. *Naunga tu ndeng'a nipeleke Lightie . . .*"

"Relax, boy. *Unataka kusaidia mathako ama hutaki?* Aren't you the man of the house?"

"I am the man of the house . . ."

Ras told him he would help him become a better man of the house. That he needn't hurt his fingers scavenging for scrap metal.

"How much will you get if you sell what you collected?" asked Ras.

"Fifty bob," said Njenga shyly, avoiding the man's eyes, not sure if Ras wanted him to pay the money to him or not. Fifty bob was way more than he could sell his scrap metal for and he wondered whether Ras would call his bluff.

Then Ras did something unexpected: he offered to give Njenga some money. Fifty bob!

"But you have to promise to help me if I ask for your help too, *ni sawa?*"

Njenga wondered what kind of help Ras would want from him, but not for too long. He could already anticipate his mother smiling at him and calling him her father. She only called him her father when she was happy.

Njenga took the money and stuffed it quickly in his pocket, as if afraid Ras would suddenly change his mind.

Ras laughed with mild amusement, snorting like a pig, satisfied that the boy had the right appetite for money.

"Meet me here tomorrow before school and I will give you something to keep for me. *Tusaidiane.* Let's help each other, *sawa?*"

But something was nagging at him about the job. Njenga remembered what his mother had always told him—that she would disown him if he ever became a gangster.

"*Ukishikwa, usiseme wewe ni mtoto wangu.* If they catch you, say you are not my son."

But something more pressing squeezed the words from his head and he remembered how much his mother tossed and turned each night praying for Jehovah to provide for them and become their husband and father.

Maybe Ras was their Jehovah. Did Jesus not say He would come like a thief?

Njenga bought chicken legs for supper that day and watched

as his mother and Lois licked the soup from their plates.

When Nyokabi asked her son about the money, he told her he'd worked extra hard *kuunga ndeng'a.*

"Thank you, my father," she said, smiling.

He had found Lois waiting alone outside their house when he'd returned home. He did not ask their mother where she had been but saw that her lips were swollen and her dress was torn. He heard her sobbing when they went to sleep.

Ras was waiting for him in Kiamaiko the next day. He gave Njenga a package.

It was a homemade pistol.

He told Njenga to put it in his bag. Told him to neither ask nor answer any questions about it.

"Unajua ma sanse hawawezi kukusimamisha juu we ni mtoi."

A *ndeng'a.* A gun.

Njenga stared at it for a few seconds.

A *ndeng'a.*

Njenga touched it and felt something running through his arm.

"Hii inaweza patia mtu shock?"

Ras laughed. He laughed like someone not used to laughing, like someone who'd just discovered laughing. Like someone who was using laughter to launch himself into an emotion he could not quite fathom.

"You are foolish but I like you. This won't give you an electric shock but it could kill you if you play with it."

Njenga took the pistol to school that day. And the next day. And the next.

He earned fifty shillings each time he took the pistol to school with him. One of Ras Kimani's boys was always waiting for him at the school gate at break time to relieve him of the package.

Until Nyalego was shot dead.

Ras Kimani's gang opened fire at Mahutini Bar and killed five people.

Njenga's mother told him that Nyalego took the first bullet.

"It was Ras and his boys. Revenge killings. That's what they are saying in the news."

Njenga stopped unwrapping the chicken legs he'd bought and listened to his mother. Something was buzzing around his head and he felt like his hands were suddenly starting to swell.

Ras Kimani was waiting for Njenga in Kiamaiko the next morning.

Njenga wanted to ask him about the Mahutini Bar killings. The words wriggled up from his stomach to his throat and hovered there, tadpoles learning to swim but drowning each time their heads came to the surface.

He gripped the package tighter than normal and jammed the zipper of his school bag as he tried to shove the pistol inside. He bit his lips and sighed when he thought of how much it would cost to repair it.

He strapped the bag to his back and waited.

"*Kuna shida?*"

"Nyalego."

"Who?"

"Nyalego. *Aliuliwa jana* Mahutini *huko sao.*"

Ras Kimani pursed his lips. "*Wacha umama.*"

"But *alikuwa* friend *yetu.* She used to help us take care of Lois."

"Listen, boy. Nobody deserves to die but everybody dies anyway. Didn't that church you go to teach you that already?"

Njenga hung his head.

Njenga took the pistol and buried it in the bush next to

the Mathare River. He did not go to school that day.

But Ras and his boys came for him that evening. His mother was working at her new job as a barmaid at Mahutini Bar.

Lois screamed when they grabbed her brother and earned a slap that sent her sprawling across the room. She landed with a thud on the floor.

They dragged him out of the house. Ras Kimani had a *nyahunyo* in his hand.

"Wapi mali yangu?" he barked, but the answer was the rubber whip he landed on Njenga's back as the boy screamed like a Christmas chicken having its throat slit.

"Rrrrrriap! Rrrrrriap! Rrrrrriap!"

The *nyahunyo* came down hard as Ras Kimani's boys watched. Ras beat defiance from Njenga's face and back. Njenga was bleeding. He could not see.

Ras asked him where the pistol was and Njenga told him.

But some defiance was still alive in him and he told Ras he could not be a transporter any more.

Ras looked at him and smiled. "Do you want to see your mother again?" he asked.

Njenga said he did.

FOR OUR MOTHERS

BY WANJIKŨ WA NGŨGĨ

Pangani

Run, Paul shouted to Samina. He was behind her. Run. Run. The sirens were getting louder. Her legs felt heavy. We need to split, he said. No, she insisted. Let's meet at home, he said. Samina knew he had run off in a different direction because she instantly felt alone. I must run. I must keep going, she thought, despite the stabbing pain in the bottom of her feet. Her vision was getting hazy as she snaked in and out of the streets of Pangani. It was as if the light was playing tricks on her, and maybe it was. Suddenly she was plunged into darkness. Like the sun had been switched off, and then her memory. She had no idea where she was, or whom she was, or why she was running. She opened her mouth. Help. No sound. She tried again. Nothing. Samina, someone called. She woke up with a start, her body drenched in sweat. Her mother Njeri was hunched over her bed, wiping her brow with a cold wet cloth like she had when Samina was seven.

There were tears on Samina's face. Njeri got to them before Samina. Next, she pulled the covers over Samina. Nightmares? her mother asked. She nodded. The nightmares started when Samina was seven and left by the time she turned nine; they had returned a few months after she turned twenty-one. Samina told her mother she did not know why the nightmares returned, but she did know. Two weeks to be precise. That's when her nightmares started replacing her life dreams.

Samina's dreams were simple. She would get a job after her accounting certification, so her mother could retire from her second job selling vegetables and fruits at the Garrissa Lodge market. Njeri's salary as a teacher at Pangani Primary School was only enough to pay for essentials but not anything extra. Take, for instance, the times when the city council decided to ration water, despite excessive rainfalls in the country. Njeri would resort to buying water from private companies rumored to be owned by government officials. Or when electricity went out, which in recent years had become routine, Njeri would need extra money to buy candles. She occasionally lamented that if Samina's father was around, it would be easier, but Samina saw no need to labor on about a father who no longer existed. That's what she told people about her father, the truth really being that he had disappeared before she was born.

This is what fueled Samina's dream to go to college. No, not her father's absence. A government employee should have known better than to impregnate a college student and then leave her. It was her mother that she always had in mind. They would move from Pangani to Nakuru after graduation, once she saved enough. Her late grandparents had spent their entire lives there. She had visited them a couple times, so she was aware of the crisp, fresh morning air and the vast lands covered in green. Pangani was dusty and loud and crowded. It was also windy, which only helped spread the odors that arose from the ditches where trash grew because the city council did not work or refused to work.

There were other options available for assisting her mother. Take her former neighbor. She dolled herself up in little dresses and visited drinking dens lined with fancy cars in Kariokor. It paid off because she moved to the blue-colored apartments across from Kimathi Street where the indoor plumbing never failed to work. Or her closest friends Satu and Batula who had worked out more efficient ways to make money. They did not harbor dreams of visiting drinking dens, or spending their hours under the sun selling things that took too long to sell, or of going to college. During their meetups on weekends, over roasted potatoes, barbequed meat, and khat-infused drinks, Satu and Batula would try to lure Samina to their holy ventures. They called them holy because they operated in abayas and hijabs. They had tried recruiting her on many occasions, but each time she declined. Samina had learned many lessons as a child about taking things that did not belong to her, let alone hiding in abayas.

Aren't you afraid of God's wrath? On no, they said, and pointed out that they had sufficient reasons for walking around in religious garb. Satu said the whistling from the young men hovering in Pangani waiting to secure jobs ceased when she was decked out in the loose-fitting, full-length robe. Batula added it also kept the police at bay. They liked to hound her, telling her to go back to the Dadaab refugee camp, as if she had not been born in Nairobi or as if her grandfather, who was of Somali descent, had not been detained for joining the Mau Mau war of liberation. Also, and perhaps the genuine reason, Samina thought: nobody could pick them out of a police lineup.

Their jobs were straightforward. Transport. The packages could easily fit into the pockets sewn into the dresses they wore underneath the loose, long abayas. Like Samina, their fathers were not present. Satu's father was killed in an armed robbery gone wrong in Runda. Batula's father had been a boxer since his youth. No one knew if the stroke that killed him was a result of the blows to his head or the fact that he passed by Satu's mother's shebeen every day. Satu's mother's homemade brew was always in demand. She mixed what she called secret ingredients into the fermented corn and wheat drinks. Next, she poured the drinks into calabashes, unlike her competitors who used plastic bags so that the clients had to struggle to squeeze the viscous, porridge-like alcohol from the corners.

A few weeks before the nightmares that had stopped when Samina was nine started recurring, Satu and Batula asked to meet up with her. They came bearing barbequed chicken, soda, and laughter. Looking at them wrestling to get the chicken off the bone and drowning it with the fizzy drinks, one would not have known they were all twenty years of age. Satu was taller and big-boned so she appeared older. Also, she had too many words in her mouth, so she spent lots of time sharing them, mostly with women in shops. Batula had fewer words but was brash, and this is one of the reasons Njeri was not a fan of this trinity. The other being that every time Samina was sent home from school for snickering and talking in class, Batula and Satu were the other culprits. Njeri would swear and shake her finger at Samina and say things she did not mean like Batula and Satu would be the end of Samina. That was years ago when they were in high school, but Njeri was still stubborn. Samina didn't concern herself with telling her friends they were not welcome in her house, but this was also why the friendship worked—because none of them bothered asking unnecessary questions. Deep down, of course, Samina was aware that her dreams did not include her friends' proposals.

On this meet-up, after the plates were clear, Satu and Batula told Samina of their latest venture, not only because it was different but because they wanted her to be part of it. Their other trusted friend had suffered an accident. Samina did not want to know the details of how he had sustained the injuries. She told them she was not interested.

That was three weeks ago, and what a difference time makes, Samina thought as she got into her bed. She closed her eyes and her brother was the first thing that came to mind. She remembered how he had come to her one morning. She tried to recall if he had been wearing a green or blue hoodie. The memories were fading with the years. She concentrated hard in order to recall his facial features, but they were evanescing. She felt herself drifting off . . . She tried to stay with Paul. She thought how good it would be to consult with him. He would have known what to do. Samina, someone called. It was Paul. Are you interested in an adventure? Of course. They stepped out onto the streets. Fifteen minutes later all they could hear were footsteps. Chasing them. Run, Paul shouted. She did.

It was his idea to go separate ways and catch up later to confuse the man chasing them down the street. With Paul by her side, Samina was brave. Without him, strength left her body. She tried lifting her legs as high up as she could muster, but her legs wouldn't obey, and her body felt as if it was under siege. Her eyes bleary now so she couldn't see past the crowds shuffling by her. She wiped her face with her hand and looked back, but he had long disappeared into the crowds. Pangani was always too crowded. Samina dashed down pavements sandwiched by tables with electronics and clothes and hijabs and cars and vendors and women and children all sharing the sidewalks, and roadways next to single-story structures built around courtyards, and multistory buildings filled with malls and bars, past those selling camel milk shipped from Garissa that her mother liked to give her at least once a week to cleanse her belly.

Half running, half walking, Samina approached her house, but darkness had crept in. She couldn't see, so she stood still. That's when she realized she did not know where she was or who she was or where she was going. Terror started filling her body, so she decided to sit on the pavement and wait. Just as her hands touched the cold concrete floor, she woke up. She sat up on her bed and wiped off the sweat with her bedsheet. She listened to the silence and then slid off her bed and tip-toed to check on Njeri. Her mother was sound asleep. She thought how her mother looked extremely small in her bed, as if she had shrunk. It's possible she had—her body was giving up on her quickly and it had been merely three weeks since the diagnosis.

A month ago, Njeri told Samina she felt a cold coming through. The following morning, she was shivering and sniffling. The painkillers did the trick, but the symptoms got worse. Two days later she could barely walk to the taxi that took her to Emarat Hospital on 6th Street. Malaria. That's what the doctor said. They brought home some tablets. After a week, they realized they were of little help. She needed to go to the Aga Khan Hospital Pangani for further tests. Antibiotics were administered and Njeri was sent back home. Two days later she was back in the hospital since she could not keep anything down, not even the medicine. By the time a proper diagnosis was made, and they realized she had bacteria eating away at her and she needed specialized treatment, Njeri's entire savings had been spent. In order to get started on the medication, a deposit was needed.

Samina decided to take over her mother's second job vending vegetables. The spot where her mother sold the vegetables was sandwiched between the popular Kilimanjaro Food Court, or KFC as it was known, and the pink and orange-colored Pangani mall. Hundreds frequented the mall which housed stalls that sold phone cards, barbed wire, and metal on the upper floor. The ground floor sold sarongs, hijabs, and other clothes. Located next to the mall was the National Farmers Bank, opposite the Horyal supermarket, so it was a strategic location.

Beside a garbage-filled ditch, she laid down a brown-and-red sisal basket. She opened it and arranged the potatoes and cabbages and mangoes in heaps of three on top of a plastic sheet in front of her. She prayed the rains would stay away. The pounding of the raindrops on the garbage-filled ditches easily awakened the smells, whose toxicity Samina often swore would kill her mother one day. She opened a purple patio umbrella to keep the sun off herself and the vegetables and waited for customers.

All this proved futile because by midmorning, the remainder of the potatoes would be shriveled, their insides sucked dry by the sun. The cabbages would rot before noon, and the carrots would wither before the sun set; the mangoes would be too scorched for anyone to eat. Samina's skin felt taut from the heat. She stayed all day, and only snuck into KFC for fish and chips, spending just fifteen minutes inside swallowing the soft, soggy, oily fries before heading back to the market.

When she went home, she fried meat and kale and made *ugali*, serving it to her mother. She saw the smile on her mother's face, and felt sure that everything was going to be okay. Besides, she had managed to save some cash, and this brought hope that had escaped her when her mother first fell ill. It was possible then, she deduced, that in a few months she would have saved enough for Njeri's treatment. So, the buoyancy stayed. When Njeri's body refused to cooperate and rejected the food or the water or painkillers and Samina had to use up some of the savings, some hope would escape, but not enough to diminish the good cheer she had managed to cultivate. She clung to it when Njeri became dependent on her because Njeri herself had not let it go, and when her strength was at its optimum, she would let Samina know she was grateful. She also swore to Samina that the illness would not last forever.

Samina hoped it wouldn't. But then there is always that chasm between expectation and reality. And the reality was that her mother was deteriorating rapidly, though this was not the reason for the recurrent nightmares. It was the phone call she had made to Batula and Satu, and the subsequent meeting she'd had with them.

During the tryst, she wanted to know everything about the heist. Satu said she had been inspired by a news story from India. This is why Satu and Batula decided to lease a stall in the Pangani Shopping Centre that was about thirty-five meters from the National Farmers Bank, next to KFC. They had rented the premises four months before with the help of their injured friend whom Samina would later learn worked at the National Farmers Bank. They told Samina that her role, though pivotal, was minor. They assured her that when her job was done she would not need to worry about her mother or where to borrow money; she would no longer need to sit under the sun all day. It's not good for your skin. Or your brains. You need a strong head to sit through accounting classes, Satu said to her. Samina could trust them. She knew this. She also considered the fact that they had never been caught.

This was not how she had envisioned their lives would turn out when she had first met her friends at Pangani Primary, a three-room school that was a couple of minutes from her house. On that first day of school, she'd woken up an hour earlier than she was supposed to. Her green uniform was too long, so her mother used a blue belt to hoist up the dress. She loved the white socks on her feet and her brand-new shoes. She couldn't wait to put books in her backpack. She hugged her mother and set out. It rained that morning on her way to school, but this did little to dampen her joy. Nothing could. Not like the past year, which had been so difficult.

For one, in the past term she had watched other kids walking to their first year of school through the window. Her mother did not have enough money to pay the registration fee. The truth is, Njeri had used all her money for their travel to Nakuru to bury Paul at her late parents' ancestral home.

Paul was nine. It had been his idea to go and take some candy from Old Johnny's shop when he wasn't looking. Samina thought it a stupid game but she went along with it for fear of being left out of future adventures. The problem is that Old Johnny did see them and started chasing them down the streets. When they parted ways to confuse the shopkeeper, Samina kept running and did not realize she had passed the street that led to her house and was approaching the junction at Kenyatta Road and Kimathi Street, which was the beginning of Ngara town. She had to turn back, but because she was frightened she decided to follow an alternative but longer route to her house where she would meet Paul. Three blocks from her home, she saw a crowd.

She asked someone what had happened. Car accident, they replied. She pushed through the crowd until she saw him. Paul. He lay there on the street, motionless. She walked over to him, sat down on the red carpet of blood that no one wanted to step on, and clung to him. She rocked him in her arms, barely supporting his four-foot frame spread out on the dirt road. The ambulance finally arrived, but it was too late.

Samina made promises to her mother. Before and after her brother's funeral in Nakuru. She assured her that she would never step foot in Old Johnny's shop. She told Njeri she would never take anything that did not belong to her. It's better to stay without. Yes, Mother. It's better to starve. Yes, Mother. She meant it.

Fifteen years later, after she had willed herself to join in Satu and Batula's scheme, she reassured herself. One time only. She told her friends it was solely because of her mother. Of course, all that we do is for our mothers, Satu responded.

Exactly three days before the heist, Samina picked up a black abaya from Batula. On that day, when the call to prayer started at the Abubakar Mosque right after the sun has passed its highest point of the day, Samina knew it was time to head out. She hugged her mother who didn't look well. Njeri attempted to smile and then suddenly reached out and squeezed Samina's hand, her eyes trained on Samina's. I should stay, Samina thought, but then tomorrow would be the same, she concluded. Her mother would still be lying on the bed, writhing. She placed some water next to her mother's bed and told her she would be back in a couple of hours. This would be the first time since her mother's illness that she was leaving her alone after the sun had gone down.

She pulled the black chiffon abaya over her head and let it drop to her feet. As she walked to the meeting place, she felt strange peeking at the world under the hijab that covered her head, neck, and ears. She paid attention to her surroundings because she was aware she was flouting something that was of value to others. Her skin flushed under her long abaya and when she thought someone was looking at her, she averted her eyes. To keep her mind off what she was about to do, she paid close attention to the passersby. She thought about how Pangani had changed over the years as she walked past a group of men in *kanzus* of various colors, and then saw Indian women in saris standing next to women in white headscarves, all waiting to buy coffee from the Ethiopian women by the roadside. Her mind, however, wanted to dwell on herself, and in a way, she started to feel that the abaya was the perfect cover, because she did not recognize this person who was going to steal from a bank.

Samina made it to the Pangani Shopping Centre and went straight to her friends' stall. Satu pointed to the extra boxes filled with dirt and advised her not to touch them or anything else with her bare hands, giving her black gloves to put on. How long did it take to dig a tunnel leading right to the bank's safety deposit box? she wanted to know. A few weeks, Satu said, her voice betraying pride. We took advantage of the drainage system, so over half the work was already done for us. The sand they dug out was put inside empty containers, which were then placed in the stall and boxes with secondhand clothes put on top. Hence, anyone who walked into their stall would imagine all the boxes were filled with clothes.

Samina looked around her. There were crowbars and metal-cutting saws and one pick mattock on the floor. It all seemed so crude and dangerous. Is this how your banker friend got hurt, by digging? Satu nodded. Batula must have noticed Samina's apprehension so she explained that the floor of the safety deposit boxes in the bank was an ordinary cement floor, so it would be easy to break.

This was not entirely true. As soon as they started, it dawned on Samina why they needed her. They suffered sore muscles. Blisters. Coughs. Itchy eyes. During all the smashing up of concrete, Samina thought only of her mother, and then the task at hand. She would take the jewelry and the cash and all the things that were stored because, she convinced herself, the owners did not really need them. If they did, they wouldn't store them away under lock and key.

Satu cried out when they first broke a hole into the cement floor. It was not too long after that they helped each other into the room. Five minutes, Satu shouted. By the time they started breaking the padlocks on the drawers, Samina was aware that her muscles felt stiff and that her breathing had slowed down. It was as if her body was numbing itself.

This is why later, she would not remember much about loading their sacks with all manner of jewelry and precious stones, or where she had left her gloves or when they crawled back through the tunnel. She was able to recall the moment when they were safely back at the stall, but this was only because Satu called out, We did it. We are free, Batula added.

Samina closed her eyes and took a deep breath and felt the air coming in through her nose fill up her lungs and immediately slow down her heart. She felt a tingling in her hands and feet as if her blood was gushing with more ease through her veins. She smiled and hugged her friends, who patted her on the back. First thing the next day, she would go out and buy the medicine. Perhaps she could flee to Nakuru and open a shop.

When Samina finally got home in the wee hours of the morning, she wanted to wake up her mother and hug her and tell her everything was going to be okay. Instead she jumped into the shower; she did not know that sometime during the night her mother had called out for her. Samina did not know that Njeri had struggled to get out of bed to reach Samina's room in order to tell her she was having difficulty breathing, or that her breathing stopped shortly after, in Samina's room.

This is where Samina found her mother, by her bed. On the floor. Samina collapsed next to her.

When the police picked her up the next day, Samina knew she could not attend the funeral or even make arrangements to bury her mother next to Paul; she wouldn't even know where the state was going to bury her. She would always wander in her daytime dreams, never sure if it was because of the abayas or because she had broken the promises she had made to her mother; in her nightmares, she kept saying no to Paul and then to Satu and Batula, but they couldn't hear her.

PLOT TEN

BY CAROLINE MOSE

Mathare

The piercing noise, when it comes, rouses us from sleep in an instant, because it sounds like the *firimbis* every plot in Mathare lets off when thieves come calling. Tired of robbers coming from Bangala on the other side of the Outer Ring Road, our community leaders walked around collecting two hundred shillings from each household, and commanded us to buy whistles. The shrill sound of one of those whistles in the night is always enough to get everyone storming out of their houses armed with machetes, kerosene, and matches. The latter arsenals are for roasting any thief to the afterlife. Every plot, as every neighborhood is called, has a head—that is, the person entrusted with the whistle. In our plot, Father was supposed to get the whistle, but when he didn't, people became impatient. Mama Mukasa in number 1 bought one and gave it to her son Mukasa, who just turned twenty.

The digital clock reads 3:12 a.m. As the time registers, so does the knowledge that this sound is not the plot whistle. It is a scream. We jump out of bed, shaking. My sister Nyah fumbles for the kerosene lamp, which is under the table that stands at one end of the room, in front of the door. We always move the table to stand in front of the door because one never knows if someone might creep in uninvited in the dead of night. Nyah is lighting the lamp, and my heart is pounding. The screams have now rent the air, a long, tortured cry:

"Uuuuuui, *Ngai fafa!*" It is the unmistakable voice of Mama Njenga, the woman who lives at number 10, at the far end of the plot near the shared long-drop toilet cum bathroom. We have usually been fascinated by Mama Njenga. She is obsessed with cleanliness and order. Her first name is Mary, and people in the plot have taken to calling her Mary Immaculate because of the way she anoints everything around her, including her front step, with bleach. Her front stoop is the only one that is consistently spotless, despite the concrete chipping off over time. Our plot has ten houses arranged in a rectangle. One side is numbered 1 to 5, and then 6 to 10 begin again on the left side, with number 10 being the farthest from the entrance. Ours is number 2, next to Mama Mukasa's number 1, which is right at the entrance into the plot, directly opposite number 6. It is now Mama Mukasa's voice we hear in the dark, following the terrible silence that has descended after that scream that has left all of us shaken.

"Enheee! What is that?" she asks in her throaty voice, a voice that carries itself like a soaring beast. We can tell she has not slept. Mama Mukasa usually goes to bed very late, after finishing her nightly sales of home brew, *keroro*, and making sure she has washed all her trade paraphernalia. This, she does in the bathroom cum toilet, next to Mary Immaculate's door, staining the area brown and wet with the dregs of her commerce. On many nights we hear the two women going at each other, Mama Mukasa's throaty voice clashing with Mary Immaculate's shriller one.

But there's no duel tonight, only a pounding silence that is cut open by heart-wrenching sobbing.

"Mama Njenga! We can hear you! We're coming out!" Mama Mukasa is shouting now, and we understand she is summoning us out of our houses.

By now, Nyah has lit the lamp, and we look around the room in the precarious yellow light. The kerosene in the tin lamp is running low, and the light emits a smoke that is oddly comforting. We see our father lying on his thin mattress at the far end of the room. He is fast asleep. Nyah does what she always does when we check up on him and slips her hand beneath his nose.

"Yeah," she whispers in the dimness to tell me he's still breathing.

Outside, there is commotion. We cautiously unlock the large metal padlock and open an inch. We peer into the passage outside. Opposite, door number 7 is wide open. We stare in surprise. Number 7 is rarely open. Its occupant is a middle-aged man we know simply as Ouko. He doesn't reveal his other name and we seldom get to see him. Some say he works with the police, others say he is on the run from the police. Yet others say he was once a robber of some renown who ran a notorious gang from the 1990s. We stare at his door because, as is typical, he is not the one who opens it. There's a young woman there, peering into the passage with us. We can see her well because of the bright security lights we call Passaris, after the woman who ran the project. She is naked from the waist up, and we stare at her pointed nipples with some fascination.

"Wooi! *Ngai, mwathani!*" Mama Njenga screams, and we peer into the passage, dropping our eyes guiltily from those tiny breasts.

"Mama Njenga, what is it?" Mama Mukasa passes by our door. She moves fast, her humongous bottom covered in a *lesso*, her top half in a T-shirt. We come out of our house and stare down the passage. The young woman at number 7 has vanished back into the dark house, though the door remains ajar. We step out into the passage and see Mama Njenga crumple to the potholed concrete. She falls on her knees and sits on them, head hung forward, shoulders shaking with agony.

Mama Mukasa hurries to her side. "What is it, *mami?*" she asks, looking around. From the bright Passaris lights hanging overhead like midnight suns, the area around Mama Njenga's corner lies in shadowy cracks and crevices.

I yank the lamp from Nyah's hands and make for the end of the passage. I lift the flickering lamp over my head and shine it past Mama Mukasa and the weeping Mary Immaculate who is sprawled on the dirty *keroro*-soaked floor. The door to the toilet is ajar, so I know that Mama Njenga opened it. Every person in the plot has a key to the toilet's padlock, and every time we use it, we are required to clean it, then lock it. I lift the lamp and peer into the toilet. And then I gasp and jump back. I can feel the people gathering behind me react.

"What is there?" Mama Mukasa asks, her knees making loud creaking sounds as she lifts her body from where she had planted it beside the weeping Mary.

I am unable to speak. Nyah saunters beside me and when she sees what I have seen, she shrieks and falls back, aghast. Others quickly come. Even Mama Mukasa's son steps out of number 1, tall with a bristling beard that makes me feel hot under my armpits every time I see him. He rarely gets animated by anything, this Mukasa, so he must sense something momentous enough to rouse him out of his mother's house. I glance to my side and see that Ouko's beautiful guest has joined our little crowd. Her nipples are now hidden behind a *lesso* that she has tied around her body just under her arms. A couple pushes forward. They live in number 8. Mr. and Mrs. Nyanjom, they like to have themselves called. Mr. Nyanjom steps forward and grabs the lamp from my numb hands and moves closer to the toilet. He whistles and speaks the name of God and shakes his head.

"*Bwana*, can you tell us what is there?" someone says, Ouko's girl, I think.

"We must call the police," Mr. Nyanjom declares.

"Eh! Why?" Everyone is pushing forward, but Mr. Nyanjom holds up his left arm with comic deference. "People, stop!"

"Waithiegeni is in there," I say, finally finding my voice. It is clear, almost loud, and its composure startles me.

Mukasa comes close to me, and I feel his breath on my neck. My heart is skipping and jumping.

"Ati, what?"

"Mama Njenga's daughter, Waithiegeni," I say, as if it is necessary to clarify who Waithegeni is. "She's in the toilet. There's blood. I . . . I think she's dead."

People gasp and push back from the ill omen I have just pronounced. I glance back at them and see them fight to register what I have told them. Beacause of the looks of confused horror I see on their faces, I refrain from giving more details of what I have seen: Waithiegeni's head lolled over, her mouth resting on the edge of the latrine.

The police have come from the chief's camp in Mlango Kubwa in their green Land Rover, or "Mariamu," as we refer to it. They announced their presence about an hour ago by knocking on the iron-sheet gate until we thought it would fly off its hinges. Why they love to knock like that, no one really understands. They are inside now, adjusting their big guns as they look around, taking in the ten doors that make up our plot.

"*Hebu angalia hiyo mwili tumalize hii kitu haraka, nataka enda nyumbani*," one of them says in his policeman's singsong voice full of impatience and contempt. *Check that corpse and let us finish this job quickly, I want to go home.* He must be the senior officer. I stare at his back, thinking he looks familiar. I turn away when his eyes gaze at mine, and fight the instinct to sink back into our house, because I do recognize him.

The sun is now up in the sky. 8:08 a.m. is what the clock said when the police arrived with their heavy knocking. It had still been dark when Mama Njenga's son Njenga returned from his nightly jaunts to find us all gathered around in shock, staring at his sister's corpse. He had only made one sound from deep inside his chest, like a suffocated screech. He held his chin in his hands for a long time, his chest heaving like it was going to explode. He entered his own house, number 9, to get an old bedsheet which he spread over his sister's nakedness. Then he declared he was going to call the police, and he departed with Mr. Nyanjom and Bosire. Bosire lives in number 6 with his wife Mwango and two children. Bosire is not a man given to small talk, though we know how active his fists can become when he is angry, and flushed from imbibing Mama Mukasa's potent *keroro*.

"*Na toa hiyo watu hapo nje, wakwende kwa kazi yao. Hii maghasia wanaenza anza leta shida hapa!*" The policeman continues to bark orders in his singsong voice. He wants the small crowd gathered outside our plot dispersed. He is squinting and sneering in the morning sun. He cocks his gun, and we all recoil at the sound. He is anticipating trouble. I know him.

Our plot is in Area Two. Between here and Kiamaiko, in the direction of the Outer Ring Road is a *baze* where young men like to sit, whistle at us passing girls as we go to school, and smoke marijuana—*bangi*, as they call it, which is quite appropriate as it looks as though it leaves their heads banged. One of those young men was found dead some weeks back, and by the time police came to cart him away, a huge crowd had assembled. One thing led to another and there was tear gas and gunshots. Five other young men died.

I remember seeing this policeman there as we dodged death and swallowed bitter tear gas that wafted in the air. He is a senior sergeant. People call him Devo, after the devil. I swallow a gasp. Of course. Devo.

One of the junior officers heads outside and tells people to get going or there will be tear gas. I peep through the slightly open gate. People are not happy. There is a hardness settling in lines on their faces as they turn away, unwilling to feed on tear gas so early on a Saturday morning, when some have not even had a cup of *strungi*—tea without milk and sugar—and leftover *ugali* or *githeri*. Times are tough, and leftovers have become rare here.

"Mkubwa," the other junior officers at the entrance of the toilet call the senior sergeant. He is looking at Waithiegeni's corpse, which he has uncovered. Njenga is there with his mother, who has not stopped weeping. Her shoulders rattle, while Mama Mukasa stands by, patting her arm and telling her to take heart. The senior sergeant moves closer, and so do we. We stop in front of number 4, giving room to the two policemen and to the third one just returning to his spot after chasing onlookers away. I hear the senior sergeant inhale, something between surprise and shock when he sees the body.

Waithiegeni is lying there on her left side, gray and still. Her body has lost color. The blood has congealed and glued her body to the floor. There are flies buzzing around her nose and lips, as though searching for moisture that is long gone. Her eyes are open and vacant. One fly lands on her right eyeball which is facing upward. Her right arm rests on the floor beside her face, the fingers halfway into the hole we *susu* into.

"When did you people find this?" the senior sergeant asks; his voice has acquired a gruff edge.

"Her mother found her at around three in the morning," Mr. Nyanjom replies.

We have now all gathered together in one crowd, all personal space set aside. We are so close that I can feel warm droplets of Mr. Nyanjom's saliva falling on my neck as he speaks. To my right is Mukasa, with his young beard and tall gait. He places a moist hand on my arm, and I feel like recoiling, but I have no space.

"*Wapi*, mama?" asks the senior sergeant. Mama Njenga steps forward. Her face is swollen from crying all night. Her braids are old, the growth at the bottom in disarray. It is clear she has not had the chance to go to the salon for a rebraid. She is disheveled, and this is not the way we are used to seeing her. "What happened?"

Mama Njenga, no longer Mary Immaculate, recounts how she came out to relieve herself and found her daughter lying there in the toilet, unmoving. "I almost stepped on her head because I didn't have a flashlight," she says, sobbing.

"You unlocked your door, and the toilet door too, yes?" The senior sergeant's voice has dropped to a gentle prod, and Mama Njenga nods as she wipes the tears off her cheeks.

"So she was not in the house?"

Mama Njenga is sobbing loudly, and does not respond.

"Mama, if you want us to help you, you will cry later." The senior sergeant is growing impatient, annoyed. He sounds like my father when he and my mother used to fight, long before she departed to be with the ancestors. Mother would cry, and Father would talk to her in that impatient voice and tell her to shut up, to stop trying to manipulate him with her tears.

He loved the sound of that word, while we found it laden with many meanings: *ma-ni-pyulaite*. Mama Njenga nods.

"If you found her in there after unlocking your doors," the senior sergeant is pointing at Waithiegeni's corpse, "it means she was not in the house, *sivyo?*"

We nod, all of us. We are entranced by that finger of his pointing at the young woman we all spoke to at one point or another in the past week. The shock of her passing, and all that blood dripping into the toilet, is beginning to hit us as we stand in the morning sun.

"So where was she, and how did she get in there?" he asks. "And who locked her inside?"

We fall back. Behind me, someone mutters a low "Mmmhhmmm!"—a sound one makes when they stumble upon a juicy realization that promises to unveil a dramatic climax. I turn my neck to see who it is. Ouko's girl. Her nipples come back into my memory and I turn away, embarrassed. I wonder, with irritation, who she is, and why she is still here. Bosire from number 6 is scratching his bare head. His wife Mwango balances their baby boy on her hips and tries to pull her *lesso* up. The left side of her face appears a little swollen, but then, that is nothing new.

"*Wewe, mama wa pombe.*" The senior sergeant now points at Mama Mukasa, referring to her by her *keroro* trade. Of course, the police know she brews liqor without a permit, because they pass by every now and then, either to drink for free or to extort money from her. She knows their game, because she has played it for decades. But a look of fear crosses her features. Her son Mukasa is too busy trying to run his fingers over my chest to see it, and my armpits are beginning to sweat because I am not sure how his fingers got to my chest, or if I like them there. I am also afraid Nyah, who is standing behind

Mukasa, might see and think this is what I let him do to me. But she is not looking at us. She, and everyone else, is staring at Mama Mukasa, who squeezes her way forward, then stops when she realizes there might be no space for her to advance to the front of the tight crowd.

"Yes?" she answers. Her soaring voice is not flying high today. Its wings seem to have been clipped, or doused with very cold water. There is a slight tremble in her voice.

"We know you go to sleep the latest here." It is not a question. "Who came in at night?"

"Njenga," Mama Mukasa says a little too fast.

"Yes, but he came in after we had found Waithiegeni," someone else speaks up. It is Gathigi from number 4 and 5. Gathigi, or Ga-things as we call him, has his wife Wanji in number 4, and his girlfriend Sweetie in number 5. Wanji has two children, and Sweetie has none. The two women are friends, though it wasn't always like this. Wa Muvea, the woman in number 3, our next-door neighbor, likes to regale us with stories about how Ga-things beat up Wanji when she tried to give Sweetie food that was laced with rat poison. Ga-things allegedly told Wanji that he would leave her to fend for herself and her children if she tried to harm even one hair on Sweetie's head. When all this was happening, Nyah and I had been in school at Kariobangi Adventist, some distance away. We missed the drama, but we understood the implication. Wanji's children were sired by other men long before Ga-things married her.

"And before that?" the senior sergeant is still talking to Mama Mukasa.

"Before that, I don't know," she says. "I was busy with my *kas-tamas.*" Customers.

The senior sergeant muses on these words and turns back

to look at Waithiegeni, who now appears to be one with the concrete floor on which she lies.

"Mama, *wacha ujinga*," one of the junior officers now casually says to Mama Mukasa. "*Sema ukweli. Nani aliingia hapa na huyu?*"

She is being urged to reveal who entered the plot with Waithiegeni. We are now staring at her moving mouth which is not emitting sound. The fear in her eyes intensifies. It is clear she knows something, but she is unwilling to say what it is. The fear in her eyes begins to infect us with its potency. I can feel hearts beating, feet shifting, sweat beginning to collect on our backs. Mukasa, silly man that he is, has refused to remove his fingers from my breast. His thumb shifts to and fro against my nipple, which has risen beneath my dress like it does after a cold shower. But he is also staring at his mother. She was the last to use the bathroom. Was it she who locked Waithiegeni in?

"*Peleka huyu mama kwa truck.*" The senior sergeant orders one of his junior officers to escort Mama Mukasa to the police van.

Mama Mukasa makes a sound of panic, but before she can move, she is being bundled like a sack of charcoal and brought to the vehicle. Mwango makes a sound from her chest that sets the child dangling on her narrow hips crying. Mukasa goes stiff beside me, but says nothing. I turn and grab that idle hand drawing circles on my nipple.

"What's going on?" I whisper to him. He ignores me.

"There's something going on here, and you will tell me what it is." The tone of the senior sergeant has changed from irritated to livid. "Everybody, sit down by your door!"

We all scramble to sit by our doors. Ga-things sits with Sweetie in front of number 5, and Wanji knows better than to open her mouth. All the children who had been told to stay indoors are called out to join their parents on the ground.

Wa Muvea only has her youngest who is three. *"Leo ni leo,"* she says cryptically. *This is the day.* The senior sergeant starts to walk among us, dodging our outstretched legs which block the passageway, as the doors across from each other are so close, sometimes we joke that two people on opposite sides can lean in through the windows and kiss without leaving their respective houses. But today is no day for jokes. Senior Sergeant Devo is here. I recall what Waithiegeni told me about a new boyfriend she was seeing, a nice man who had promised to marry her. Davy, she had said his name was. But now I'm convinced she meant to say Devo.

We are all seated on the potholed concrete. The senior sergeant has been asking us who was with Waithiegeni last night, who saw her come in, who she was friends with, but none of us are talking. We are scared now. Everyone has a key to the toilet. Someone must have opened it for her, and then locked it behind her after she was lying there, her blood flowing into the pit, her body as naked as the day she was born. Someone removed her clothes, slit her throat, and locked her in there. One of us. We stare at each other with suspicion. All eyes end up on Ouko's girl. She is new, so she becomes the focus of our suspicions. She seems to know this, because she has this sardonic half smile on her lips. She sits with her legs out, crossed at the ankles, arms across her belly, chest thrust forward, her back resting easy against Ouko's door, number 7. She stares at the senior sergeant, who is on his walkie-talkie.

"Over and out," he says, and lowers the black gadget from his mouth. Then he stares hard at all of us. "Someone here knows what happened to this young girl, a very innocent person who was supposed to sit for her KCSE in two weeks."

I feel a jolt of panic crack through my groin. Of course, the end-of-high-school exams are going to start in a fortnight. I am to sit those exams, but I feel inadequately prepared. Waithiegeni was to sit those exams too, but I know she had stopped going to school because she was sneaking off to see "Davy" all the time. We had spoken of this. We had a shared dream of maybe going to a famous polytechnic in the city center once we were through with high school. Walking distance, we had said, so all we needed to do was find a way to pay the school fees. Before she had let Davy fill her head with romance and a good life of raising children, Waithiegeni had wanted to be an artist. Her skills with a brush, or a pencil and pen, were amazing.

"You!" My heart starts to beat like the rotors of those police helicopters that fly by low at night with a big shining light, when I realize the senior sergeant is addressing me.

"Yes?" I hear myself saying.

"She was your friend," he says, as if he is revealing a secret. "Where was she last night?"

I shrink back. I want to say, *I would think she was with you,* but I dare not. She and I used to leave school and walk to Moonlight with our friend and classmate Waceke. Moonlight is in the *ubabini* side of Area Four, which means Waceke and the older brother she lived with had electricity. We would go there to listen to *Sundowner* on the radio as we did homework. Then we would walk back to our plot, Waithiegeni and I. When she started to skip school, I couldn't go to Waceke's house alone. I didn't like the eyes her brother used to nibble me with, and it was unsafe to walk home from Moonlight alone.

I open my mouth to say I don't know, but I realize he has

lost interest in me. He is telling one of the officers to bring back Mama Mukasa.

Mama Mukasa returns—there is blood dripping down the side of her mouth, and her eyes are no longer visible. Her usually fleshy face is now swollen round like the moon, and has swallowed up her eyes. We all gasp in unison at the sight.

"Ehee?" the senior sergeant grunts, as if to say, *This is your last chance.*

"Mummy, *sema ukweli tumalize hii kitu!*" Mary Immaculate is wailing from her corner, urging Mama Mukasa to say what she knows, once and for all. She has taken up that keening cry again.

The senior sergeant turns back and tells her to shut up or they will make her cry forever. She quits her weeping abruptly.

"Inaonekana msichana alikuwa na kijana ya huyu mama usiku," one of the officers reveals.

"Hmmmh!" Ouko's girl sits up at this news, while we all turn to stare at Mukasa with surprise and some shock. Apparently, he was the one who entered the plot with Waithiegeni last night. His mother was trying to protect him, and we wonder what they did to her in the truck to make her reveal this. Right now, she turns her misshapen and bleeding visage toward her son, and there is a tear slipping out of her right eye.

"I always knew this *chizi* boy was a *klinja!*" Njenga has roused himself from a stupor and is roaring from his door, hurling insults at Mukasa. He has never liked Mukasa, but still, we are taken aback by his screaming. All this time, Njenga had been sitting there, staring at his dusty sports shoes. They have a faded *Connate* label on the side, but one cannot be sure because those shoes have walked many miles and have seen a lot of stitching to hold them together.

"*Kijana, kimya!*" the senior sergeant warns Njenga to be

quiet, but Njenga leaps up and charges toward Mukasa, who is now half-crouched on his heels like a stray dog about to take a hurled stone. Njenga gets as far as our legs, which we pull back because he looks like he will trample them, when the senior sergeant hits him with his gun. Njenga falls back, his face bleeding. He lands on Ouko's girl, and both of them let out cries of pain. Njenga holds his face with both hands, while Ouko's girl hugs herself and pulls her knees into her chest.

"Let us hear from the young man," the senior sergeant says, then turns to Mukasa.

"Officer, I just opened the gate for her, I was not with her," he wails. I notice the way his Adam's apple is bobbing up and down with fear, and I feel a little nausea rising up my throat. Maybe he is a *klinja* after all . . .

"Were you on the outside or inside when you opened the gate?" The senior sergeant's voice is changing, and I am unsure what its lowered timbre is all about.

"Outside," Mukasa replies. "I snuck out when my mother was serving customers, and then I entered with Waithiegeni so my mother would think we had been together."

Mama Mukasa's round face is beginning to twitch with annoyance as she regards her son. Even swollen, the threat of a beating later is written in clear lines on her face.

"Ehee. And when you saw her outside, was she alone?"

Mukasa looks away, and that is all the answer needed.

"Who was she with, boy?"

Mukasa doesn't want to answer, but he looks up and sees his mother's swollen face and the threat written all over her body, and he sighs. "She was with their father."

It takes a moment to register that he is pointing at both Nyah and me, and that is when we realize our father is not with us on the potholed concrete. But at this point, we are beyond thinking as Njenga, his mother, and Mama Mukasa jump up, screaming and beating their thighs, as my sister and I cower in front of number 2, speechless.

We are back in our childhood home in Nakuru where we grew up. My mother was a nurse at the general hospital, and this accorded us a small flat in the staff quarters at the foot of Milimani. We are running away from an irate man who keeps calling us *nugu*, monkey, as he gives chase. Nyah and I are in full flight, the laughter dead on our lips. We were up in the trees, just playing, and we threw a small stone that caught this man on the head. We laughed, and he didn't. We are running toward the line of maize plants, where he is sure not to follow. We disappear into the maize field, and dive low to the ground, trying not to pant. We can hear him contemplating whether he should run after the monkeys. He eventually gives up and leaves. And that is when we realize we are sitting neck deep in *thafai*, the stinging nettle . . .

They ask us where our father is. There is shouting and screaming directed at us.

"Leave them alone!" Wanji shouts from nowhere, stilling the commotion.

"Those girls are raising themselves with no mother and with a father who doesn't even talk to them," Sweetie says, coming to stand by us. "Moraa and Nyakerario are good girls."

We are both in tears now. The senior sergeant boots our door down and enters with his rifle drawn. We start to scream, because we know our father is asleep on the floor, and if he does not respond, he will be shot. The police are inside our small house. I can hear the lamp breaking, followed by the stench of spilling kerosene. If someone is careless, they could start a fire. I break free from Mama Mukasa's grip and jump into the dark shack. The senior sergeant is turning our father around so he can see our father's face. Then the senior sargent jumps back, a small cry on his lips.

"You!" he exclaims. The two men stare at each other. Father says nothing. The senior sergeant appears to lose all his verve. He lowers his weapon, comes out of our house, and goes back to the scene of the crime.

We are all breathing hard, wondering what is going on. We see him lift the sheet that is covering Waithiegeni. He pulls it back, and most of us turn away from the sight of her naked grayness. Except for me. I watch him look at her. I watch him shake his head. Then he pulls the sheet back up and tells his officers to take Waithiegeni to the mortuary. Everyone falls silent as she is lifted onto a black polythene sheet. Her head lolls a little, but her eyes remain open. The senior sergeant tries to shut her eyes but fails. Mama Njenga cries at full volume. This time the senior sergeant lets her be. Njenga follows his mother and sister to the police truck. Then they are gone.

After a minute or two, Ouko's girl enters number 7 and comes out with a bucket, some Omo detergent, and bleach. Then she proceeds to wash the blood off the floor. We stare at her in disbelief.

"I am pressed," she says simply as she starts to hum, scrubbing the floor.

Waithiegeni is buried the day the KCSE exam starts, at the Langata Cemetery. I do not go, because I am taking the exam. For me, and for her.

On the last day of exams, I spot Senior Sergeant Devo near Huruma Primary. He is in his van, the one that took Waithiegeni away. I duck so that he doesn't see me, and walk on home.

By now, whispers have come and gone that Waithiegeni had been heavy with Devo's child, and that Devo has a wife and three children. No one knows how Waithiegeni died, but Mary Immaculate is back to scrubbing her floors, and Mama Mukasa is back to making her brews. I don't talk to anyone, not even our silent father, about what Devo saw underneath the sheet—the blood, the tissue, and the tiny limbs that lay by Waithiegeni's legs.

HAVE ANOTHER ROTI

BY RASNA WARAH

Parklands

Anamika was nervous as she drove into the 1960s art deco bungalow, on 6th Avenue in Parklands, that Dr. Shirin Manji had converted into an office. The entrance was through the type of verandah that Anamika, and probably the psychiatrist herself, played in as a child, with its terrazzo floor and quaint pillars that seemed to evoke a misplaced grandeur.

The office was sparse but cozy. There were no pictures of family on Dr. Manji's desk. Anamika noticed that she did not wear a wedding band and suspected she was single.

Dr. Manji had the kind and concerned face of a doting aunt. Droopy brown eyes with a twinkle of mischief framed by wavy hair that had a tinge of whiteness emerging in a shapeless fringe that covered her forehead. She was slightly overweight but pleasant-looking. She had been recommended to Anamika for the sole reason that she was Asian. She didn't look much older than her patient; if they had met under different circumstances they might have even been friends.

"Why are you here?" asked Dr. Manji as Anamika settled into the beige velvet sofa that smelled slightly of mildew.

"I don't know," Anamika shrugged. "I don't want to be here, to be honest. I find talking to psychiatrists a waste of time and money. I am only doing this because my employer is paying for it."

If Dr. Manji was taken aback by her client's candor, she did not show it. The doctor at UNHCR, the United Nations refugee agency where Anamika worked, had suggested that she might be having a nervous breakdown after colleagues found her crouched under a sink in the office bathroom. The kindly Canadian medic from Toronto who had left a thriving practice to help out the world's refugees—but who ended up treating highly paid self-indulgent UN staffers—gave Anamika a couple of tranquilizers and names of psychiatrists and psychotherapists in Nairobi who he believed could help her.

Anamika had initially resisted the idea but eventually relented when her childhood friend Winnie suggested she give a woman psychiatrist named Dr. Manji a try. "Only an Asian woman can truly understand another," she had advised. Anamika wasn't sure. When two people are too much alike, they can't help each other—because they know the sins of their tribe too well, and are adept at hiding them, not just from themselves, but from each other too.

Besides, she found the whole concept of talking to a complete stranger about intimate details of her life to be unnatural and unnecessary. Psychiatrists coax patients to remember things they have carefully stowed away and forgotten. Why exhume that which is already buried?

Excavating memories can be a delicate and risky maneuver. Quite often the temptation is to bury the memories in the hope that the pain they cause will go away. Anamika had managed to bury these memories for most of her adult life. Then, shortly after Raage's death, the memories resurfaced like a tsunami, particularly when she was drinking, which was pretty much every day.

They say people drink to drown their pain; Anamika's

drinking precipitated more pain. Not only were her memories more vivid when she was intoxicated, but they also resurged like episodes in the 24 TV series: *Tick-tock, tick-tock, tick-tock, tick-tock—bang!*

One evening she was home alone watching a Bollywood movie. Shah Rukh Khan had just confessed his undying love for Kajol through a song-and-dance routine in the Swiss Alps. Then, suddenly, whoosh, images of Raage's lifeless corpse swirled in her head. Then other more cheerful images surfaced: She was on her way home from school, gathering tadpoles in her compass box from the stream near her house on 2nd Avenue in Parklands. She brought them home, hoping to see them grow into frogs. Of course that didn't happen; the tadpoles died in her dripping compass box, their lifeless forms lying on their backs in utter surrender. Or when in the twilight hours, she and her two younger sisters would trap fireflies that lit up the garden in bottles, hoping that their bright neon-green light would illuminate their bedroom at night. Or Diwali nights, when the whole neighborhood was enraptured in a blaze of firecrackers, as the sweet smell of *jalebis* and *rasgullas* wafted from every corner.

Anamika's childhood was comfortable but cloistered. Racially segregated neighborhoods like Parklands offered an illusion of safety, but the suffocating norms and traditions of Indian family life created internal frictions and spawned rebels who couldn't wait to escape. In those days, everyone knew their place—the Indians lived worlds away from whites-only enclaves in Karen and Muthaiga and the dingy slums of Majengo and Mathare where the African working classes eked out a subhuman existence. The pecking order was clear: Europeans/whites first; Indians/Asians second; and Africans last. Unfortunately, not much changed in the years after Independence despite the desegregation of schools and the rise of a post-Independence black elite. On the contrary, a new type of segregation based on class and tribe emerged.

Anamika had no African friends until Winnie, the most clever girl in class at the mixed-race primary school they both attended, came along and imposed herself on her one morning after Miss Patel's math class. Winnie insisted on sitting next to Anamika in the games room, where segregation was enforced even in the types of games the girls played. The Indian girls always went for group activities like rounders, while their African counterparts preferred athletics. Winnie and Anamika's friendship blossomed.

After the office bathroom sink incident, Winnie—who was now a successful lawyer—suggested that Anamika write down her feelings, and when she was finished, burn every page in a symbolic act of redemption and forgiveness. It didn't work. Erasing memories from a page does not erase them from the mind.

We all have secrets that we do not wish to share with anyone because they are too shameful or too painful or because they remind us of the person we once were but which we do not want to remember anymore. It's called self-preservation. It is how the human species has evolved. If we remembered everything, from the moment we are violently ejected from our mothers' warm and comfortable wombs into the harsh and cold world, we might never get on with the task of living. So we choose to forget, or at least to remember passively.

Which is why Anamika was so baffled and scared when her fleeting memories flashed in Technicolor. At one point she thought that she might be losing her mind. The notion that she might actually be insane, or worse, a hopeless alcoholic, occurred to her when she began seeing images of a smiling Raage standing next to her bed in the middle of the night.

Their first encounter had been at a training workshop for midwives where Raage was hired as an interpreter by a local NGO. He was fluent in Somali, English, Kiswahili, and Arabic, and also knew a bit of Italian, the language of his nation Somalia's former colonial master.

Raage did not have the dark, lean good looks of a typical Somali; he could pass for an Arab or a Swahili from Kenya's coast with his light-brown skin and soft wavy hair, which could be attributed to his mother's side of the family, whose ancestors settled in Mogadishu from Persia some one thousand years ago.

"My mother's family were Reer Xamar, the original inhabitants of Mogadishu," he explained to Anamika. "Unfortunately, they were overrun by the pastoralists, who didn't care much for urban life. These plundering pastoralists, my father's people, destroyed my city." The latter wasn't exactly true; Raage's father had held a senior position in Siad Barre's government and was hardly a camel-riding nomad. But clan-based feuds between urban warlords with a pastoralist mindset had no doubt played a part in decimating a city that was once so beautiful that it was referred to as "The White Pearl of the Indian Ocean."

Raage's ability to laugh at himself and the predicament his country was in was what first attracted Anamika to him. "Don't be fooled," he had warned her. "We Somalis are born actors. We know how to hoodwink people." Months later, when the friendship had deepened, he told her he loved her. She believed him.

But underneath that cheery, carefree facade lay a deeply tormented soul and, as Anamika would learn belatedly, a frailty that rarely bubbled to the surface. Most Somalis, whether born in the throes of civil war, or the relative calm of exile, grieve for their fallen homeland. Unprocessed trauma is the term for it, and Raage had all the hallmarks of the condition, which Anamika could neither decipher nor treat.

Instead, Anamika had her own cries for help. Raage listened patiently, with the wisdom of those who have known real suffering but have survived through sheer resilience and optimism. *How selfish of me*, Anamika would scold herself the next day, *to reach out to a refugee who has nothing and to expect him to comfort me. What must he be thinking?* She could not possibly compare Raage's trauma with her own feelings of unrootedness. A century after her great-grandfather was recruited in India by the British as a station master for what was then known as the Uganda Railway, Anamika still did not feel like she belonged in her country of birth. Her and Raage's mutual feelings of "not belonging" to this place called Kenya is probably one of the things that drew them to each other. That feeling of being, but not really being. Of claiming spaces, but not being *of* those spaces.

The first time Raage reached out to kiss her, it felt like they had both found a home. Raage clung to Anamika afterward like a toddler latches onto his mother. Even though they were both in their thirties and had been in relationships before, that kiss felt like first love, an intoxicating mix of broken innocence, curiosity, and longing.

They mostly met at a café near her office, where many Somali refugees and their families gathered as they waited for one document or another to be processed by UNHCR. One day, as they sat having coffee, Raage pointed out a young Somali woman wearing a full-body black hijab. "You see that woman over there? She is a Kenyan Somali but pretending to be a Somali refugee, just so she can be resettled in America. A genuine Somali refugee in Dadaab sold her his lottery for $10,000 dollars." *Lottery* was the term used by refugees who had secured resettlement in a third country.

"Do the people in my office know?" Anamika asked with the naïve incredulity of a young Western aid worker stationed in Africa for the first time.

"Of course—they also get a cut of the money. In fact, they are the brokers for this sort of deal. But it will be hard for you to prove—for you guys, all Somalis look the same." Raage let out a loud chuckle.

As their friendship deepened, Raage confided that his younger brothers had settled in Minneapolis a few years ago, but they had never quite adjusted to American life. Two had turned to crime and were in jail. Another had been shot dead by a white supremacist in a street fight. Raage did not speak much about his family after that, and Anamika did not ask too many questions. But she knew they were a source of much anguish for him. What she did not anticipate was that Raage would suffer a fate similar to those of his brothers in America.

Initially, Anamika did not make much of Raage's absence from their usual haunt. At worst, she reasoned, it may be that he had been arrested in a police swoop. He had had many such brushes in the past, but always came out of it laughing.

"Saved by *Baba*," was Raage's way of explaining that he had offered a five-hundred-shilling bribe to a policeman to win his freedom. *Baba*—Swahili for *father*—referred to the image of the nation's leader that stares out of every currency.

Raage lived and died as a refugee but he didn't see himself as one. "Somalis are nomads," he often told Anamika. "We cannot stay in one place too long. Our home is wherever our camels take us. I am in Kenya, so this is my home for now.

But I will go back to Mogadishu someday, buy a house, and live there permanently." One day, out of the blue, he asked Anamika if she would go with him to the city of his birth. The question stunned her, not only because she had never entertained this idea, but because it seemed so absurdly optimistic.

Like most Somali refugees who escape to Nairobi, Raage led a subterranean existence, teaching English and Kiswahili to other urban refugees at a local community center during the day and working as a cook at a Somali restaurant at night, all the time trying to escape the snare of the notoriously greedy police officers who Somali refugees refer to as "human ATM machines" because of their penchant for demanding bribes. His fluency in English and Kiswahili often enabled him to pass for a Kenyan Somali, which is why he was so eager to teach Kenya's official languages to other Somali refugees.

As the week progressed, Anamika started worrying that something more sinister than a police arrest was keeping Raage away. By the end of the week, she was sufficiently alarmed to seek him out at the restaurant where he worked. The grim news awaited: Raage had suffered an asthma attack as he slept. His neighbor Abdi Mohamed, who everyone knew was from the Puntland region in Somalia, but whose recently acquired fraudulent Kenyan ID showed he was Osman Hassan from Garissa—had found Raage lying on the floor of his tiny bedsit. He had died instantly. An uncle and some neighbors had already buried Raage in the Muslim cemetery nearby.

Just as so many aspects of his life had remained secret, so had Raage's illness. "If we tell you our secrets, how will we be able to charm and disarm you?" he had once said. Anamika wondered when her secrets would consume her too.

* * *

In her ten years of practice, Dr. Shirin Manji had never encountered a patient like Anamika. Her mostly white and Asian patients tended to be much older, usually bored or disillusioned middle-aged women searching for meaning and purpose in their lives. A few were troubled teenagers dealing with addictions or the stresses and demands of modern life.

Despite her relatively young age, Anamika appeared self-assured and confident. Her smart bob haircut and perfectly manicured nails belied a woman who was always in control, one who could not let her guard down even in the midst of a crisis. But the cracks began appearing when she started to talk about her childhood home in Parklands. Was she a victim of incest or sexual abuse? Or was the pain she was experiencing the result of a rebelliousness that had taken its toll on her psyche and was now erupting as anger and depression? Dr. Manji was determined to get to the bottom of her angst but Anamika proved to be a tough nut to crack. Psychiatrists often use a method known as "free association" to pry open long-forgotten memories from patients. Patients are asked to associate an image with something they know or remember. The job of the psychiatrist is to find patterns that may lead to clues as to the reason for the patient's mental condition.

In Anamika's case, seemingly unrelated memories came flooding back like a badly edited movie. In the first scenario, she was having a conversation with a cousin, who had confessed to her that her grandfather used to fondle her when she was a child. In the next scenario, she saw her uncle putting his hand under the housemaid's skirt just as her mother was walking into the kitchen. All hell broke loose that day. The maid was fired but no one said anything more about the incident.

That was how it was in Anamika's family home in Parklands. No one spoke about anything too personal, especially a topic as delicate as child abuse or illicit sexual relations between Indians and Africans. In Nairobi, apartheid did not just manifest itself physically but mentally as well. People chose not to see what they did not want to see, or that which made them uncomfortable.

When Anamika was growing up, residents of Asian neighborhoods could go through an entire day without seeing people of other races. They shopped at the local Indian duka that sold everything from spices to safety pins. They hung out with each other at community halls or at the temple on weekends. Indians—who were collectively referred to as Asians after the Indian subcontinent was partitioned and a new nation called Pakistan was born—stuck with their own kind, as did the whites. They shared intimate domestic spaces with their African servants, but did not really know them. They bought *dhania* and okra from Wanjiku, the *mama mboga* who heaved her vegetables in a large *kiondo* from Kiambu to Parklands every morning, finding customers by going house to house. Everyone knew Wanjiku by name, but no one knew how many children she had or how many hours she had walked to reach Parklands.

This inability or unwillingness to connect with those of a different race or class became evident to the eight-year-old Anamika when Wanjiku stopped coming to her home in Parklands to sell vegetables. Neither her mother nor her grandmother knew where to look for her or who to ask about her whereabouts. Later they learned from a neighbor's maid that Wanjiku had died of a disease that was left undiagnosed for too long—perhaps because she was too busy working or because she did not have the money for treatment.

The void left by Wanjiku was never filled; by the time she

had disappeared from their lives, housewives in Parklands had started shopping at the swanky new Sarit Centre mall, where one could even pick up plump imported oranges from South Africa, a delicacy that Wanjiku had not been in a position to offer.

After Independence, racially zoned areas were desegregated but apartheid never quite went away—another type of segregation based on class replaced it. The colonial administration was gone, but the colonial mentality remained. Waiters left their ten-by-ten-foot hovels to work in five-star hotels with heated swimming pools; domestic workers cleaned houses with four bathrooms but in their slum shacks they only had access to pit latrines. Tycoons who made fortunes after buying off white settlers' farms at throwaway prices looked down on their impoverished brethren who fought in the war for Independence. No one questioned the hierarchy of privilege; everyone knew his or her place. But underneath there was seething anger—which sometimes erupted into physical violence—that no one dared to acknowledge.

"We are all underwater creatures," Winnie once told Anamika. "We live below the surface of the water, only coming up for air when it is absolutely necessary. Showing our true selves is too scary for us Kenyans. We never grew comfortably into our skins, maybe because we have been told for so long that our skins are ugly, not white enough. We always wear masks because knowing too much about our true selves may make us loathe who we have become." Anamika loved Winnie because she always spoke her mind, which was so rare in this city of make-believe.

Speaking one's mind was particularly taboo in Parklands, which is probably why Anamika struck up a friendship with the fiercely outspoken Winnie. Girls were taught to be silent, uncomplaining, obedient. Stepping outside the boundaries of the little bubble the residents had created for themselves meant inviting danger, especially of a sexual kind. Yet everyone knew that the boys and men in this neighborhood were crossing these boundaries all the time. It was common knowledge that teenage Asian boys lost their virginity in the hidden brothels and bars in seedier parts of the neighborhood. Gangbangs in these brothels were a coming-of-age ritual among Asian adolescents. These same nice, well-brought-up boys then went on to marry nice, well-brought-up Hindu virgins.

But when it came to food, well, they could talk about it all day. *Samosas, bhajias, chevda, jalebis, rasgullas, mishkaki, chicken tikka.* Housewives in Parklands learned how to make all these when they were girls and competed fiercely with each other over who made the best *kheer* and whose *pakoras* were the tastiest. The fragrance of *biriyani* from a neighbor's kitchen was enough to ferment jealousy and start tongues wagging. "What happened in Usha's house last night that made her cook *biriyani* today?" a housewife would ask a neighbor. "You think her husband beat her again? Is that why she has been wearing sunglasses all day even though it is raining? And did you see the new Peugeot her husband bought her last month? Wonder how much beating she had to endure to earn that. She always cooks *biriyani* after a thorough beating, have you noticed?"

In Anamika's childhood home, like in most Punjabi households, food was not just a passion but the very reason for existence. Her family not only obsessed about food the way an addict obsesses about the substance he abuses, but talked about food all the time. Perhaps talking about it prevented them from confronting their own pain or reality. Often food or talks of food became substitutes for meaningful or uncomfortable conversations.

It was the conversations—or the lack of them—that Anamika remembered most vividly, especially in the days after Raage's death. She recalled how talks at her childhood dinner table were dominated by how well the curry had been cooked or how nice and soft the rotis were. If she dared bring up a topic unrelated to food, such as how the headmistress scolded her in front of the whole school, or how she was bullied in the playground, or that she had tried to kill herself the previous day by swallowing twelve Panadols, the topic would quickly turn back to food. "Have another roti!" was a common response from her mother, or, "Can I give you some more *daal?*" There was no tragedy in her family that food could not soften.

Sometimes food was used to forestall a much-needed discussion, such as the one Anamika should have had with her mother when she began menstruating. She got her period fairly early, when she was just eleven. But because she was still considered a child (though her breasts had started to grow at an alarming rate), she was ashamed to tell anyone about it. Luckily she had seen her older cousins use cotton wool during their periods so she snuck into her grandmother's bedside cupboard and stuffed her underwear with a bunch.

She hid her period from her mother and grandmother for two whole days, until her grandmother discovered soiled cotton wool on the bathroom floor and decided to make a public announcement just as her father walked in from work.

"Anamika got her period!" she yelled, much to the consternation and horror of her father. Anamika burst into tears and ran into her room, swearing never to come out until the periods stopped. What seemed like an eternity later, her mother—an attractive woman who had tolerated years of humiliation for bearing three girls and no son—came into the room with a tray of food. "Here, I made you *pakoras,*" she said.

The woman-to-woman conversation Anamika was expecting didn't materialize, though her mother did tell her that now that she was menstruating, she should keep away from boys and not eat ice cream. (To this day she has never understood the bit about the ice cream.)

It is no wonder that she always had a difficult relationship with food. Friends told her that when she ate, it was as if she was at war. The knife stabbed the meat, the vegetables were mutilated, and no bit of the plate was left without wounded morsels of food. Perhaps because she found eating so traumatic, she was also allergic to cooking.

But then maybe food was how her family expressed love. There are many words for love in Indian languages. Urdu and Hindi have at least three words, each with a connotation that is unique to that word—*ishq* is a playful and passionate kind of love, *muhabbat* is a deeper and more enduring kind, and *pyaar* is a universal word for love, one that you can apply to your lover as well as to your pet dog. But these words are rarely spoken. A husband rarely tells his wife that he loves her; the language of love is spoken through the body—a meaningful meeting of the eyes, a slight touch of the hand, a smacking of the lips after a good meal. Often "I loved the chicken curry" is code for "I love the person who made this chicken curry." Saying no to a second helping can cause deep hurt and distress. "You don't love me? Is that why you are not eating?"

Associating food with love was always problematic for Anamika. She could see that the extra helpings of love that her family were getting were seriously impacting their health—her father was a gentle and hardworking man who made a living as an accountant at a big insurance company, but he had weight issues that led to diabetes, which eventually killed him. Anamika and her sisters were overweight when they were kids. Yes indeed, they were loved a lot. Her younger sisters went on to marry men who also loved food—and whiskey. The youngest divorced her husband after five years of marriage because the whiskey got in the way of the love.

The piece of land in Parklands where Anamika's family home once stood is now occupied by a towering office block, the result of a property boom and gentrification that have consumed almost all the old bungalows in Parklands. Gone are the art deco verandahs and red Mangalore tile roofs, as are the frangipani and mango trees that littered every garden.

Where can Anamika go now to rekindle memories of her grandmother's storytelling, or the fragrance of her mother's special chicken *biriyani?*

It was Anamika's fourth visit to Dr. Manji. As during all her sessions, she quickly settled into the velvet sofa that was positioned across from Dr. Manji but at a slight angle. A box of Velvex paper hankies sat on the small coffee table that separated her from the psychiatrist. She noticed that it had been recently used—one mangled wet hanky lay on the floor beside her.

In the earlier sessions, Dr. Manji had already asked the standard questions about her childhood that every psychiatrist is programmed to ask. Anamika had told her, rather unconvincingly, that hers had been a magical one, with picnics in the Ngong Forest on weekends and beach holidays in Mombasa during Christmas. No big dramas. Lots of food and laughter.

"No violence or abuse that you can remember?" Dr. Manji had asked.

Anamika had told her that apart from beatings from her mother—which Indian mother doesn't beat her children?—she couldn't remember being physically violated.

"What about sexual abuse?"

"Apart from that time when my drunk uncle's hand landed on my breast, I really can't think of any other incident. Why are you asking?"

Dr. Manji scribbled notes in her large red notebook, letting out little sighs now and then, like a child who is forced to do her homework instead of being allowed to play outside. After a few minutes of note-taking, she looked up, her face a little pensive. "I should have asked this earlier," she said, "but are you in a relationship?"

Anamika didn't know what prompted Dr. Manji to ask this question. It seemed a rather dramatic shift from her earlier line of questioning. "No, I am not in a relationship and I am not married."

"Any reason why? Not that I think it is not okay to be unmarried. I am not married myself. I just want to know if it is a deliberate choice."

"Didn't find a nice Indian man." She hoped Dr. Manji would detect the sarcasm in her voice.

"Not even a boyfriend?"

"Uhhm. Yes, but he's dead now."

"Asian?" Strange question to ask, Anamika thought, but then completely relevant in the Kenyan context.

"No, Somali."

Dr. Manji's plump hands curled up as if she were suppressing a thought. She glanced up from her notebook, and gave Anamika an inquisitive look.

The room went silent for a few seconds. The response had clearly startled the psychiatrist, but she continued with her probing after mustering a poker face.

"Did your family have a problem with that?" Again, a completely relevant question in the Kenyan context.

"No, they didn't."

"Really? That's unusual."

"No, it's not that. My parents died a few years ago and my sisters, well, I just didn't tell them. Raage was Somali after all, and a Muslim."

"What part would they have had a problem with, him being a Muslim or a Somali?"

It struck Anamika that Dr. Manji was herself a Muslim, an Ismaili, so she responded as tactfully as she could: "Being Muslim might not have mattered if Raage hadn't been a Somali to boot. You know how we Kenyans view Somalis, especially now with al-Shabaab and all that. One of my distant relatives was killed by al-Shabaab terrorists in the Westgate mall attack. Besides, I just didn't think it was necessary to talk about it since Raage and I had no plans to marry."

"When did Raage die?" Dr. Manji asked after a long pause.

"Two months ago."

"Is that when you had the nervous breakdown?"

"I wouldn't call it a nervous breakdown, but yes, I did start drinking a lot. And then there were the nightmares."

"Tell me about Raage."

"What is there to say? He was a Somali refugee. Grew up in Mogadishu and then fled with his family to Kenya in 1992. His father was killed in Mogadishu at the start of the civil war. His mother raised four children by herself. He was the oldest. He ran away from the Dadaab refugee camp to Nairobi. We met through my work with the refugee agency. A self-made, proud man. Died of asthma partly because no hospital in Nairobi would admit a Somali man without an ID."

"Do you blame yourself for his death?"

The question took Anamika by surprise. "No. What do you mean?"

"I mean here you are working for a refugee agency, and

you could not do anything for this particular refugee. Perhaps you feel guilty?"

"He didn't want to be helped. He was too proud. He wanted to live in Kenya, but Kenya does not issue citizenship to Somali refugees. So what could I do?"

"Did Raage ever ask for your help?"

"No, and I don't know where you are going with this line of questioning."

"It is clear to me that Raage's death was a turning point for you. I am just trying to see if there is any connection between his death and . . ." she paused, "your—your own feelings of . . . worthlessness."

The clock on the wall behind Dr. Manji's desk seemed to be ticking louder. Anamika wondered what she had said that made the good doctor believe that she felt worthless.

"I do not feel worthless," she stated firmly. "I'm just having a rough time right now dealing with Raage's death."

Then, quite unexpectedly, tears begun soaking Anamika's cheeks. She reached for the Velvex, feeling slightly embarrassed about crying in front of a near stranger. Her sobs sounded like a strangled wail.

Dr. Manji noticed that the teardrops were drenching Anamika's neck and soaking her white silk shirt.

Then, the *Eureka!* moment. In psychotherapy, they call it a breakthrough. It occurred to Dr. Manji that Anamika was not mourning Raage as much as she was mourning her own demise, many years ago in Parklands, where talk of food had replaced meaningful conversation, and where trapped fireflies and tadpoles came to die. She was grieving the loss of home, just like Raage, a home whose memories now lay buried in the foundation of a sterile office block in Parklands and in a heap of blood-soaked rubble in Mogadishu.

The clock announced that it was five p.m. The session had ended. Dr. Manji closed her notebook, looked up at Anamika, and smiled.

PART III

THE HERDERS

BELONGING

BY J.E. SIBI-OKUMU
Westlands

I f the robbery involving the Haywoods had been an inside
job, the common analysis in such circumstances, then the
two prime suspects lacked motives. Both were insiders, as
they lived on the Haywood compound, in the secured domestic servants' quarters. These comprised two separate rooms,
each with space enough to fit a bed, a gas cooker, and a few
other personal belongings, stacked up to make movement
possible. As for amenities, the occupants shared a long-drop
toilet as well as a space to have a cold shower. In the enclosed
yard, there was a concrete sink for washing laundry by hand.

In one of the rooms lived Hannah, the house help. That
was the politically correct term, which had replaced *house ser-
vant* and *house maid*. Hannah was a family institution, having
been with the Haywoods from two years after they got married; long enough to have played a significant part in raising
their son and two daughters, now adults and parents themselves. Hannah had grown-up children of her own but her
husband had died.

In the other room lived Dixon, the gardener, a young man
of twenty-three, who had taken over the job from his own
father after his retirement.

There were two regular outsiders. One was Muthoni the
vegetable lady, or "Mama Mboga," who came by once a week
to offer a choice of cabbages, onions, tomatoes, and especially

sukuma wiki, the kale that did, indeed, "push the week along" when money was tight. She carried her offerings in a heavy bundle strapped to her forehead and supported on her back. The other was Enock, the night watchman. He had been the mainstay on the compound for the last four years, only relieved during weekends, every fortnight. Should the need arise he could call for unarmed reinforcement from his firm by pressing one of two panic buttons strategically positioned at opposite corners of the main house, after which a support vehicle was guaranteed to arrive within minutes. The Haywoods had two buttons inside the house as well. Security was an issue.

The Haywoods lived in Westlands, described alongside Muthaiga, Karen, Langata, and Lavington as one of Nairobi's earliest upmarket and multiracial, "leafy" suburbs.

Westlands rarely drew attention to itself. Every once in a while, an incident worthy of public interest did occur there. Sometimes there was agitation within Deep Sea, the slum or "informal settlement," on its periphery. Either accident or arson would set its highly flammable dwellings and kiosks ablaze, with vermilion flames visible from a distance and thick smoke billowing up to the sky. But Deep Sea had a capacity to rebuild itself within months.

Sometimes there was a concerted push to get rid of *chokoras,* who were ruining the look of the area through their unkemptness, their glue-sniffing, and their begging.

Sometimes there would be gridlocked traffic jams because major arteries had been sealed off to accommodate the arrival or departure of a visiting head of state.

The name Westlands could bring back disturbing memories of Professor Wangari Maathai's fight to save the Karura Forest, also on its periphery. Or it could call to mind Westgate,

Kenya's own 9/11-style experience when, in September 2013, a late-morning raid on a shopping mall of that name had left more than sixty people dead.

Richard and Felicity Haywood were Kenya Cowboys, or KCs, that is to say Kenyans of mainly British origin. They still worked as partners in their own accounting firm in central Westlands and had a reputation for philanthropy. They made it clear to every guard who was posted to them that they were against the idea of their home being some sort of no-entry military zone. Everyone was welcome, they insisted, without protracted interrogation. That was how human beings were meant to live, they believed. And that was why they did not consider the added expense of taking on a day guard. In the daytime, their main metal gate remained open.

On the night in question, a Wednesday, Enock was on duty. The Haywoods were always reassured by his trusty presence. Enock, a married man in his late thirties whose young family lived away from him in a village in Ukambani, rented a tiny mud-walled room in Deep Sea. He would walk to work every evening, to begin around six. It took him about half an hour to get to the Haywoods'. For the past year or so, a bypass under construction had cut right through Deep Sea, branching off from the Limuru Road to merge into Ring Road, Westlands, there from colonial days, which was now to be expanded into a dual carriageway. Just past the Shiv Temple, Enock would turn right onto Eldama Raveen Road, signposted ahead of him by a city council painter who had not known how to spell *ravine* properly. He would go past the Mystique Restaurant, famous for its *koroga* or self-cooking option for patrons. On either side of him would be the homes of well-to-do local and expatriate Africans, Asians, and Europeans. It had not always been thus, for in pre-Independence times, Westlands had been a segregated whites-only section of Nairobi. The Haywoods lived a short distance from the West Wood Hotel and the About Thyme Restaurant, both toward the end of the road. Enock always carried his uniform with him and changed in the DSQ (domestic servants' quarters) shower room. Without it, he held no menace, being of very slight build. But once he put it on, he looked very much the part.

At around seven thirty, Enock registered headlights at the gate. He let himself out through a side opening. The car was a white four-wheel drive. Two men were sitting in front.

"*Habari?* Can I assist you?" Enock asked.

"Yes. We have come to see Mr. and Mrs. Haywood," the driver explained. He spoke in a deep baritone.

"You are from where? You have not been here before," Enock challenged.

"Yes, we have," the driver answered. "*You* were not here. Mr. Haywood used to be our teacher. We have come to take him and Mama out for dinner. Mr. Juma is my name. And this is Mr. Kizito. You can tell them that."

Kizito leaned over to be more visible, smiled at Enock, and cupped his hands together as if in supplication, a sign of humble greeting.

"That's okay, *sah!*" Enock accepted. He went back to open the whole gate. Normally, he would have thought twice about letting the two men in without first going to seek confirmation, because the various races usually kept to themselves when it came to socializing. But the Haywoods were different. All sorts of people came to visit them regularly. And from the way Juma spoke English it was evident that he was a very high-class man. And he had identified himself and his companion, very openly.

Enock let the car drive in and closed the gate after it. The car continued along the cobblestones then made several turns to face the gate before stopping. The two men got out. They were dressed in dark suits and red and blue ties. Juma was the much taller of the two. He looked like a bouncer. Kizito was not as huge.

Enock walked up to the car. "You know the way?"

"*Ndio!*" Juma declared. Up to this point, Kizito had said nothing.

"*Sawa,*" Enock said, and walked back to his shelter beside the main gate.

Juma and Kizito were glad that things were going so well. There was an alternative plan if the guard behaved differently. Juma went ahead of Kizito.

The Haywoods' house was built on one acre of land whose lower boundary was marked by the Mathare River, once notable for its clear waters but nowadays more for the plastic containers that bobbed along it. The Haywoods' property was on an incline. The DSQ and garage were at the driveway level but to get to the Haywoods' house and its surrounding garden, Juma and Kizito had to walk down a series of steps, introduced by a wooden barrier. Once they had gone past it, Caesar, a black Labrador and one of the household pets, ran up to them. He let out a growl, followed by some squeaky barks, then came up to smell them and leap at their trousers. Juma kicked Caesar out of the way and the dog yelped. The two men walked confidently to the front door, which was behind a padlocked grille. Juma rang the bell. Once, only. About half a minute later, a key turned.

Haywood opened the door and found himself face to face with two unfamiliar men. The taller one was pointing a handgun at him.

Juma sized him up. Haywood looked taller than he actually was because he stood so upright. He had the physique of a young man and only his graying hair and beard revealed his age.

"Mr. Richard Haywood, I presume," Juma said knowingly. "Open!"

Haywood did as he was told. Taking another key, he first opened the padlock, then the security grille, and stepped back diffidently to let the two men in.

"Give me the keys!" Juma ordered. He locked up and kept the keys.

Felicity Haywood showed surprise when her husband came in with two unfamiliar African men. She was sitting on a scarlet-red sofa reading a novel, but she stood up immediately, as if to acknowledge the entry of superiors. Bach's cello suites, interpreted by Casals, were playing soothingly but unobtrusively from a CD. Felicity had auburn hair that was tied in a bun and she was wearing dark-rimmed spectacles. Dido, the cat, was a silent onlooker, lying in a basket on a drinks cabinet.

"Good evening, Mrs. Haywood," Juma said. "I have a gun." The weapon was not visible in its belt holster covered by his coat. "And my friend has one too. Don't do anything stupid. *Sasa,* hand over your cell phones."

Haywood's mobile was in his pocket. His wife's was in her handbag, on a side table. Juma gave them to Kizito, who switched them off before placing them in the side pocket of his suit.

"May we sit down, madam?" Kizito asked, speaking for the first time.

"Yes. Do sit down." Felicity was trying hard to hide her

fear, calling to mind what she had often heard: that in these situations it was best to keep the other people talking and get them to relax.

"Thank you," said Kizito. "Do join us!"

Soon they were all seated, Richard and Felicity beside each other on the sofa and the two strangers in armchairs, opposite them.

"Very good. They call me Juma. And this is Kizito."

"And you, Mr. and Mrs. Haywood, are fellow Kenyans," interjected Kizito. "That makes me very happy. So rest assured: we will not hurt you. Unless, of course, you make us." His voice was higher-pitched than Juma's and he spoke very deliberately, like a politician addressing gullible *wananchi*. "When did you become Kenyans?" he asked.

"We were both born here," Haywood responded. "My wife and I are third-generation."

"Ah! The children of our colonial masters?" Kizito said.

"In a manner of speaking."

"And where did you go to school?"

"The Prince of Wales, now Nairobi School," Haywood answered.

"What a privilege," Kizito said. "But our past is past. We are now in the same boat. Except that those whose grandfathers served the wishes of *your* forebears have now taken over. But they are worse than the white man. Now, it is the turn of the sons and daughters of home guards to oppress the sons and daughters of freedom fighters. We must not forget our history. Wouldn't you agree, Mr. Haywood?"

"I have no great interest in politics."

"Oh, but you must! You must! Everything in life is political," Kizito rejoined.

"Kizito!" Juma cut in. "That's enough! *Wacha maneno!*"

"Don't worry," Kizito countered, "there's nothing wrong with getting to know each other a little better."

Juma looked quickly at his watch.

"Mrs. Haywood . . . Felicity, if I may," Kizito went on, "you haven't said a word. Where did *you* go to school?"

"My parents were farmers," Felicity proffered. "So, I first went to the Hill School, Eldoret, and then I boarded at Kenya High."

"Ah! The *Boma*! The enclosure for beautiful females like yourself. What a privilege for you too, Felicity!" Kizito said. "Unlike you, the two of us went to maize-and-beans schools. But I hope that our roots do not betray us?"

"No, not at all," Felicity quickly replied. "You both speak very good English."

"Count me out!" Juma protested. "I am a secondary school dropout!"

"Do you speak Kiswahili?" Kizito asked.

"Not as well as we should," Haywood said. "We were never taught it at school."

"What about you?" Kizito asked Felicity.

"*Kidogo*," she answered.

"*Kidogo?* A little is not enough," Kizito scolded. "Look at the effort *I* have made to try to master *your* language. I have a degree in English literature. But it has done nothing to help me to find a job. Or at least a proper job, which could allow *me* to live like *you*. In a house like *yours*, one day. So, much against my will, in order to survive, I have ended up in your living room. Anyway, like I said, there's nothing wrong with getting to know each other a bit. It would be nice to have a cup of tea and continue chatting. In fact, I would love to look through some of the books in your wonderful library—"

"Enough!" Juma snapped.

"*Sawa*," Kizito conceded.

Haywood was trying his best to put on a brave face but every cell in his body was filled with fright. He was trembling slightly. He looked across to his wife, who had cupped her hands in front of her mouth and was holding back tears. He had never had to act courageous in front of her before.

"Take what you want. But please don't hurt us," Felicity entreated.

"I am sure it won't come to that," Kizito reassured her. "You can trust me." He walked up to her and kissed the palm of her hand.

"Kizito, stop fooling around! There is no time to waste!"

For all their bravado, Juma and Kizito seemed equally agitated. Kizito kept pacing around, picking up ornaments and then putting them down again. And Juma kept glancing at his watch.

Husband and wife stood up. It was at this point that Felicity made an unexpected request, all the more so because she made it in Kiswahili.

"*Wacheni pete zetu ya harusi, tafadhali,*" she said.

"How interesting," Kizito remarked, "that someone who can say, *Leave us our wedding rings, please,* in such perfect Kiswahili professes to speak the language only *kidogo*? Is this a case of false humility?"

"I get by," Felicity replied.

"Ah! The English love of understatement!" Kizito said.

"No. Quite seriously," Felicity said, making another attempt to ease the tension. "My husband and I appreciate that, however regrettable your intrusion, this whole matter could take on quite a different tone were it not for your understanding. We thank you for promising not to hurt us. Take what you want. But just leave us our wedding rings. That's all I ask."

Kizito smiled and said nothing.

"These *wazungus* are very funny *peepo*," Juma noted. "Everything is so lovey-dovey to them. Sorry, though. We will take the rings!" He glanced at his watch again.

Haywood reached across to help his wife remove her ring. Then he removed his own and meekly gave both to Juma.

"*Sasa*, any money in cash? And bring out your ATM cards. Write down the PIN numbers!" Juma instructed.

Haywood handed over his wallet and Felicity her purse. Haywood wrote down his own PIN number and passed the piece of paper and ballpoint pen he had used to his wife.

"The correct information," Juma said. "Remember, any *nyoko nyoko* and I'll cut off this man's penis and make him smoke it like a cigar. Do you understand?"

"Yes," Haywood replied.

"We understand. Please don't hurt us," Felicity said.

"No," Juma said. "With you, Mrs. Haywood, we can have some fun together."

Kizito held up the keys and motioned everyone out. He took out his gun but concealed it under his coat.

They went past Dido the cat, now walking about but still in a separate world.

Upon seeing his owners, Caesar the dog stood up and wagged his tail as he accompanied them to the car.

Haywood thought he saw a curtain being pulled aside in Dixon's room, which had some lights on. But that may have been wishful thinking. Hannah's lights were already out. As they got into the back of the car, the thought entered both Haywood's and Felicity's minds that it may have been stolen and the license plate changed to read, *KAZ 581 N.*

Enock was still beside the gate. At ten o'clock, his supervisor would come for a routine check and Enock would begin hourly walkabouts at midnight, carrying his baton and shining his flashlight. His beat ended at five every morning. As he opened the gate for the white car to exit, he was not at all suspicious. The two men had not stayed very long. And there they were taking out their teacher and his wife for dinner, as they had explained.

"*Asante*," Kizito said through the side window closest to the guard.

"*Sawa, sawa*, Enock!" Haywood added reassuringly.

Enock saluted them as the car drove out.

At around ten to eight, there was still a lot of traffic on the roads. They did not head, as the Haywoods might have thought, to Deep Sea. Instead, Juma turned right on Eldama Raveen Road, left past the bank building onto the lower end of Peponi Road, then drove straight ahead. The car headed past the Westgate Shopping Mall, repaired and fortified since the terror attack.

A confusion of thoughts invaded the Haywoods. Foremost among them: were they going to come out of all this alive? Felicity wondered whether she would ever see her grandchildren again. Then she wondered whether she had turned off the oven. Haywood wondered what he could do, proactively, in this situation. As a mental diversion each of them resorted to identifying landmarks along the way, reminiscent of the observation game they had played with their children on their way to school, or on safaris. After a couple of minutes of driving, they came to the Sarit Centre.

The car turned right at an intersection and then left onto Waiyaki Way, heading in the direction of downtown Nairobi, past what was once the landmark Westlands Roundabout, now sealed off as part of supposed improvements in traffic flow. A bit farther down, Juma took a slip road and made a

U-turn that put him back on the highway, but going in the opposite direction, toward Naivasha, the nearest sizable town.

"Where are we going?" Felicity asked.

"You talk too much, woman!" Juma snapped. *"Nyamaza!"*

"Don't speak to my wife like that!"

"Don't you talk to *me* like that!" Juma shot back. "Or you will see!"

Silence reigned from that point onward, at least for the Haywoods.

Juma and Kizito continued to have animated exchanges in the English and Kiswahili hybrid known as *Sheng*. The Haywoods couldn't follow everything but they registered disagreement on what to do next. The farther along they went, the more Juma drove like a maniac. Felicity thought that she was going to vomit. Juma turned left on a bypass to take the Escarpment Road. With no streetlights, it became impossible for Haywood and Felicity to get their bearings. Eventually, the car stopped in forested terrain.

"Time to get out and stretch," Juma said. It was his turn to pull out his gun.

"And then for the blindfolds and then into the boot for *Bwana* Haywood," Kizito said. "Just like in the movies. Felicity will remain in the backseat with me."

Haywood felt his powerlessness even more keenly.

The Haywoods were blindfolded with colorful *khanga* cutoffs. This was particularly uncomfortable for Felicity, because of the added pressure of her spectacles. She was made to lie across the backseat, facedown. Haywood was made to get into the boot, facedown.

Juma started the car. They drove at breakneck speed and stopped, then drove at breakneck speed again and stopped, for what must have been an hour or more. Juma and Kizito lit up a marijuana joint, after which their exchanges became even more animated and contentious. Felicity had only tried a joint once, at her high school. She found the smell absolutely nauseating and wished to God that it would go away.

Felicity's prayer was answered a bit later. The car came to a halt. Someone got out and walked away, followed by an interlude of silence. After what seemed like an eternity, the person returned to the car. Juma and Kizito talked to each other before one of them walked away once more.

How strange, Felicity thought, that she and Richard were going through an experience that was visited upon a significant number of African Kenyans every day but which *mzungus* like her would take as a sign to leave the country immediately. Haywood wondered what they should do, if they survived the ordeal, to have Juma and Kizito apprehended? He could go to the Spring Valley Police Station and have the incident recorded and a report issued to him, for a small bribe. But he knew that nothing much would happen after that.

Both Haywood and Felicity were trying to find an explanation for the sudden lull in events.

Actually, Juma had driven the car back toward Nairobi and into the Westlands area. It was Kizito who had first walked off to make a maximum withdrawal from an ATM machine beside Sky Park Plaza on Waiyaki Way. Then he returned awhile later to make a second maximum withdrawal five minutes after midnight, it being a brand-new day.

Juma and Kizito took out 400,000 shillings at the ATMs. That was close to four thousand American dollars. Not a bad outing. But it had to be worthwhile for them: robbery with violence was a serious crime in Kenya. If found guilty of it, Juma and Kizito could spend decades in prison. Unless, of course, the police pumped bullets into them in an ambush, long before any trial.

Once Kizito was back in the car for the second time, Juma drove past the rear of the Sarit Centre and turned left onto School Lane. He stopped the car some distance along a darkened path just short of Westlands Primary School.

Juma opened a side door and the boot to let Felicity and Haywood out. He removed their blindfolds. "Okay, good *peepo*. It's time for us to say goodbye."

"*Si* you are fellow Kenyans," Kizito stated. "You know how to get back home from here, don't you?"

"Yes, we do," Haywood answered, although he couldn't quite tell where they were.

"Ahead is School Lane which, as good citizens, you must take every time you go to vote," Kizito said.

"Mama Felicity," Juma began, in an effort to prove that he, too, was capable of charm, "I don't want to be remembered as the bad one. Here . . ." He reached into his trouser pocket and presented Felicity with the two rings he had taken earlier. "*Sasa*, off you go!" he commanded.

Haywood and Felicity started walking, hand in hand. They turned left to head back to Karuna Road. It would take them half an hour at most to get back home.

"*Kwaherini*," Juma and Kizito called out, waving to the couple as they drove past them.

The Haywoods said nothing in reply. They were speechless. They saw the car turn right to continue along School Lane. It let out two hoots of farewell, then disappeared.

THE HERMIT IN THE HELMET*

BY NGŨGĨ WA THIONG'O

Kawangware

This saga took place during the colonial era, when whites owned our soil, water, air, and, well, our bodies, and even tried to own our soul. Our soil and soul. And because most of you were born after Independence, stories about those colonial days may sound like fables. So, if you find this tale hard to believe, I won't blame you. If I had not been there and saw it all with my own eyes, I would not have believed it either, no matter from whose mouth.

Kanage, the subject of our tale, was a respected teacher in the elementary school called the Whetstone of Wonders (WoW), located in Wonder Village. Some nicknamed him Mr. Wonderful, and others, Kanage Son of Wonders. He had an incredible crop of dark hair, multilayered curls of soft shiny blackness, the result of diligent grooming with comb and oil.

His reputation, though, resided less in the color and softness of his hair than in his knowledge of English. He spoke it through the nose, like the colonial white settler owners of the language. It was said that his English was so difficult, or *conk*, as some pupils would say colloquially, that even some white owners of the language were left shaking their heads in disbelief, having tried but miserably failed to figure out what he meant. Nobody had actually seen or heard him speak to any white person, so none of us knew where or how the rumor

* Translated from Gikuyu by the author.

started. Some people surmised that Kanage himself started the rumor, for he became visibly upset when people doubted the veracity of such tales. What most irritated him was the lack of opportunity to engage the owners of the language in public view.

The opportunity came unexpectedly. And all because of his church and voice. Wait. Let me explain.

Kanage and Salome, his wife, were faithful churchgoers. Accompanied by their son and daughter, Gacagĩ and Gaceri, they were often the first on the holy premises and the last to leave. They remained a regular faithful foursome, until the children became teens, and developed other uses for their time. The church was named after Elijah, the prophet said not to have died and been buried like other people, but that when his time came, his clothes turned into wings of glory and, in broad daylight and with people cheering him on, he flew to heaven.

There were some who denied that version and asserted that Elijah ascended to heaven in a horse-drawn carriage of fiery flames. *Fiery flames without the horses burning?* some asked doubtfully. The dispute deepened with years, the arguments nearly driving some of the disputants crazy.

Kanage was in the camp of those who claimed Elijah ascended to heaven in a fiery carriage, but Salome was among those who claimed that Elijah's clothes turned into wings of glory. The dispute over the manner of Elijah's ascendancy almost split the church in two.

Well, let me first fill you in. Church divisions did not begin in our times. And I am not just talking about the original parting ways between Orthodoxists, and Catholics, or later between Catholics and Protestants. During the colonial days, the churches, even those within the same camp, used to split into sects, which would vie with each other for which had more followers, especially followers with deep pockets, every church and sect claiming that God was on their side. Some even claimed that angels visited their churches regularly, but that they could only be seen by those without sin.

Samuel Solomon TT, for Truth Teller, the leader of the Church of Elijah, believed that the best shepherd holds the herd together in the same kraal. He asked that both factions listen carefully to hear what the Book of God said about Elijah's ascent to heaven. So he opened the Bible and read out: *And it came to pass that as they continued on and talked, that suddenly a chariot of fire appeared with horses of fire, and separated the two of them; and Elijah went up by a whirlwind into heaven.*

But no matter how much Samuel Solomon TT read the Bible, no faction would budge. *You have heard for yourselves,* they said, *he was lifted by wind, the horses just met him in the air, just an escort, he entered heaven as he was.* The others would counter: *Didn't you hear the scriptures? Didn't you hear about horses and chariot and fire?*

Samuel Solomon TT, or Double T as young people called him, beseeched his followers to end disagreements: what was important was not whether he went up in a chariot, or his clothes, but the fact that Prophet Elijah went to heaven in public view. If the manner of his going to heaven, in a carriage or in his clothes, was what was important, God would have let Solomon know.

His words touched Kanage deeply, which made him want to sing. Oh yes, his voice! It was soft like castor seed oil. Whenever he got an opening to show off its pitch, low or high, Kanage would seize the time and break into song. And that was what he did: lead in a call-and-response.

What matters is not how Elijah went to heaven
What matters is that he went up there
The heavenly doors opened and let him in
He dwelt therein with God.

And as the others responded, they would jump up and down; it felt as if their voices would split the iron-corrugated roof.

Up in heaven
Even we
Powered by faith
We will fly there
Up there in heaven.

Far from abating, the disagreements deepened till some of the congregants, especially the more affluent, swore to leave the Church of Elijah, or the Church of God Is God, and form another, the Temple of God Is the Savior, to be named after Prophet Elisha. This threatened to split many homes. Even the house of Kanage and Salome.

Salome threatened to join the new Church of Elisha, or the Temple of God Is the Savior, claiming that it would be the best for those who wanted quick riches, but Kanage swore never to leave the Church of Elijah, for it was the Church of God Is God. The new tensions made Solomon set a special Sunday for prayers for the unity of the church.

And on that day, Solomon kneeled down before the congregation and besought God to do a miracle in public view to show how Elijah ascended to heaven, so that tensions within them would cease, and all the people would come to know truly that the Church of Elijah was the true church. He called upon God to remind the people that Elisha was Elijah's follower, his son really, and a child does not defy their father.

I was there, in the church, that Sunday. Samuel Solomon prayed nonstop for nearly the whole day, till sweat drops fell from his face to the floor, and in no time formed a stream. After he was done, he told us to be patient and wait for God's miracle, but he was quick to remind us that God cannot be ordered to do this or that, He does his will as He wills. He might reveal the truth after one day, or a month, or even after several years, what was important was for them to wait patiently and without hasty splits.

His words so moved Kanage that he broke into another song, with the others joining in the chorus:

> *God is never commanded*
> *God is never bribed*
> *God does not marry*
> *God does not get married*
> *God is not pushed around*
> *God wills what He wills*
> *When He wills*
> *His wonders are done*
> *Done done done dane done*
> *Done done done dane done.*

Samuel Solomon was overjoyed by Kanage's support, and he proclaimed that the words in the hymn were actually God's own, through the mouth of His chosen vehicle, Kanage himself.

The praise pierced Kanage's ear, the spirit seized him again, and he raised his voice in song:

Wash my soiled soul
Whiten it bright
Wash my soiled soul
Whiten it brighter than stars
Wash me my soul
Whiten it whiter than snow.

At first, even Salome, his wife, was taken aback, but then she joined him in the last lines. And then it happened. Just as he finished the song, who should enter the church?

A white man.

Yes, that fatal morning an Englishman came to our church, and guess what, he wore a pith helmet, the kind we called a basin. We had seen similar helmets worn by the governor of the colony, as he toured the provinces and then sat in a high chair before adoring hundreds, with native dancers beating the drums and doing aerial acrobatics, but that was only in pictures. This white man dwelled among us. Whatever its shortcoming compared with that of the governor, for us in our village, it was the first time that we were seeing a similar headgear at close quarters. It covered his entire head, including his hair.

Samuel Solomon Double T beamed with happiness. Already, he could imagine his church's fame spreading village to village, region to region—nay, the whole colony.

And immediately, the preacher made the stranger a guest of honor and invited him to sit in the front row, near him. The visitor nodded his acceptance of the honor, took the seat, the helmet still on his head. But he did look a little surprised when Solomon added that because he was now their guest of honor, he would be given time to talk to the congregation. When Kanage heard that he would be the interpreter, he jumped up, saying, quite loudly, "Yes, yes." Even though interpreting was a big honor, Kanage would have loved a conversation between the two of them, so that the whole assembly could see him defeat an Englishman in spoken English.

Englishman: I am Smith Livingstone

Kanage: *I am Maker of Living Stones.*

Englishman: I flew here . . .

Kanage: *I flew myself here . . .*

The helmet still on his head, the Englishman said he appreciated the honor; he was really on a study tour on the state of Christian worship in the rural communities and this church's architecture had caught his eye. The church building had a steeple, like some of the Gothic churches in Europe, and it was really this that attracted him to the church. How had such a style reached the rural areas of this colony?

Who does this white man think he is? I wondered. *To visit us simply because of a steeple?* Or maybe it was Kanage who was not interpreting correctly.

He then asked us to open the Bible to the Book of Matthew, the text that says: *Blessed are the meek: for they shall inherit the earth.* After which he gave a short sermon. The text, he said, called upon people to reject the machete-armed gangsters who spread terror under the pretext of demanding freedom. The freedom of the soul was the true and everlasting freedom and for that all one needed was Faith, Cross, and Christ.

After the service, and looking very holy, the Englishman mingled with the congregation, even shaking hands with some. And all the time he was taking pictures of the church, particularly the steeple, from different angles.

When his turn to shake hands with the guest of honor came, his first ever with a white personage—he had never shaken the hand of a white man before—Kanage was all meekness, but once he grasped the white hand and shook it vigorously, muttering something through the nose, he would not let go. Even when the Englishman tried to free his hand, Kanage tightened the grip, making us all wonder: *How is this going to end?*

I was torn between the spectacle of the handshake and the steeple. For some reason I had never paid any particular attention to it until the Englishman mentioned it as what drew him to our church. I realized that it was indeed unique to this church. The steeple ended in a spire. I wondered if there were any documents relating to our church's origins. When my eyes turned to Kanage and the *mzungu*, I found the pair still locked in the handshake, the Englishman trying to free his hand and Kanage tightening the grip on it.

And then to my utter astonishment and that of the entire congregation, Kanage burst into a hymn of pure pleading joy:

Pass me not, o gentle Savior
Hear my humble cry
While on others Thou art calling,
Do not pass me by.

Savior Savior
Hear my humble cry
While on others Thou art calling
Do not pass me by.

"My son, what can I do for you?" the Maker of Living Stones asked, obviously moved by the man's devotion. He was still struggling to disengage his hand, without seeming to, but Kanage would not let go.

"In church you said ask and it shall be given?"

"Yes, yes, my son, and also knock and it shall be opened. What can I do for you?"

We pushed and shoved one another trying to get a better position from which to witness more clearly this battle between a white and a black hand. We also enjoyed the English sounds coming out of the noses of Kanage and Livingstone.

"Can I please wear that which you wear on your head, for a moment?"

"What, this?" the *mzungu* asked, a little astonished, touching the helmet with his left hand.

"Yes," Kanage said, "it is beautiful, it looks holy."

"This is for the sun . . ."

"But you wore it right through the service?"

Suddenly the *mzungu* saw an opportunity to disengage his hand with dignity. "Okay," he said. With his free left hand, he took off the helmet and put it on Kanage's head.

Smiling with all his teeth, Kanage immediately let go of the handshake to adjust the helmet, enjoying being the center of attraction and general envy.

Kanage was about to give the helmet back when he beheld the *mzungu*'s hair. It was silky and silvery, and it fluttered gently in the wind, as if about to fly. Kanage was struck dumb with an insane admiration of the flying hair. He even forgot that he was handing back the helmet, and he held it in the air, frozen.

"Would you like to keep it?" the Englishman asked, thinking that the freeze had something to do with Kanage's reluctance to give up the helmet. "I have a spare one in the car."

"Yes, yes," Kanage said, as if in a dream.

It was a sight to see, the Englishman walking back to his Ford Model T, his head uncovered, Kanage, under a sun helmet, a step or two behind, and then Salome behind him, then the crowd of congregants, with laughter and all sorts of comments, following. The Ford Model T had an open roof, and as the guest of honor drove away, his silky hair could still be seen fluttering in the wind.

Oh! For hair so soft that when blown by the wind it flutters like the wings of an angel about to fly!

Kanage went home, a hero of sorts, but so possessed with the one desire and unquenchable longing that he walked slowly, wondering how he could possess such hair. Or was it a longing for the impossible? He sighed: *Oh for hair that can fly.* The solution lay in the helmet. In bed, he took it off and hung it where Salome could not trample on it accidentally. In his head trying to figure out how he could make his hair grow silky. And then suddenly he saw the light.

The condition of the Englishman's silky hair had something to do with its being shielded from the sun by the pith helmet at all times. Kanage thought that if he too kept the helmet long enough on his head, his hair would grow equally long, soft, and silky. And from that day, he never took off the helmet, in public at least.

At first his wife and their two children, Gacagĩ and Gaceri, were amused. The neighbors too—they saw it as a fad, a passing cloud. The village nicknamed him Bwana Ngũbia, in full Bwana Ngũbia Kanage, but which he himself anglicized to Lord Gofear Carnagey. Then he got himself rebaptized with the new name. Later Mr. Ngũbia, or Lord Gofear, or Lord Carnagey, or Lord Gofear Carnagey, acquired an old bicycle, and this suited him fine. A two-wheeler was not exactly the same as a four-wheeler, but to him it was the equivalent of the Englishman's open-roofed Ford Model T.

The hidden, like the forbidden, always excites curiosity.

In time we became very curious about his hair. How did it look under the helmet? Had it turned silky like the English-man's? It became a game to see if we could ever catch Kanage without the helmet. Even children stalked him. Sometimes, people would visit his house unexpectedly under all sorts of excuses, asking for this and that, water to drink even, but they never caught him without the helmet.

Inside the house or his office he would first ensure the door was closed. He would then hang the helmet on the wall. But let somebody knock at the door: Kanage would rush to put it on, once bumping his leg against a desk, another time his forehead against a post in his house. Thereafter, he in-stalled extra locks so that if a caller turned up unexpectedly, it would take his wife some time to fiddle with the door, which bought Kanage the moments to get to the helmet and put it on.

Except for the terror of being caught with his hair uncov-ered, Kanage was otherwise quite satisfied, nay delighted, to hear people talk of how well the helmet sat on his head. Some said: *This helmet is exactly like the ones the whites wear!* Others, *No, Kanage's is special. The Maker of Living Stones once wore it.*

And then arose a few domestic complications. Salome wanted a sun helmet of her own. But they did not know where to get another one. Oh, if only the Englishman had brought his wife along, that way the Kanages would have inherited two helmets. They decided to wait for his return, but soon became impatient. When he did not return to the church, Salome de-manded they share the one they had—Kanage wear it for one week, then Salome would wear it for the other.

Kanage would not hear of it, not because he would not have liked to share, but for fear of exposing his multicurled black hair, even for a minute, before it had lost its curls and grown long and silky. Salome got irritated. She rebelled. She said in that case, she would be opening the door immediately when anybody knocked. And to show that she meant it, she had all the extra locks removed.

He decided never to remove the helmet. At work and at home, in the bathroom or toilet, walking or sitting, he had it on. In bed, too, he kept it on. Salome decided to wait till Kanage was deep in sleep, snoring, and then she would take it and try it on, walk about, or simply look at herself in the mirror, just to see how it sat on her. Once, hearing him snore, she decided to remove the helmet to try it on and also to see what change may have come to his hair. But Kanage woke up as from a nightmare, clutching his helmet in both hands. He was sweating.

"What's the matter?" Salome asked innocently. "You just woke me up!"

"A nightmare," he said. "Satan was trying to remove the holy crown from my head."

Salome fetched a Bible with a big cross on its cover and placed it on his side of the bed. Kanage went back to sleep, but his two hands were still clutching the helmet.

When he woke the next morning and found himself safe from the nightmare, Kanage broke into a hymn about the dangers of sleep:

> The fruits of sleep
> Let us take care
> We don't get our hair shorn off
> The source of our power
> Like Samson who lost his hair
> All because of sleep.

Thank God everything was in its place. And then doubts.

How could he be so sure that his hair was still on him? He became curious about the condition of his hair. He wanted to see if there were any changes to it, in length, shape, color, or texture, whether indeed it had had grown long and silky and brown. The desire became irresistible.

Kanage stood in front of a mirror and tried to take off his helmet. It wound not move. He tried again. It would not move. He shouted for Salome. Even she could not move the helmet: it was stuck to his head; it had become part of his body.

"This is no longer a joke!" Salome exclaimed, but what she wanted to do was laugh out loud, though she did not succumb to the desire. As for Kanage, this was a horror: this was not the change he had been looking for. Should he go to a barber or an artisan to help him remove it? Or should he simply rush to the hospital, the emergency ward, for its surgical removal . . . ?

But wait! This was a miracle. The light in his eyes where she expected tears took Salome aback. He thought of telling her about his sudden revelation, then changed his mind. He had just realized his great good luck.

Now he would be able to sleep and even snore without the fear that Satan would remove it. There was no chance of anybody ever finding him naked, as he liked to say about a head without a helmet. Maybe the process of hair changing color and texture begins with the helmet growing roots in the head. He composed a song:

A helmet for a hat in and out my hut
Nothing hurts my heart's joy
No harm to a hermit with a helmet.

He wished he could meet the Maker of Living Stones again, because only he could really explain this phenomenon. Or could it be that Kanage's helmet was especially blessed? Oh, how could he meet with the Maker of Living Stones? Just to let him know that the helmet he inherited from him was especially blessed? Or that Kanage had so taken care of it that it grew a life and had become one with his body? But the Englishman never came back to the area.

And then a new worry begun to tarnish Kanage's new-found joy. Now that the helmet had become one with the body, how would he know the current condition of his hair? Whether or not the black curls had turned brown and soft and silky and straight? He would be like everybody else: not able to look at their heads, except through the aid of a mirror. And being stuck to the head, the helmet would not let him even touch his hair? But his head was his and he had every right to know what grew on it!

An even more intense desire to know how his hair looked seized him. He turned over ways by which he would outwit the helmet. He tried standing for long periods in front of a mirror, but all in vain. He tried to place the mirror on the floor, to see if he could detect the reflection of any part of the head not covered by the helmet. Even a few strands of hair would have satisfied his curiosity, but alas, it was not to be. The helmet covered the whole head and whatever grew on it.

And then one morning, in front of the mirror, he noticed that the helmet was bigger than when he first wore it. *What?* Were his eyes deceiving him? Was the helmet growing? He asked Salome if she could see any difference between the helmet then and now. *Yes, yes, wonders will never cease*, she exclaimed, *it is growing!* He could not believe it. A living helmet? His helmet had become alive? And it grew like any of his other organs?

Kanage and Salome talked of how they would keep this from Gacagĩ and Gaceri, but alas, the children had heard everything. They came out of their room and surrounded him, asking him if he could let them play with the helmet, shake hands with it, or else just touch it. Eventually, reluctantly, he let them touch it. *Please take it off and let's play with it, like with cats.* It would not come off, and they went back to their room, disappointed. But their curiosity had given Salome a brilliant idea, and she told it to Kanage.

"My grandmother told me this story. There was once a little man, John Gakuhĩ, a bearded grown man with the body of a child. His owner, John Showman, a white man, a hunter, had apparently got him in a forest from faraway Congo. He put John Gakuhĩ in a cage, like an exhibit. People lined up to see him, and paid for it. Showman, the white owner of the black exhibit, took the exhibit on a tour in many countries and he made a lot of money, enough to buy himself a plantation in the colony.

"Rumors said that finally some furious young men said that John Gakuhĩ was not an animal, and they organized themselves and plotted to capture Showman, free Gakuhĩ, and then put Showman in the cage for show, so that John Gakuhĩ would also raise money from the white exhibit. But Showman got wind of it and stopped the exhibition. Yet others say that Showman simply starved Gakuhĩ to death, soon after the income from the exhibition had secured him a plantation.

"My idea is this! The Englishman who gave you this helmet is a maker of living stones. And you, my dear, have nurtured this helmet to life. He makes living stones; you make living helmets. Maybe we can put you in cage and exhibit you in the market, and charge money for the sight. We may end up owners of a plantation."

"And who would pay money to see a helmet?"

"A helmet that grows? Before our very eyes? Who would not want to see this marvel?" she argued back. "If now they follow you in the hope of catching sight of your hair, what about when they hear that the helmet has a life? We can put up letter boards: COME AND SEE THE MAKER OF A LIVING HELMET. Who would not want to witness this wonder?"

Kanage wouldn't hear of it. He was not going to play an animal in a zoo. "I want all talk of an exhibition to end," he told her.

But it did not end.

Rumors say that it was Salome who hinted to a neighbor, who hinted to another, who hinted to yet another, and so on, till the whispers became a roar. Others said no, this was not so, that it was his children who bragged to others about Daddy's live helmet. People began to talk about the miraculous transformation of the helmet from a thing to an organ, some intensifying their praise of him as Kanage the Maker of Living Helmets. Some even claimed that there were plans for an exhibition of Kanage in an open field.

The more the Kanage family denied the rumors, the more they whetted people's curiosity. *Where there is smoke, there is bound to be fire*, people would say. He became an object of everybody's gaze; wherever he went, people would cast eyes in his direction. People started stalking him, and no matter how intensely he tried to shoo them away, they still followed him or just cast their eyes in his direction, muttering, *Look at the helmet growing on Kanage's head.*

In school the children could hardly listen to what he taught, they were more interested in his growing helmet. Some asked him to let them touch it, but he would not. Others asked "innocently" if helmets could really grow. Like plants? Animals? Did they breathe, did blood flow through them like in other limbs? Could helmets breed little helmets? *Ask your biology teacher*, he told them. Was it true that he was going to be an exhibition? *I don't want to hear more nonsense*, he barked at them.

One day Kanage went home early just to get away from the incessant questions from his students. As he tried to pass through the door, his helmet got stuck against the frame. He shouted for Salome to help. Fortunately, she was harvesting some potatoes in their backyard. She tried to push him. Then she squeezed herself through and tried to pull him from the inside. Nothing doing. She then left the house, and after some time she came back accompanied by a carpenter. The carpenter went about his work in silence; he widened the entrance, and Kanage was finally able to pass through. Salome asked the carpenter to widen all the other doors in the house. Fortunately, the doors into the classrooms were wide enough to let him and the helmet through.

The helmet now looked like the conical roof of a rondavel, a huge mushroom, or an umbrella. Always under the shade—good for the skin, no sunburns, he would say. But soon the helmet became too big for the newly expanded doors into his house. He started sleeping outside. Very good, it was like camping in the open, Kanage told Salome. Fresh air, at all times, he added. Protected from the sun and the rain, he did not need a house and a roof.

In time, the helmet grew too large for the door into the classroom. So he held his classes outside, and lectured his students about the importance of fresh air.

Soon word reached the press about a growing helmet. With their cameras, pens, notebooks, and cameras, reporters descended upon us. Scientists too.

I know very well what you young people are asking your-selves: *Did they video him with those camera phones?* You would love to see them, wouldn't you? I feel like laughing at your questions, but you are not to blame. In those days there were no videos or phone cameras, no iPhones and all the digitals you use today.

Kanage decided to go into hiding. He wrote a letter to himself, as if it came from a doctor, giving himself sick leave, and Salome took it to school.

"And don't you tell anybody about my hideouts," he in-structed her before she left.

He first fled into the forest of Kawangware.

But in the forest, the helmet kept getting caught between trees, impeding his movement.

"I will flee into the desert," he confided to Salome. "Like the prophets of old, like John the Baptist."

Salome became his only human contact. Even though she felt sorry for Kanage, she was happy that she had not been able to get the helmet she had so desired. It was not good for a home to have two prophets, let alone the two being forced to live in the desert.

His sudden disappearance raised eyebrows. People started asking questions first to themselves and then to each other. Rumors of his death started. *But we never heard anything about his funeral,* some said. *He was buried in secrecy,* others added. *Why in secrecy?* others would ask. *Don't ask unnecessary ques-tions. Don't you know that Kanage is a man of property? Maybe he is . . .*

And thus began another more sinister rumor: that Kanage was bewitched to death.

Let me say that even I did hear the rumors. Some said they had sighted sorcerers flying on saucepans. They had started with their beloved teacher. Now these sorcerers would end up killing the whole village. Sorcery must be uprooted, some demanded. But who would dare to murder wonderful Kanage, the teacher of their children?

Some started casting silent glances at Salome, seeming to ask, *Where is your husband?* Others whispered among themselves: they had always known that the woman had odd ways. Some even jumped to the side when they met her on the road. In church, too, nobody would sit next to her. Salome went to seek help from Solomon the Truth Teller. When he saw her, he dashed inside and came back with a big Bible, and clutching it close to his chest the whole time, he talked to her. Even after Salome explained that Kanage was simply hiding, the preacher seemed to harbor some doubt, and would not let go of his shield against the devil. In the end, Salome confessed that her husband was hiding in the desert.

The mention of desert triggered a revelation in Solomon.

"Like the prophets of old?" he said.

"That was what he told me."

"Are you sure?" Solomon asked.

"And he told me not to let anybody know about it."

"Except me, his preacher," Solomon said.

Salome and Solomon kneeled down and prayed for Kanage. They hoped he would receive great revelations in the desert; he must not forget the Church of Elijah.

Solomon helped her write a press statement denying the rumors of Kanage's death. But it did not say anything about his being in the desert: they did not want the reporters to flock there and interfere with Kanage's conversations with God.

But the statement only intensified the rumors! *Who does she think we are! She claims he is not dead and yet she won't tell us where he is!*

I must say that even I did hear rumors of murder and witches and ominous talks of what to do with witches that disappeared their husbands. The witches had started with their beloved teacher; they would soon overwhelm the village and the region. *Nip it all in the bud,* some said, hinting that the woman had always behaved strangely.

The intensity of the backlash alarmed Salome. She did not even consult Solomon, and early one morning she was back in the wilderness confronting Kanage.

She threatened to divorce him if he did not free her from the helmet madness. He had to appear in public to end all the rumors about her having murdered him and satisfy everyone's curiosity. She was tired of being looked at as a witch, and he knew very well the fate meted to witches, real or imagined: arson. What would happen to their children without a roof over their heads? And being teased everywhere as children of witches? And you know the saying, *Mtoto wa nyoka ni nyoka? The offspring of a snake is still a snake?* Do you want your own children to be called snakes, just like the one that deceived Adam and Eve long ago and brought sin to the world?

Kanage loved his wife and children. He agreed to appear in public and end the rumors which now threatened the very existence of his family. Salome went back to Solomon. It was then announced that Kanage had been in the desert to find himself.

And so the day was announced when the Hermit in the Helmet, as some press now called Kanage, would appear in public. He would appear on a Sunday on the grounds of the Church of Elijah.

Newspapers had a field day with screaming headlines: *THE HERMIT IN THE HELMET FOUND IN THE WIL-*

DERNESS. THE HERMIT IN THE HELMET TO APPEAR
AT THE CHURCH OF ELIJAH.

Even I, the teller of this tale, got to the church very
early, and, speaking nothing but the truth, I have never seen
a crowd that big. The entire region had congregated there
to hear what God had told Kanage. Even members of the
other churches abandoned theirs and flocked to the Church
of Elijah. This did not particularly bring joy to the leaders of
these churches, but even they were forced by curiosity to flock
there. Yet what seemed to anger their hearts was the sight of
so many reporters with cameras. The Church of Elijah would
outshine theirs. Still, all were united in the questions: *Where
is Kanage? How does he look like?*

And then we saw something like a big mushroom; no, like
the conical roof of a rondavel; no, like a big umbrella—fact is,
I don't know how to describe it—but I saw it walk toward us,
Salome leading it or seeming to pull it with the straps of the
helmet, almost like a rider and her horse.

Well, wonders will never cease. It was Kanage, but the
mushroom helmet had swallowed his entire body, except for
the two tiny feet that carried it. Not a sound from the crowd.
Lost for words, we just waited, then gave way as the mushroom wobbled through, till it stood amid us. Not able to see
his mouth, the reporters thrust microphones under the mushroom. Some of us did not even believe that there was really
a mouth down under the mushroom, except when, after the
words *testing, one, two,* we heard some sort of English sounds
coming from his nose. Our beloved Kanage was indeed the
Kanage under the mushroom.

He had hardly begun to speak when came a breeze. Some
said it was the spirit trying to speak out, but others said it
was the demons, like those that once escaped into the belly

of a pig in the times of Jesus. But there were no pigs around. Which created a little panic among some who feared that, not seeing any pigs to enter, the bad spirits might enter people's bodies. Then the breeze turned into a gale and then a whirlwind, really big winds that carried everything into the sky. And then marvel of marvels! The wind blew the mushroom helmet into the sky. We saw it rise and rise, and now, underneath the mushroom, could be seen Kanage's feet, like those of a man parachuting up and up and up, till he became a silhouette against the clouds.

Salome jumped up and down as if she wanted to follow her Kanage to heaven. "Don't leave me, don't leave me behind!" she cried out, and then fainted. Solomon fanned her with a Bible, until she finally came back to life. In gratitude, Salome burst into a hymn and others joined in:

> *I will fly from the Earth*
> *Floating above it I will witness*
> *Wonders never before seen*
> *Being done on the Earth.*

People raised their arms heavenward, jumping up and down as if they also wanted to follow Kanage. Some repented openly for having harbored thoughts of Salome bewitching her husband to death. She was a woman truly blessed, and if she should follow her husband to heaven, they hoped she would not forget them during any conversations with God.

Solomon was all for encouraging people to sing and dance, and then he begged for silence.

"God works in mysterious ways," he said. "His wonders to perform; He can use the winds even, to bear His message. Now the same good Lord had chosen the Church of Elijah as the grounds on which to strike a miracle, with all the eyes of newspapers and the radio present." And then he opened the Bible and once again read a few lines from scriptures concerning Elijah's own flight to heaven: "*And it came to pass, as they still went on, and talked, that, behold, there appeared a chariot of fire, and horses of fire, and parted them both asunder; and Elijah went up by a whirlwind into heaven.*"

People kneeled down to pray in gratitude at the miracle of their teacher going to heaven in clear daylight. They did not close their eyes for they hoped to see him enter the gates. But the clouds swallowed him.

Exactly the way Kanage used to tell us, some said, recalling the disagreement that had plagued the church about the manner of Elijah's ascendancy to heaven, but conveniently forgetting that Kanage had been on the side of horses of fiery flames. Others claimed victory: *He has used Kanage to prove we were right all the time; that Elijah went to heaven the way he was, driven by the wind only.*

"You saw it all with your eyes," Solomon said. "Kanage's flight to heaven, and Salome, his wife, coming back from the dead. I have always told you that our church is the one truly blessed by the Lord. Since our own Sir Gofear Carnagey was given the holy helmet by the Maker of Living Stones, I always knew that it was a sign that he was the chosen vehicle for God to show His power and to show that our church is the one truly blessed. So, now, let us all behold St. Peter opening the gates of heaven for Gofear Carnagey to enter."

Samuel Solomon broke into another hymn. The open-air congregation joined him, their eyes still fixed heavenward.

> *They pray to the Lord*
> *They pray to the Lord*

May I come to you?
May I come to you?
Yes, Come in
I am waiting for you.

And then the wind subsided, the clouds moved. And we saw the mushroom descend, slowly, parachuting down. *Who? What? What's this all about?* Had St. Peter denied him entry into heaven? Was Peter showing his Catholic bias against Protestant churches? Maybe blinded by all the incense burned in Catholic churches? And those of Catholic faith protested: *Stop maligning the true church. St. Peter was anointed by Jesus Himself to be the founding rock of the universal church—us, Catholic!*

All the same, despite the conflicting claims, it was still a sight to see. Our eyes were glued to the mushroom, as it descended slowly. With people pointing at it, children jumping up and down, we waited for the wonder unwinding before our very eyes, and all in the light of day.

Some recalled the words of the Maker of Living Stones: that he flew himself there. Kanage was doing exactly as the white man had done. And then we remembered that the Maker of Living Stones had come in car, a Ford Model T. But others were able to explain this! The white man had flown down with his car, and so to each their own opinion.

And then the wind broke out again, and blew off leaves, and forced trees to bend. We saw the mushroom turn this way and that as if dancing, or displaying acrobatic aerial maneuvers.

Just as it turned upside down so that the conical top now faced the earth, the wind suddenly stopped blowing, the mushroom umbrella hurtling down through the air, toward where we stood, the cone crashing into the ground. Kanage's scream almost split all our ears. Clutching his Bible, Solomon ran to the place, all of us following him. He bent down over the helmet. All we could hear was Kanage's voice pleading: "Please take me out! Please take me out!"

Solomon whispered in his ear and told him it was his sins that had barred him from entry to heaven; but he would absolve him of whatever sin he might have, then would pray so that the doors of heaven would open for him as they did for Elijah. He should be prepared to return to heaven.

"No, no, I want nothing to do with heaven," Kanage said in panic.

"Please don't bring shame to your church! Fulfill God's will! Like Elijah! Look what the Lord has done for you. He got you a free helmet, like a crown. Then He led you into the wilderness like John the Baptist. Please go back to heaven," Solomon urged, and blessed him with the Bible several times, just to remove any remnants of sin from his soul, including the sin of refusing to return to heaven.

"No! No!"

And just at that moment yet another gust of strong winds came and blew the mushroomed helmet back into the air, Kanage screaming out, "No! No!" till his voice faded into silence. And once again we watched him, until, like before, the clouds covered him.

Solomon turned to the crowd: "This time around, the gates will open. Be patient!"

We waited, as before.

And then the wind subsided, and out of the clouds we saw the mushroom reemerge, returning to earth.

It looks as if Kanage has been rejected, murmured someone in the crowd. *Well, at least he will be able to tell us how the doors of heaven look. Gold, diamond, silver, or a mixture of all?*

And just as we were trying to speculate where he might land, there blew a little extra wind. So instead of landing where we were, the mushroom was caught by the church steeple. For a moment it hung from the spire, with Kanage still crying: "Free me! Free me! Our people, please!"

And that was when another miracle happened. Kanage managed to disentangle himself from the helmet; he jumped out and landed on the ground on his butt. The helmet remained hanging from the steeple. And when a moment later he stood to speak, he said one sentence only: "Thank God, He has given me back my own head."

And up to this day, people still argue and often disagree about what he could have meant by *given me back my own head*. Some claim that Kanage was talking about his good luck, because the way he had hit the ground with his head the first time could have broken his skull into pieces. And the second time, the steeple saved him: he fell on his butt, without a scratch. Others said he meant the proverb: *Borrowed jewelry burdens the borrower's neck*. Others said no, he meant another proverb: *Don't lose your old garment for a borrowed one, however shiny.*

But no matter what pressure the curious brought to bear upon him, Kanage would not dispute or say anything about what he saw at the gates of heaven. In church, he never turned his eyes to the steeple where the helmet still hung. The leaders of the other rival churches told unflattering stories about Kanage and the Church of Elijah, claiming that what made Kanage run away from heaven and refuse to return was the fact that what he was actually shown were the gates of hell, where those who worshipped in fake churches would burn forever. *That's pure envy*, the adherents of the Church of Elijah countered.

Many people claim that sometimes the helmet moves from the steeple to other centers of worship. At various times, it has been seen on the roofs of Catholic cathedrals, Jewish synagogues, Buddhist temples, Muslim mosques, and Sikh gurdwaras, but eventually it returns to its base: the Gothic steeple. Even today, if you go the Church of Elijah when the helmet is not on its wanderings, you can still see it hanging from the steeple.

TURN ON THE LIGHTS

BY STANLEY GAZEMBA

Kangemi

A cool breeze blew over the market and stirred the dry polythene sheets strapped down on the deserted stalls lining the road. On the breeze was the strong smell of yesterday's cabbage and potatoes the market traders had left on the huge dump spilling into the road for the city council to collect in the night. There was no one about at that predawn hour and the breeze had a ghostly ring to it as it whistled over the tattered strings of polythene trailing from the sides of the sagging stalls. And like a twine rope that peters to the thin end, the putrid smell gathered momentum and passed under the bridge. And then the task, seemingly complete, promptly lost steam and fanned out into the heavy dawn air. The band of street boys curled up in their dirty long coats under the bridge hardly stirred as the wind echoed through the enclosed place. Instead they dug in even closer, a glue-smudged nose tucking into the warmth of a fecund anus here and a corny toe into a gaping mouth there, just like a litter of abandoned puppies, gracefully indifferent.

The drone that had sounded in the distance drew closer and soon twin light beams stabbed the whorls of mist drifting from the Limuru direction and swept toward the little roadside settlement. The night country bus swung to a stop and the door opened, the cabin lights coming on.

"Kangemi, *haraka!*" called the sleepy conductor hugging

himself in a warm pull-neck sweater worn over his brown, Michuki-issue road uniform. He reached behind the door where he hung his key-boot on the frame of the back of the forward seat and raced around to the rear of the bus. As he struggled with the bent metal rod and swung up the boot door he glanced casually about the seemingly deserted stage. *Where were the damn* chang'aa mamas? He was not about to be delayed here waiting after he had completed his part of the business. In any case, he was going to tell the driver it was getting too dangerous. Just the other day he had heard a rumor while he was hanging out with the boys at the downtown country bus station that they were marked, that the police were onto this bus, waiting to pounce. All the same, he could not deny that it had been a lucrative side business.

The two bundles of rags that had been squatting in the shadows a little distance from the curb came to life when he started offloading the luggage. Hardly a word of greeting was exchanged as the two elderly women stacked the gunnysacks together, counting them off carefully. A shadow loomed in the window above the boot as a passenger who had sprung awake pressed his face to the misted glass pane. Seeing that it was not his luggage being taken off the bus, he promptly lost interest and went back to sleep, tucking into the raised collar of his night jacket.

Having ascertained that everything was in order, the shorter of the two women reached into the folds of her worn *lesso* and pulled out a knotted end of the cloth which she pried open with her teeth. Inside was a bundle of notes that were pressed into a tight ball. The conductor snatched up the little fistful and ran back onto the bus, hardly stopping to count. Like a coconspirator taking his share of the spoils of a shady night business, he seemed impatient to shut the door and shouted at the driver to speed off.

"*Pato, hao wamasa wanalia je? Ama wanaleta kujua kaa jana?*" asked the driver, stifling a yawn in a cupped hand.

"*Zii. Wako poa,*" said his conductor, snuggling back into his seat.

"*Sawa.*" The driver slammed his foot down on the accelerator as the bus groaned in protest.

Soon after it zoomed off, the lone passenger who had disembarked took up his bag and clutched it to his side. As if full of indecision now that the bus had left, he glanced briefly at the two women and then ran across the road, eyes wide, ears cocked for muggers waiting in the sagging market stalls. At that hour Kangemi was as still as a tomb, with hardly a hint of the bustle that erupted during the day. In the far distance, like a bright eye glowering over the sleepy slum, towered a yellow light hoisted up on a tall mast. The council had started erecting the masts to light up the slum's alleys. From that direction, too, sounded the faint rumble of the early goods train, steam horn blasting a faint *toot-toot* as it approached Ndonyo.

Working with surprisingly supple hands for their age, the two women soon had the luggage nicely crammed into two bigger gunnysacks which they hoisted onto their backs, placing the broad band sewn into the custom-made bags over their foreheads in the manner of the Kikuyu *mboga* women. Adjusting the knots of their *lessos*, they took off at a labored trudge in the direction of the bridge, hanging onto the taut bands to steady the swinging jerricans in the bundles. One of the snoring street children stirred when the women went past and opened one eye, yawning lazily. He eyed the women for a while as if debating whether to make a solo go at an early catch. On second thought he gave another indifferent yawn into his hand and then, sucking the goo-spattered glue bottle back into its customary place under his upper lip, he snorted and went back to sleep.

The two women made their way slowly along the drizzle-slicked highway until they came to a point where a narrow path cut through the bushy grasses up the slope to the rusty *mabati* shops lining the highway in that part of the slum known as Sodi. They steadied themselves by holding onto the knee-length grass on the side of the path that reeked of the urine the *busaa* drinkers, returning from the countless shebeens lining the road, had splashed there the evening before. It was a steep climb that sapped the breath out of them, but still the two didn't stop to rest. It was as they crossed the *marram* road running along the line of shops and entered a darkened alley that the faint beam of a low-battery spotlight played briefly across their way and then snapped out. Shortly after, two figures in long dark coats detached themselves from the shadows with a familiar cough.

"Hee, mama, *naona leo mmebeba kabisa!*" (I can see you are well loaded today!) said the first figure. "*Leo tutakula na kijiko!*" (Today our pickings will be fat!)

"He-hee! I tell you they carried everything, *afande, kila kitu!*" said the second shadow with a soft laugh. "*Leo wazee watakula mzuri!*" (The drinkers will have a party.)

The two cops had been waiting in the shadows for a while and had carefully observed the cargo as it was offloaded from the bus.

The two women stopped and lowered their sacks to the ground with soft sighs, the one at the front wiping the thin sweat that had broken on her lined brow.

"Ehe! Mama. So today we do not eat, eh?" said the first cop, advancing toward the luggage, the short automatic rifle tucked under his arm glinting faintly in the dawn light.

He shined his flashlight briefly on the gunnysacks, keen eye quickly assessing the contents. *"Pheeew!"* he whistled softly, summoning his comrade with a wave. The two women stood by silently, hugging their *lessos* about them from the chill that whistled through the alley. The bigger one at the front wore a look of tired resignation. She had hoped that by taking this longer route they would bypass the two cops, who she knew would be loitering at that hour in the vicinity of the police booth built on the raised verge next to the bridge, waiting to solicit bribes from early risers.

"You know that we haven't sold anything at this hour, *afande*," she said, crossing her arms over her chest in the manner she adopted when dealing with a customer who wouldn't pay.

"Now, you know that that is none of our business, mama. In any case, I think we have spoken too much already," said the taller cop, reaching under his coat where his pair of handcuffs was hooked to the belt. "How about we go back to the station and talk from there, eh?" he dangled the steel cuffs in front of her. "Is that the way to talk to an officer?"

"You are right, *afande*. These women are starting to get too friendly with us—it must be the soft way we keep talking to them. Perhaps they need a little straightening to know that we are officers of the law. They have become *kisirani*." The second cop had taken a step back and raised his gun to hip level. "They think we live on empty words, eh? And look at this one; she is an old woman who should be taking care of her *mzee* back up-country. The age of my own mother she is."

"And yet she is still selling fire to young men in the city. Mama, don't you have a home in Kakamega?" added the other officer cynically.

"It is problems that make me sell this brew, officer. I do not take pleasure in it, as you seem to think," said the older woman, squaring up to the sneering cop in a rage. "I was brought up on the proceeds of this brew, young man, and I have educated my own children on the same. And now I am even having to raise my daughters' children on it, and yet you call it play, officer? You think I have that husband you speak of to help me raise the children he sired? Eh? Don't you have respect for an elderly woman, *kijana*?"

"Now, don't you pour out your problems on me, mama," said the taller officer, his spine stiffening. "I didn't tell your *mzee* to run off on you. Neither did I tell your daughters to become *malayas* here in Kangemi, understand?"

"These women are joking with work, *afande*," intervened the other officer, who had been silent throughout the exchange. "They have the nerve to talk rudely to an officer even when he does them a favor. Let's take them to the station. That is where we will complete this *biashara*—what do you say, *afande*?"

"You're right," said his partner, dangling the cuffs. "Let's go. We do not live on empty stomachs, you know. Now, *jiteteee haraka haraka*, mama, before we go." A menacing tone had crept into the officer's voice. "We don't have all night. We have some other work to do, you know!"

In an instant the mood had changed. Now cold menace hung on every word.

"First you pass under the bridge in an attempt to throw us off. And on top of that you have the audacity to tell us you haven't sold anything yet—you think we are children, eh? You think we stand out here in the cold for nothing? I tell you to-day you will carry this luggage on your head. We shall take you to Mkubwa. You will sing, you mamas. *Mtaimba!*"

"Wait!" said the other woman, reaching into the folds of her *lesso*. The cop who had started hustling the first woman paused, a cold smile playing on his lips in the chilly dawn light.

"Now, what do we have here? *Ngoja, afande.*" The cop switched on the flashlight only long enough to register the color of the proffered money. And then his lips peeled back as he broke into a soft laugh, the type the fox might have used with rabbit's children when negotiating with them to open the door. "What is this you offer us now, mama, eh? You think we are schoolchildren who eat *peremende*? Ha! You are joking. Put your load on your head. NOW! We will go for a short walk."

"What was it, *afande*?" said the other cop, inching forward.

"*Ati*, two heads is all she has."

"With all this *mzigo* here she has only two heads? Ha ha! These old mamas are joking indeed. I think we have been too lenient, they are taking us for fools. Mama, pick up your luggage, now! Or you want me to let the dog loose on you, eh? Maybe that will hasten you up." He took another step back into the darkness, where indeed a huge Alsatian crouched, tethered to a fence post. There in the shadows the beast was dark as the devil himself. And as if on cue it gave forth a deep, low, blood-curdling growl. "Eh? Mama, you want to give the fangs of our other *askari* here a little exercise?"

"*Pole, afande*," pleaded the woman, sinking to her knees and raising her arms. "I didn't mean to be rude to you."

"All right, talk nicely. Keeping in mind there are three of us. In any case, I still want you to put your load on your head as we walk. We are wasting far too much time arguing."

In the end the women had to turn themselves inside out to appease the cops. And it was a good forty-five minutes later that the cops released them. By then they were at the lower end of Kasarani, close to the murky green river that separated the slum from the affluent Loresho. Day had already broken, and the occupants of the leaning shacks straddling the river like a horde of dusty flies competing over a putrid mound opened their rickety doors one by one and peeked out as if to reassure themselves that the shanties were still standing; that the city council hadn't flattened them as they slept. The day guards working in the affluent estates neighboring the slum popped up on the dusty paths, joined by the casual hands headed to the industrial area.

Mama Pima lowered her load to the floor and sank into a battered armchair, letting out her breath as her heavy arms flopped over the stained bare-ribbed armrests. "This is robbery. Robbery in broad daylight!" she said to her trading partner, who had also lowered her load and was perched on a rickety table. She took off her bright nylon headscarf and brushed a hand through her unkempt gray hair, wiping the moisture on her brow with a stubby thumb. Both women held their heads in their hands and regarded what was left of the delivery. Besides the money they had taken, the cops had also made off with four of the five-liter jerricans.

"They are worse than thieves, those sons of dogs!" said the other woman, drying her moist face on the edge of her *lesso*. "Just how are we expected to make up for what they took— and what will we even make for ourselves?" For the first time since she had left her babysitting job in the Mountain-View estate eight years back to venture into this business, she had doubt about their future. Though of wiry build, Khasiani was the one who had always retained her resolve whenever this happened. It was often her wise counsel that had reined in the burly and short-tempered Mama Pima wherever the vagaries of the trade weighed down on them. "I don't see us getting anywhere if this persists. We are doing all the work, only for the *askaris* to come and reap all the rewards!"

"This is a huge problem," said Mama Pima, jaw working in thought, her gaze trained on the jerricans stuffed in the gun-nysacks. "That was our entire profit those sons of dogs took. It leaves us in a fix. And we must find a way out. We have to eat too."

On the mat beside her a child stirred and rose on one elbow, eyeing the visitor across the room with sleepy blinking eyes. The little one beside her stirred too and cried out in pro-test, poking his brother in the ribs with an elbow.

"Shut up, you two!" glowered Mama Pima. "Can't you see we are talking here? Now you'll start asking for tea. And yet your mother doesn't even know how you eat!"

The child who had been scolded, not wishing to draw any more of his grandmother's wrath, tucked back into the thin blanket and was still. They all knew better than to talk back to their grandmother when she was in a foul mood.

Khasiani waited as Mama Pima mulled over the problem, her moist brow glowing, loose rounded cheeks puffed out, shiny eyes roving over the smoky rafters of the *mabati* hut. The rapid arithmetic going on in her head was evident in the fleeting expressions on her dark face. "We have no choice," she said at length, gazing steadily into the eyes of the other woman. "We have to call in the *daktari* to do his work. We must get those four jerricans back and at least three more on top if we hope to pay Franco for the delivery and keep some-thing for ourselves."

The other woman met her host's stare with a knowing one of her own. They had been a long while together in this busi-ness. "You are right," she said, nodding. "We must get the *dak-tari*. I only hope he is not too drunk already to mix the *dawa*."

"Well, knowing him, you must leave immediately so that

you catch him still at Shiro's. I hear he has moved in permanently with the widow. Go now. Our first customers should
be arriving soon, you know the Securicor *askaris* got their advance yesterday—it is still hot in their pockets."

As Khasiani rose, throwing the folds of her *lesso* over her
shoulder, Mama Pima stood too and moved toward the dark
corner where the cooking utensils were stacked on a rack,
bellowing at the little bundles stretched out neatly side by side
on the floor to get up and dress for school.

The *daktari* slumped over the corner table at the bridge-side
pub and called for another round of drinks, banging the beer-
slopped table for emphasis. His glazed eyes were bloodshot
and hooded, a cigarette dangling in the corner of his mouth.
He had barely had time for a quick nap after his night duty
at the city morgue before he was rudely awoken by Shiro, announcing the early visitors. And as he headed off to make his
first kill for the day, so had gone his chance of catching up on
some sleep.

He gazed into his glass and idly twirled the frothy residue,
bellowing at the waiter to hurry up. The woman accompany-
ing him drained her glass and threw her arm around him, idly
caressing his bony shoulder as she trumpeted a hearty belch
into his ear.

"You must have made a big fortune today, *daktari*," she
said, a hiccup causing her words to slur and gargle, her heavily mascaraed eyes watering in the thick cigarette smoke. Just
like the *daktari*, she too had been up all night, drinking at
Manyatta Pub with an old friend who had popped into town
after a long absence trucking clandestine cargo to and from
the Somali border.

"Money? Who needs money?" said the *daktari*, breaking into a wheezy laugh that reverberated in the dank hall like a backfiring farm tractor as his hooded eyes swept the bar. "Look," he continued in a conspiratorial tone, moving closer to the woman and opening the breast of his well-worn suede jacket, "I have enough here to buy the whole of this bar rounds for the entire day. You think I am another useless Kamau talking big, eh, woman? You joke with *daktari*? This is a real Makerere University–trained doctor here . . . he-heee! Don't joke! I have money, my dear. And sure, I will have even more tomorrow. Heh! You joke with *daktari*? . . . " A squirt of saliva escaped the gap between his huge browned teeth and laced through the air, spraying the woman's rouged cheek. "*Weeeee* . . . you think I am some cheap fellow who drinks *kumi kumi*? I am a man of substance, my dear. A man of means who lives on his imagination!" He beat his hollowed chest for emphasis, squaring up his angled shoulders. "I, *daktari*, schooled with President Kibaki, he-heee! I drink bottled beer, my dear. Let those hopeless folks who have no money drink sisal juice and formalin—it serves them better! In any case, it only makes the morgue attendant's job easier . . . he-heee!

"And you know what?" he edged closer, his face lighting up, "this time around I fixed the poor bastards real nicely. I bet the first one in line will be knocked flat out on the first glass . . . he-heee! Anyway, that is a story for another day. Now, come closer, my dear, and give *daktari* a hug. Today we celebrate good tidings, you and I . . . Waiter! . . . *Jinga* waiter, can't you run when you are summoned?"

Back at Mama Pima's it was a full house. The regulars were well perched in their places in the cramped room, which reeked so strongly of the spirit liquor that one patron jokingly cautioned anyone against striking a match lest they blew the place up. They were all nodding their satisfaction to themselves as they downed the contents of their glasses. The room was abuzz with murmured conversation, everyone conscious of the fact that the cops might arrive on their impromptu raids at any moment. Occasionally the conversation got animated and the host had to ask them to be quiet. As for Mama Pima, she wore a satisfied smile on her face as she dipped her right hand in and out of the money bag hanging around her neck for change. Indeed, the *daktari* had laced the drink well like he had assured her. All the customers were satisfied. Unless the cops interrupted, this was certainly going to be a good day for her and Khasiani.

That was until one of her patrons rose up to relieve himself in the narrow tunnel behind the house. He was an old regular who rarely stumbled on his long feet, however strong the stuff was. There was a roar of laughter as the old man swayed, his hands groping about for support. He took another step and stumbled, his right leg cutting across the way of his left like a newborn calf's.

"Mugo, walk like a man, *bwana*!" called one of the other patrons, laughing at what he perceived as a stunt from the old man. "You just got here. Don't you pretend you are drunk already!"

"Ha! Mugo has never been one to wet his pants. A tough old stud he is. Mama Pima's stuff must be really potent today," quipped another patron from the other end of the room.

Somehow the unsmiling Mugo managed to find the door and stumble his way out into the corridor.

It was quite awhile before Mugo came back. In the meantime, Mama Pima and her assistant continued making their rounds, doling out measures in a tiny measuring glass from the plastic bottles they clasped underneath their arms.

Soon, someone else stood up to go pee. And when he similarly stumbled and groped about with his hands, it ceased being funny. In any case, they were all experiencing this strange giddiness in their heads.

"Mama! *Washa taa!*" called someone else from the far corner, his hands moving about, clawing at the air. "Turn on the light, old woman. You want to chase us away and yet we are only getting started? Well, I am not budging until I have another drink!"

Mama Pima had been in the act of refilling her bottle from one of the jerricans stashed away underneath the bed. She paused, looking around at her customers. "James, what's the matter with you?" she asked, even as it started dawning on her.

"I cannot see you, mama. It is all dark in front of my eyes!"

It was barely midday, and the sun was crackling on the rusty corrugated iron overhead, baking the dusty streets outside.

Her hand flying to her open mouth, the host retreated back into the bed area that was partitioned from the sitting area with an old *shuka*. Her mind was racing as she searched frantically for her money bag in the clothes trunk. Outside the old man who had gone for a pee slipped in the slimy drain trench and fell with a heavy thud against the *mabati* wall, sprawling downward.

THE NIGHT BEAT

BY NGUMI KIBERA

Mukuru kwa Njenga

N ow going to two o'clock, the night was as dark as sin; the darkness was only broken by faint light coming from some shanty here and there. There were the usual night sounds of Mukuru kwa Njenga: a sleeping resident snoring fitfully, a curse and a scuffle, but so far, nothing untoward. That is, unless Corporal Senga was to count a few minor incidents.

One was when he and Sergeant Odieki had come across a couple canoodling in an alley. They had paused just long enough to catch their breath before dismissing the two cops as inconsequential in their current arrangements.

"We take them in?" Corporal Senga had asked.

"What for?" the sergeant had responded.

"Why—for indecent behavior, sir."

"Then by daybreak you will be needing a trailer to haul *all* of them in. Now hurry up, corporal. We've got a lot of ground to cover."

The second incident was when they surprised three young men smoking pot. The startled culprits had scampered through the maze of alleys, stepping on sleeping mongrels, which in turn scattered away yelping as distant ones howled in commiseration until the night was one big choir and half the slum was awake cursing.

"Let's get them!" Corporal Senga had said again, starting after them, his cumbersome G3 rifle cocked.

Sergeant Odieki had sighed. "You really don't get it, do you? Which area were you assigned to?"

"Kilimani."

"That figures," Sergeant Odieki had scoffed, walking on. "Corporal, try to remember this is not Kilimani or those other uppity areas where you book drunks for pissing on fences. We are here for the *real* bad guys."

"Yes sir," the corporal had said, suitably reprimanded. And next time they stumbled upon another startled couple, he did nothing more than frown. Nor did he make a mention of the whiff of *bhangi* hanging in the air.

"Once you have been on this beat long enough, you will come to realize it's futile trying to arrest every petty criminal in the valley, unless the idea is to empty it," Sergeant Odieki said, now in a more friendly tone.

"How long have you been on the beat, sir?" the corporal asked as they sloshed through raw sewage crisscrossing their path, running in rivulets, and stumbled over unseen ditches and rocks.

"Three years."

"Three years! Doing *this*?" the freshly recruited youth asked.

"Well, I did traffic for three years before that."

"*Traffic!*" Corporal Senga stared at the sergeant in the semi-darkness. Then his voice lowered into a longing whisper: "I hear that is where the money is."

"If you have no qualms fleecing the motorists," the sergeant growled, his mind reluctantly back on his days flagging down motorists and pinning them with violations, hopelessly trying to reach his target.

The corporal remembered the meetings later after the shift. Often it was in some bar-cum-restaurant, and he and his fellow traffic cops would fall over one another competing for the boss's favor, buying him *nyama choma* and Tusker. Then the day's collections would be quietly passed under the tables. He remembered the nodded approvals when he met his targets, and the cold warning looks, and the final threats: *Corporal, pull up your shorts or your ass will soon be warming the chair back at the reporting desk. You might even find yourself doing beats in the Northeastern Province where you have to be constantly on the move lest your ass got shot off!*

"Why did you leave?" persisted the young recruit.

"Enough questions, corporal," said the sergeant stumbling on, and Senga hurried to catch up, swearing to himself never to fail if given a chance.

The cop's word was the last at the magistrate's court. Corporal Senga could always color the nature of the offense, real or imagined, until the difficult motorist had to choose between the slammer or spreading "something small" around to the magistrate, the clerks, and Corporal Senga.

Their heavy boots alternatively pounding gravel and sloshing through the endless muck, they marched on, Sergeant Odieki's face still grim. He was now recalling his sudden transfer to the desk to handle the Occurrence Book. It had come just after he got married—at a time when money was needed most.

He remembered how devastated Edith was knowing they were stuck at the bottom of the ladder, destined to live in a cone-shaped tin shack while her husband's fellow recruits resided in modern apartments. Some had cars, and others even pieces of land. Yet others had built, or were building their own houses.

He remembered how she had borne it bravely at first, encouraging him when he was low. Then later, he was the one doing the encouraging, telling her things would work out, that sooner or later some boss was bound to recognize his dedication and kick him upstairs. It was useless. Edith had already withdrawn into herself, and while she dutifully made his meals, she hardly spoke to him.

Thinking of this depressed him. If there was anyone he had loved, it was Edith. Her parents reluctant at first, wondering how he could feed a wife; he had waited two years, and when he graduated from Kiganjo Police College, he had given the proposal another shot.

"So where will you be located?" her old man had asked him.

"The traffic department, sir."

The old man's hard glare had softened. He had seen enough potbellied cops manning roadblocks while the thin ones did neighborhood beats bearing heavy G3 rifles looking for illicit brewers and other petty criminals. His daughter would be well cared for.

After months of silence, Sergeant Odieki had figured that if Edith had a child to keep her busy, she might cheer up. Two years later, it was time they both visited the doctor to find out why she was not conceiving.

"And how do you intend to support a bigger family when you cannot even afford supporting just the two us?" she had flared, speaking a complete sentence for the first time in weeks.

Deflated and wounded, he had not uttered another word until rumors started circulating that she was having an affair with one Senior Sergeant Lagat at the camp. He confronted her and she turned away, confirming the rumors had substance. He slapped her and she sneered at him with such loathing that his anger dissolved into shock, then despair, then finally acceptance.

After she had fled—no doubt to Senior Sergeant Lagat—he threw her things out, in the process discovering a packet of birth control pills. Then, before his fresh anger and shock were over, there was a loud bang on the door and two policemen stood there to make an arrest for domestic violence. Following his short stint in the stinking cells, they moved him from the desk to night shift, his area being the sprawling slum where the only thing certain was trouble.

Up ahead, a scream rent the air. "Alert now," he warned, flicking the safety catch off. "Could be a robbery."

They stalked toward where the scream had come from, Corporal Senga all set to make his first arrest. Then he cursed quietly at female laughter coming from the shanty.

The sergeant signaled and they burst inside, at first blinded by a TV screen showing porn, nevertheless registering that there were about a dozen assorted characters in there.

"Police! Freeze!" Sergeant Odieki shouted uselessly. Already there was a scramble for the back door, and the sound of breaking glass. "Don't shoot, you fool!" he roared, hitting the barrel of his gun just as the corporal fired. The bullet flew heavenly, together with a chunk of the tin roof.

The sergeant stared at the hole, then at the back door. It was still swinging after the last customer. Finally, he turned to the large woman seated on a torn seat staring up at him with no fear. On the table were some CDs. He flipped through them, then turned to an array of illicit gin on a makeshift bar.

"I am taking these away as exhibits," he said, sliding a few bottles into his blue raincoat.

At the crack of dawn, they staggered past the last shanty overlooking the magnificent office blocks which had recently come up around Mombasa Road. At that early hour, only a few vehicles were on the road. Then they spotted a crowd gathered.

"Some murder, I bet," the sergeant said.

It was chilly and almost totally dark in the alley where the victim lay after being mugged. The first person to arrive was an office cleaner, and she almost stepped on him. "*Ngai!*" She jumped back gasping, then hurriedly threw a *khanga* over him, according him some dignity.

The next one along shook his turbaned head, muttering: "*Werry* bad."

Soon, the crowd of city workers was milling around the body, craning their heads to see, while thieves searched their pockets.

"*Aliwekwa ngeta*," one of the thieves offered knowingly.

"A proper stranglehold, from the look of it," agreed another, his hand busy in someone's pocket.

"Is he dead?" someone asked excitedly, sounding hopeful, but the victim was still alive. He was dreaming he was hiding from deadly men, and could hear distant voices approaching. He was struggling to run but his limbs were nailed down. Then one of the killers was grabbing him.

The dream snapped and he shot up screaming, throwing off the *khanga*, looking around wildly, then up at over a dozen strange faces staring down at him.

"Kindly give him some trousers," someone said, addressing a *mali mali* man who was on his way to peddle secondhand clothes in the streets of Nairobi.

The *mali mali* mumbled something about hard times, so there was an impromptu *harambee*, people contributing whatever they could to buy the victim a shirt and trousers, in the process some of them discovering their pockets had been picked.

A commotion broke out instantly amid shouts of *Thief! Catch him!* Then blows were rained on one of the culprits as two others tore down the alley, disappearing around a corner.

"Let's burn him! *Weka taya!* Someone fetch a tire!" one person called out.

Another shook his head in disapproval. "You nuts? Right next to the highway? It's bad for tourism!"

"Where am I?" the victim asked after a semblance of calm had returned.

"In an alley," said the cleaner unhelpfully.

"You got robbed," said another person.

"Who are you?" asked a third.

"I'm the chief accountant at Leaknot Pipe Manufacturers," the victim replied with some pride despite his possible concussion as he massaged his bruised neck. He searched his pockets, suddenly remembering his money, and forgot them all, shooting to his feet. "*Ngai!* My money!"

"Cops!" someone warned, and they turned to see the two policemen approaching. They stared for a few hesitating seconds at the pickpocket sprawled on the ground, not sure if he was alive, then at the victim, and fled. None of them wanted to give the story of how it all happened, or who did what.

Sergeant Odieki and the corporal reached the crime scene breathlessly. "You're under arrest!" the sergeant informed the robbery victim, who was standing rooted to the spot. Then he studied the pickpocket on the ground, covered in dust.

"I can explain, sir," said the accountant.

"You will have all the time to do so at the police station."

"Now up, both of you!" snapped Corporal Senga, kicking

the accountant, then the pickpocket, feeling like a cop for the first time since his graduation.

They prodded the two captives toward the police camp three kilometers away. Then, half an hour later, a closed-cabin police pickup came by, headed for the city. The commandant's wife and kids were in the backseat looking all smug.

Sergeant Odieki nudged the two suspects harder with his gun, his mood foul afresh. They went staggering ahead while he took another swig of the illicit gin and threw the empty bottle into the bushes.

"Saw that?" the sergeant growled, turning to Corporal Senga. "That was the big man's madam and kids on their way to work and school. Next time you figure you need police backup, try to remember police vehicles have loftier things to do."

Corporal Senga nodded grimly, ticking off another compelling reason why he *must not* allow himself to wither away doing beats. According to the regulations, cops on the beat were supposed to be dropped in their areas of operations, then picked in the morning.

Sergeant Odieki went on, telling him about more ills at the station, freezing in his tracks as a courier van came racing from the industrial area, shooting past other motorists recklessly. Its full lights were flashing, then it braked sharply at the roundabout, its tires screeching, and the sergeant saw its window on the passenger side was broken and the security wire mesh covering it had been torn off.

A man was waving a gun at the stunned motorists, motioning them to give way. Then the man saw the cops and the gun swerved in their direction.

"Dive!" Sergeant Odieki yelled, dropping into a ditch, the corporal following suit as bullets razed the grass around them.

The corporal recovered his senses and shot back, but if he hit anything, only the Lord knew. Sergeant Odieki fired a volley as the van broke out of the jam, shooting forward. It careened, hitting a post and a bus stop, then all was eerily silent for long seconds.

The two cops climbed out of the ditch and moved forward warily, guns at the ready. The hissing of the radiator spewing steam was the only sound coming from the vehicle.

"Go check it while I keep the crowd away!" Sergeant Odieki shouted, the two captives forgotten.

The corporal approached the van, no longer feeling like playing tough cop. He peered inside and gasped. The gangster was sprawled over the gear stick and the driver's head lay on the steering wheel. Both were obviously dead. The corporal turned to the rear compartment. There was another man, this time a uniformed one, lying on the floor, also dead, but this was not what shocked Corporal Senga. He was staring at piles of money in an open safe.

Then he snapped into action, yelling: "Keep the crowd away, sergeant!" He scrambled to the back of the vehicle and hurriedly unfastened the belt of his trench coat.

He scooped the bank notes, frenziedly stashing them into the deep inner pockets, then froze for a second as distant sirens caught his ear. Finally, his pockets bulging, he jumped out, slamming the door of the van and hurrying to join the sergeant who was still busy waving his gun to ward off the gathering crowd.

They were sitting at a table inside the police canteen, now dressed in civilian clothes, Sergeant Odieki nursing his drink, the only thing that kept him going nowadays.

Every now and then, Corporal Senga stole nervous glances at him, wondering if he had spotted him taking the money.

"What's the matter with you?" the sergeant snapped at last, irked by the recruit's strange looks. "Never seen dead bodies before?"

Corporal Senga stared down at his feet swallowing a lump, then geared himself for the final lie. "There was at least two million in the van!" he whispered.

The sergeant stared at him. "Corporal!" he hissed, looking around self-consciously. The other officers were busy with their own conversations. "Corporal," he hissed again, now gripping the sides of his chair, "why the hell didn't you tell me? You *let* it all go?"

"Sir," the corporal said apologetically, "I thought you wouldn't want to know—seeing how you dislike dishonesty, unlike the other cops—"

"Fool!" The sergeant slumped back against his chair, breathing hard.

"Sir, it seemed the right thing to do then," the corporal went on warily, and Sergeant Odieki nodded glumly, looking deflated.

"Young man," he said finally, "when you and I were doing the beat last night, I was ticking off points why *I* should never have allowed myself to be allocated the beats! Then, just when the big break comes, *you* blow it!"

The corporal blinked, shocked. "I'm sorry, sir. I feared how you would react if I suggested we take some money—"

The sergeant gripped his bottle, growling from deep in his throat, his face purplish: "Corporal, get lost!"

"I'm sorry, sir—"

"I said get lost before I cause actual bodily harm!"

Half an hour later, seated smugly in the backseat of an Uber, the corporal watched the Athi plains unfolding as the vehicle raced toward the sprawling maze of residential houses where he was certain it would be a miracle if the cops found him. By his side—*not in the boot, hell no*—was a large bag containing his entire legal worth as well as four million shillings he could never account for.

Back at the police canteen, Sergeant Odieki was through cursing at Edith and Senior Sergeant Lagat, and harboring specific thoughts of harming Corporal Senga. He was now through cursing the world at large, and was idly watching the seven o'clock news on the small TV anchored to the wall a safe six feet from the dartboard.

A commercial was trailing off, then the newscaster with heavy makeup was back on. *"And now for the latest update."* She smiled winningly but Sergeant Odieki's mind was settled darkly on his sad life—courtesy of that fool corporal. Still, looking at her, he could not help wondering if she would ever develop a worry wrinkle in her life. What he was as certain as hell of was that *she* had never stepped in the kind of muck he had been sloshing through on countless nights.

"It has now been confirmed that the security van hijacked by two robbers along Mombasa Road early this morning was carrying six million shillings, not two. The police now suspect . . ."

Sergeant Odieki choked on his beer. *"Six* million?" he whispered, then with a gasp he sprang up, knocking away the drinks, ready to sprint into the darkness after Corporal Senga.

A burly officer stood in the doorway. "Thought I might find you here. You're under arrest, sergeant!"

"I can explain, sir."

"I'm sure. You'll have lots of airtime for it back at the station. Perhaps you will even tell us the whereabouts of the stolen money and your junior colleague." The senior sergeant narrowed his eyes at him dangerously. "One Corporal Senga? His mug shot is all over the film we recovered from the van's security camera. How much did you share?"

Sergeant Odieki shook his head violently, gagging on the word *none*.

"Move on—to the station!" the senior sergeant barked, prodding him with his baton, sending him stumbling forward, his pistol at his fat waist, within grasp.

At the gate to the station, the senior sergeant stopped, his manner changing abruptly. "Sergeant Odieki," he sighed, "I have known you since our graduation days. You are a good man."

Sergeant Odieki's eyes widened with surprise.

"You might not remember but we joined the forces at about the same time, even did traffic like you for a while."

Sergeant Odieki was dumbfounded as he now remembered the paper-thin recruit who could not shoot straight. The man had turned into a barrel, and the long thin face the sergeant remembered was round as a ball. "I remember you!" he said with fresh hope.

"Sergeant, considering the money in question, I cannot see how you can wiggle out of this one—"

Sergeant Odieki groaned in despair

"—unless I talk to the top brass."

"*Please!*" Sergeant Odieki responded.

"He will need a cut of the money you stole. I don't see him accepting anything less than 1.5."

ABOUT THE CONTRIBUTORS

STANLEY GAZEMBA's debut novel, *The Stone Hills of Maragoli*, won the Jomo Kenyatta Prize for Literature in 2003. It was subsequently published in the US as *Forbidden Fruit*. He is also the author of two other novels, *Callused Hands* and *Khama*, and a collection of short stories, *Dog Meat Samosa*. His articles and stories have appeared in several publications including the *New York Times*, a Caine Prize anthology, and the *East African* magazine. Gazemba lives in Nairobi.

Drix Photography

NGUMI KIBERA has written over twenty-five books to date, ranging from preteen to adult. He is a past winner of the Jomo Kenyatta Prize for Literature and a Burt Award. Prior to taking up writing as a near-full-time occupation, he held senior posts in various major companies mainly in marketing, an area he finds quite in tune with his creative bent and love for travel.

PETER KIMANI is a leading Kenyan journalist and the author of, most recently, *Dance of the Jakaranda*, a *New York Times* Notable Book of the Year. The novel was nominated for the Hurston/Wright Legacy Award in the US and long-listed for the inaugural Big Book Awards in the UK. He has taught at Amherst College and the University of Houston and is presently based at Aga Khan University's Graduate School of Media and Communications in Nairobi.

Boniface Mwangi

WINFRED KIUNGA is a Kenyan writer who enjoys creating historical fiction and sharing her childhood stories. Her background working with refugees has greatly informed her recent literary work. When she is not writing, Kiunga enjoys reading all kinds of books. Her greatest desire is to retire to an island—any island so long as it is not Robinson Crusoe's—to read and write but mostly to just lie and swing on a sturdy hammock.

Josiah Matthew

KINYANJUI KOMBANI, "the banker who writes," is a creative writer, banker, learning solutions specialist, and entrepreneur. Kombani was the recipient of the 2018 CODE Burt Award for Young Adult Fiction. He has also been recognized with the Outstanding Young Alumni Award by Kenyatta University and was featured in the "Top 40 Under 40 Men" survey for his contribution to Kenya's creative writing scene.

CAROLINE MOSE is a Nairobi-based writer and lecturer at a local university. She studied at Oxford and the University of London. Her earliest reading memories include being terrified by the fictional worlds of Stephen King, which birthed in her a subsequent desire to create similar worlds. Alongside her academic duties, Mose is completing her debut novel, which she hopes will impact the nascent genre of African epic fantasy writing.

Paul Munene

KEVIN MWACHIRO is a broadcaster with eighteen years of experience and is now building a career as a writer, podcaster, and poet. He was the editor of *The Invisible: Stories from Kenya's Queer Community* and was part of the editorial team for *Boldly Queer: African Perspectives on Same-Sex Sexuality and Gender Diversity*. His first play, *Thrashed*, appeared in *Six in the City: Six Short Plays*. Mwachiro is a Nairobian who now lives in the coastal town of Kilifi.

Sami Sallinen

WANJIKŨ WA NGŨGĨ is the author of *The Fall of Saints* and is the former director of the Helsinki African Film Festival. She has served as a columnist for the Finnish development magazine *Maailman Kuvalehti*. Her essays and short stories have appeared in *St. Petersburg Review*, *Wasafiri Magazine*, *Auburn Avenue*, *Chimurenga*, the *Daily Nation*, *Pambazuka News*, and *Chimurenga*, among others.

Francis Nderitu

FAITH ONEYA is a Kenyan writer and journalist, presently with the Nation Media Group. Her work has appeared in the *Standard* and the *Daily Nation*, among other media outlets. Her short fiction was first published in the *Fresh Paint* anthology in 2012. In 2018, she published her first children's book, *The Girl with a Big Heart*. She lives in Nairobi with her daughter and is working on her first short story collection.

Samson Mutisya

MAKENA ONJERIKA won the 2018 Caine Prize for African Writing for her story "Fanta Blackcurrant." Her work has appeared in *Wasafiri* and *Urban Confustions*. She is featured in the forthcoming anthology *The New Daughters of Africa*. Makena is working on a short story collection titled *Direct Translation* and a fantasy novel.

TROY ONYANGO is a Kenyan writer and lawyer. His work has been published in *Ebedi Review*, a Caine Prize anthology, *Afridiaspora*, and *Kalahari Review*. His short story "The Transfiguration" was nominated for the Pushcart Prize in 2016, and he won the fiction prize in the inaugural Nyanza Literary Festival Prize for his short story "For What Are Butterflies without Their Wings?" Onyango is currently a student in the creative writing MA program at the University of East Anglia.

George Kitavi

J.E. SIBI-OKUMU is a published playwright, poet, and columnist. He has also had success as a French-language teacher, broadcaster, and actor. Sibi-Okumu has played many leading roles onstage and appeared in *The Constant Gardener*, *Shake Hands with the Devil*, and *The First Grader*, among other films. He narrated the audiobook of Peter Kimani's *Dance of the Jakaranda*. Sibi-Okumu's submission for *Nairobi Noir* is his maiden effort at short story writing.

NGŨGĨ WA THIONG'O, one of the world's best-known living writers, is a novelist, essayist, playwright, activist, and cultural theorist. His work has been translated into more than thirty languages. Thiong'o has received a dozen honorary doctorates and is a perennial nominee for the Nobel Prize for Literature. He has taught at Amherst College, Yale, and New York University. He's presently Distinguished Professor of English and Comparative Literature at the University of California, Irvine.

Najam Quraishy

RASNA WARAH is a Kenyan writer and journalist. She has worked for the United Nations as an editor and has also contributed to various publications, including Kenya's *Daily Nation* and Britain's *Guardian*. She is the author of five nonfiction books, including *UNsilenced* and *Mogadishu Then and Now*, and the editor of *Missionaries, Mercenaries and Misfits*, which critically examines the role of the aid industry in Africa. Warah lives in Malindi with her husband.